PRAISE FOR *STONING THE DEVIL*
BY GARRY CRAIG POWELL

'STONING THE DEVIL is a mesmerizing read. You will not find another book like this one. Powell has an astonishing ability to create characters with swift and haunting power. His intricately linked stories travel to the dark side of human behavior without losing essential tenderness or desire for meaning and connection. They are unpredictable and wild. Is this book upsetting? Will it make some people mad? Possibly. But you will not be able to put it down.'

Naomi Shihab Nye

'These linked stories are utterly mesmerizing and exotic. With a keen ear for dialogue, and a sensibility of the best Conrad, Kipling, Orwell and Achebe, Powell pulls off a masterful feat.'

George Singleton

'Garry Craig Powell's *Stoning The Devil* interweaves narratives of sex, power and identity through a feminist lens, with all of the *contradictions* and myriad facets that perspective affords. This episodic novel–each chapter of which is complete unto itself–is first and foremost a work of lush and vivid prose. Various formal innovations, from the epistolary opening chapter to the syntactic feat of the chapter entitled "Sentence," demonstrate Powell's technical virtuosity. It's this skill that allows him to capture the Gulf landscape's severe beauty, alongside a wealthy city's urban sheen and excess, with clarity that feels neither detached nor heavy-handed. While the Gulf in general, and the UAE in particular, almost function as their own characters in the book, it's those souls who suffer and thrive in the foreground whom Powell trains his, and in turn the readers', attention on. The characters which inhabit Stoning 's pages are sensitively drawn and attuned readers will find themselves quickly invested in the lives of Badria, Fayruz, Alia and all the other "players" of this novel.

'Even now as I write this, weeks after reading this book, I am still haunted by the story and the traumas that befall Badria, and Fayruz–two characters who seemed to me to embody traditional Western feminist ideals of power (…)

Stoning The Devil does not shy away from controversy, nor does it provoke for provocation's sake. Barbarities and hypocrisies of both Islamic and Western cultures find their complexity–in these stories as in real life–through the individual human being. Powell's sensibility, as well as sensitivity to loaded imperialist rhetoric and post-colonial politics, offers some truly inspired and nuanced passages that work within that charged linguistic space to fret the limitations of "enlightened" thinking. Powell plays with the practice of exoticizing, in small and profound ways, but what is ultimately gratifying here is that what we're left with are not just concepts or too-easy epiphanies, but real people, written with a skeptic's compassion and a poet's clarity.'

Paula Mendoza

Garry Craig Powell

Garry Craig Powell grew up in a working-class family in Aylesbury, Buckinghamshire, when it was still a pleasant market town. He attended Aylesbury Grammar School and completed his first degree at Cambridge University. He also has an MA from Durham University and an MFA in Creative Writing from the University of Arizona. He has spent his adult life outside Albion – running his own language school in Portugal, then teaching English at an Arab university in the UAE, and finally as a professor of Creative Writing at the University of Central Arkansas. (He recommends that writers do not waste their time and money on such courses.)

His linked collection, *Stoning the Devil,* which is set in the UAE, was longlisted for the Frank O'Connor International Short Story Award in 2013, and the Edgehill Short Story Prize the same year. He believes literature has a vital role to play in the defence of Enlightenment values. Garry Craig Powell lives in northern Portugal, and writes full-time. He plays classical guitar, and loves hiking in the mountains. *Our Parent Who Art in Heaven* is his first novel.

For more information, visit his website, www.garrycraigpowell.org and follow his Facebook author page, www.facebook.com/gcraigpowell

Our Parent Who Art in Heaven

A Novel

Garry Craig Powell

Flame Books

First published in the United Kingdom by Flame Books
Isle of Skye, Scotland
www.flamebooks.net

Cover illustration by Nick Ward. Cover template design by Zack Copping. Author photograph by Dayana Galindo. Formatting and typesetting by Vivien Reis and Susan Flowers.

Printed and bound in Great Britain by Clays Ltd., Elcograf S.p.A.

9 8 7 6 5 4 3 2 1

ISBN 978-1-7399164-0-4
E-book ISBN 978-1-7399164-1-1
Audible book ISBN 978-7399164-2-8

For my mother

'In times like these, it is difficult not to write satire.'
Juvenal

'Who will guard the guards themselves?'
Juvenal

'Satire is a sort of glass, wherein beholders do generally discover everybody's face but their own.'
Jonathan Swift

'Fools are my theme, let satire be my song.'
Lord Byron

'Satire is moral outrage transformed into comic art.'
Philip Roth

ONE

As Long as You Make Me Happy

Another blissful day is beginning, Huw thought, as he made love with his wife that mild morning in March. *Yet another in a series of blissful days destined to last forever.*

Half-closed in rapture, Miranda's honey-coloured eyes gazed into his, and she gripped his arms. Huw saw her as a pre-Raphaelite nymph: lissom and pale, her face pure and plaintive. The purring sound she made was perhaps at variance with her virginal appearance, but Huw found it both fetching, and flattering. As he redoubled his efforts, a faint frown appeared on Miranda's brow, which invariably signalled the approaching cataclysm.

Birdsong and the perfume of azalea blossom poured through the open window.

It was eight o'clock, breakfast was over, and Owen was on his way to Tocqueville Junior High, so Huw and his wife were free to bellow like cows in labour. They roared—and kept roaring—and roared more.

'Do you think the neighbours heard us?' said Miranda

afterwards in her Delta belle accent. Although she was in her late twenties, her voice was still girlish, soft and high.

Huw collapsed by her side. 'Unless they're stone deaf, I should certainly think so.' She giggled; he neighed with laughter.

'I thought you Brits were buttoned-up,' she said. 'Cold. Repressed.'

'That's the English,' Huw said. 'I'm Welsh.'

'Isn't a Welshman a kind of Englishman?'

'So you will insist,' Huw said. 'But we're not alike. Look you, I grew up on a dairy farm in Cardigan Bay; my parents spoke little English and my grandparents none at all.'

'I know, honey. You've told me tons of times. You're a wild Celt.'

'An uxorious one,' he said, relishing the Latinate word. 'I love you.'

Her honey-brown eyes glistened. 'I love you too,' she said, stroking his hair.

Oh, lucky man! At the pinnacle of happiness, what more could he desire? Only the infinite extension of that happiness. And this was where, like most mortals, he made a fatal mistake. Huw was intelligent and cultivated, but not, sad to say, a wise man, although he was not far off fifty. The Fates bless the virtuous with happiness, he believed. Forever, naturally.

'I hope you will always stay with me,' he said, confident of her response.

Did she frown or sigh? Not at all. 'I'll never leave you,' she said, still smiling, but with a glassy look in her eyes, 'as long as you make me happy.'

Faintly at first, Huw heard the sinister bowing of basses and cellos, that ominous sawing that often presages a storm in the early films of Ingmar Bergman. Now he knew: his wife's love was conditional. *As long as you make me happy.* It was no different, of course, from the attitude of most people, in these enlightened times: you stay with a partner just so long as it is pleasurable or to your advantage: then you break the contract and seek another, better, companion. It is commerce: each of us has a quantifiable market value. And yet Huw had believed, with a naivety that stunned him now, that his paragon of a wife loved him as he loved her, without reservations, for as long as they lived. That was what they had vowed, on their wedding day, beside the white columns of the mansion in the Delta. *I take thee, Huw, to be my wedded husband, to have and to hold from this day forward, for better, for worse, for richer, for poorer, in sickness and in health, to love and to cherish. Until death do us part.*

'What?' she said, sitting up. 'What's that funny little smile?'

Had she meant those words? Apparently not. 'Nothing.'

'Don't lie to me. It's that twisted, bitter smile you have sometimes.'

'I can't help it, my love.' He turned away to hide the tears in his eyes.

'Did I say something wrong? I *told* you I won't leave you, silly.'

'As long as I make you happy.'

'Don't worry about that. You do make me happy. And you always will.'

She kissed his lips, briskly, with that glassy look again. *You must believe her*, he told himself. But could he still do so? For seven years he had been happy in this American Eden—and now the bearded tyrant of the Old Testament was kicking them out.

What had Eve murmured to Adam as she handed him the apple or whatever it was? *I'll always love you—as long as you make me happy. But woe betide you if you ever bore me.* Was it something like that? Was that the darker part of primordial knowledge? Not simply of our mortality, which is bearable, but of the faithlessness of those we love, which is not.

*

That afternoon, while he was speaking to his Creative Writing class about generating suspense in their stories, a beam of sunlight burst through the neo-Georgian window, which was not unusual—but then something very odd happened: gold-edged clouds invaded the classroom, and fat chuckling babies gambolled on them, and blond angels flew in, blowing trumpets, and a Michelangelo man with immense muscles and a grey beard held out his palm, arresting Time. The trumpets were baroque, Handelian, and a choir sang. *Tempus abire tibi est.* Latin. It is time to for you to leave. But time to leave what?

And was this an epiphany? Surely that was clichéd if this were a supernatural event?

His students froze like figures in a painting. Elise, the most beautiful girl in the class, or in any class, probably, was staring at something below the table—her phone, doubtless. Walt, an overweight boy with an inflated sense of his own intellect, was smiling at some secret thought. Others had the glazed eyes of kids who played too many video games. The better students, such as Jordan, the fey, frail lesbian with short-cropped bottle-blonde hair, and Charleston, the black student who led a Marxist study group, were gazing at him with an intensity which might indicate their intellectual hunger. Or maybe they were just on drugs.

Two insights struck Huw: first, that teaching Creative Writing to people who read little but Harry Potter and comics was a waste of time, so maybe the choir was telling him to leave the academy; and second, that although Time was on pause, as in *The Secret Miracle,* the Borges story they were discussing, he could still think, as the protagonist Jaromir Hladik could when he faced the Nazi firing squad. If so, were the students *compos mentis*, too? He observed them; could they observe him? If so, what did they see? A middle-aged white guy whose posture proclaimed his boredom, while a despicable glint of lechery lit up his face?

Next, assuming that he was not deranged, could he use this unique event to complete his own masterpiece, the way Hladik had used his year-long reprieve before the rifles to compose his verse drama, *The Enemies,* in his head? Huw's Modernist retelling of *The Mabinogion* had been stalled for years. Hladik had asked

God for a year, whereas Huw had not asked for Time to be halted at all. It had just happened. How long did he have? What if this tableau were frozen forever? Could the universe grind to a stop? It might get boring, even with Elise to look at in perpetuity. *Scribe, scribe, scribe,* the choir sang. Write, write, write.

Non te amat, the choir sang now. She doesn't love you. Elise? Of course not. Miranda. *Uxor tua, non te amat.* Your wife does not love you. Could he believe that? No.

And would he ever see Miranda and Owen again?

He did not have to wait long to find out. The drone of a lawn-mower drowned out the dying blasts of the angels' trumpets. The chubby babies with their tiny wings rolled out of the windows, using the clouds as slides, and God gave him one last frown, probably for ogling Elise. Then he heard a voice intoning some bloody rubbish about scenes being battles, with a winner and a loser. It was his own voice. The tableau came to life: Elise was furiously texting under the table, Walt's eyes closed in joyful surrender to his inner joke, and Charleston pointed a pencil at Huw, like a knife. It was time to leave. He had let his opportunity slip.

'Good God,' Huw said, 'did anyone else notice that?'

For once even Elise glanced up from her phone, puzzled.

'I mean, did Time stop a few moments ago? It wasn't just me, was it?'

Jordan said: 'We all get the metaphysical game Borges is playing with the reader.'

'Yes, yes, but did Time actually stop for a minute or not?'

Students giggled. 'Maybe you're overtired,' said Walt with an air of condescension.

'What's he been smoking?' Frank—or was it Hank?—said in a stage whisper. A tall, curly-haired lad with the lean physique of a rugby scrum-half, a swagger and a quick smile, he stood out among the misfits of the Creative Writing programme as oddly normal. His classmates shunned him. No one sat near him or chatted to him before class.

The rest of the hour passed as usual: the students 'critiqued' stories, a sci-fi by Charleston, in which an enslaved proletariat revolted against the capitalist cyborgs who controlled them, and a fantasy by Elise, whose fashionista protagonist found fame and romance thanks to the help of a squad of gay and trans elves, who had the diction of rappers. Although the sunbeam had evanesced, wisps of cumulus cloud lingered in corners of the classroom, veiling glass-fronted bookshelves and the sparkly 'Celebrate Diversity' poster. Comments on the workshop stories ranged from 'Dude, I loved this' to 'I totally identified with the main character' and 'It was awesome when you killed the boss robot, Charleston' (echoed later by 'It was so cute and hot when you kissed the Maharajah, Elise'). Huw was half-listening. He strained his ears to hear distant scraps of laughter, the beating of great wings, and plucked strings, almost out of ear-shot. Harps, lutes, lyres? Or some twit furtively playing a game on their phone? Was he going bonkers?

'You mean the protagonist, not *you*,' he said. Bloody hell, that silly prat was him!

'We identify with her,' said Truman, who last year had still been Trudy.

'It doesn't matter whether you identify with her.' That awful voice of his, badgering, bullying, professorial. He hated it but could not help himself. 'A writer's got to be able to create characters you can connect with even if you don't have a similar background.'

'Well for me it was totally awesome,' said Truman, blushing.

'But *what* was awesome about it? Be specific. General praise doesn't help.'

Again for a moment Huw saw Michelangelo's God leaning across his desk, his long hair and robes swept back by a scorching wind, his forearm muscles as prominent as ropes. His index finger extended towards Charleston's pencil, which still pointed at Huw. From the vast vaulted ceiling of the Sistine Chapel, came a booming, thunderous voice:

'Your problem is that you don't read. Your inspiration comes from television, video games, and movies. You aren't writing about people with real problems. Why not? Why do you write? Because you have something to say? Or do you just want to be J.K. Rowling and live a glamorous life?'

The students gazed back at him with baffled, hurt expressions.

'What about you?' said Jordan, with a touch of defiance. 'Why do *you* write?'

'Because you want to be famous, right?' Elise said. 'You want to be somebody.'

Huw shook his head. 'Not at all.'

'Have *you* got anything to say?' asked Broome, an ageing black-haired Goth.

That stumped him. Well, did he? Broome scowled—she disliked him, he knew, but she had a point. Was this that other cliché of the creative writing class, the *inciting incident*?

'I don't know,' Huw said, meekly for once. 'I don't know why I write half the time.'

'You just have to keep at it,' Walt piped, in adenoidal tones. His cheeks dimpled in a complacent smile. 'Follow your dream.'

Disney. What was the damned dream? To create a perfect work of art or to be seen to have created it? To be creative or admired? Echoes of the trumpets, or maybe tinnitus, bounced from the barrelled ceiling—but in the Sistine Chapel. Not here.

'Yeah, totally,' Elise said. 'That's what inspired my story.'

A pity she's not as bright as she is beautiful, he thought, *and that she's the daughter of the President of Oxbow State. What's more, she's my student, and a quarter of a century younger. Oh yes—and I'm married. Happily married. There is that, too.*

Come back to the class. Should I address the Disney dream?

No, to argue against that would be fruitless. His students, who had accepted the Disney dogma, would only think he was ranting. Already they were looking at him with anxiety, as actors regard an actor who has forgotten his lines. Jordan, in denim jacket and jeans, her legs wide apart—the word *manspreading* sprang to mind—came to his rescue.

'If you're not feeling well, we could quit a few minutes early,' she said, leaving her lips open, following the fashion photographer's rules: open mouth equals sexual availability and vulnerability. Probably she knew she was cute but was unconscious of the irony of posing in attitudes dictated by the sexist patriarchy.

'I'm not exactly unwell,' he said. 'It may sound pretentious, but I've had an epiphany. Are you familiar with that term?'

'I've heard of it,' Charleston said. 'But I don't know what it means.'

'Have you read James Joyce?' Blank looks greeted the question. 'No, I suppose not. You should all read *Dubliners* at once. An epiphany is a moment of sudden clarification or understanding, usually at the end of a story, often in place of a climax, which Joyce considered rather crude.'

'Hey, I dig climaxes, personally,' said Frank or Hank.

This caused giggles, an eye-roll from Jordan, and a sigh of derision from Charleston. Elise was one of the gigglers.

'Either I have just had a hallucination—and I haven't been smoking anything,' Huw said, 'or something unprecedented outside the pages of fiction has happened.'

'Life is imitating art,' Charleston said earnestly.

'Or you were so into the story,' Jordan said, 'that it affected your notion of reality.'

'Would you say you're a suggestible person, sir?' said Elise. She was sitting very near him in a short kilt and even behind the table he could see she was scratching her thigh.

Did she mean him to see? 'I am a bit suggestible,' he said.

'The logical explanation,' said Walt with an air of triumph.

Might the students be right? Could it have been a hallucination? 'Look, if you'll forgive me, we'll take Jordan's suggestion and finish early. I apologise for my strangeness today. I'm not sure what came over me. I'm sorry if I sounded rude.'

As they stumbled out, most of the students already had their phones in their hands. Charleston and Elise approached Huw's desk.

'Hey, man,' Charleston said, 'no need to apologise. You're right, we don't read enough. Capitalists feed us on video games and superhero movies, so we can't tell the difference between fantasy and reality.' His pencil still made stabbing motions at Huw's chest. 'Our minds are so full of that shit that we can't think at all, man. All we want to do is get high and buy more of their stuff.'

'Exactly,' Huw said. 'Write about that.'

Charleston's forehead crinkled. 'I can write about *that*?'

'Absolutely. You can and you must.'

Charleston gave him a rare, disarming grin. 'Thanks, man.' He barely glanced at Elise, even though she was beside him in a minikilt and a tight turtle-neck that disclosed dangerous curves. Might he be gay? Or just shy? In any case, he was gone.

'What can I do for you, Elise?' Huw said, keeping his eyes firmly on her face.

'I just wanted to say it's all good, and I don't think you're nuts. It's cool that you're suggestible.' She paused—meaningfully, or awkwardly? 'Do you like, believe in astrology?'

'Not really, I'm afraid.'

'Pity. I can cast horoscopes and read the cards. I could tell your fortune.'

'That's very kind of you, Elise. Let me think about it.'

'Sure.' Out she flounced, doubtless aware that he was admiring her pert arse.

Outside the campus resembled a scene in some film by Joseph Losey, shot with filters to intensify the greens. Rolling lawns dotted with oaks and magnolias, Georgian style buildings with porticos and pediments, a fountain with a peristyle of white Tuscan columns—supporting nothing—and flower-beds of geraniums and wisteria. Kitschy but attractive, it aimed to resemble an Ivy League university. Huw was fortunate to have a job here. And what did it consist of? Talking about things he loved, to people who had chosen to study them. Many of his students were talented; a handful were brilliant. Aside from his teaching hours, he chose when he worked. So why did he feel so dissatisfied lately? Why had that bizarre experience befallen him? Was it a message from God—to pause, arrest the flight of Time and reflect on the meaning of his life? Or simply what the kids called a 'brain-fart'?

Before he could answer these questions, his colleagues Melvyn and Frida appeared, walking towards him—Melvyn, in jeans and trainers, with a mop of uncombed hair and a grey goatee, ambling with the loose-limbed gait of a stoned teenager, and his wife stomping alongside in a purple voodoo robe that contrasted with her pasty white face. The robe sported stars, comets, moons, palm trees, panthers, and silhouettes of feline African women. Below its fringed hem, she wore desert combat boots. Piercing her snub nose, a gold ring glinted.

Melvyn gave him a warm smile. 'Coming to the reading tonight, buddy?'

'I had forgotten all about it,' Huw admitted. 'What's her name again?'

'Savanna B. Manley,' said Frida. 'A great rider.' Huw pictured a woman with six-guns and a cowboy hat. But she meant *writer*, of course. 'You gotta be there, Huw.'

Was there a whiff of menace in her tone? As director of the Creative Writing programme, Frida had always been kind to him, even motherly, but of late Huw had sometimes caught a gleam of annoyance in her pondwater-brown eyes, and irritation in her voice. Might he have offended her in some way? Nothing came to mind. And yet she narrowed her eyes at him like Clint Eastwood in a Spaghetti Western. As she tramped away, picturesque and incongruous from the red bristles on her nearly bald head to the desert boots, her panthers prowling through the fronds of the forest, her black Amazons lurking and prancing with spears, the fringe of her dress shaking to the beat of tribal dance, an icy current tingled in the Welshman's spine. First Miranda, now Frida. But he dismissed it. Over-tired, that was all.

Don't worry, boyo, he told himself. *You are invincible.*

He was wrong about that, as he was about nearly everything that year.

TWO

So Incredibly Human

At seven-thirty Melvyn was seated in the tiered lecture hall. The whiff of marijuana smoke hung in the air, wafting from the students' clothes and unbrushed bird's nests. Predictably, Frida and Savanna B. Manley were late—whenever Melvyn was not with her to nip her heels, Frida was unpunctual—and already the students were showing signs of restlessness. Scrolling through their phones, glancing at the entrance, and even taking the extreme step of talking to each other. Vocally. In person. Without using their thumbs, without acronyms or emoticons. The two girls sitting behind and above him were talking about his wife, either unaware that he could hear them, or indifferent. The latter, he decided.

'Like, where do you think Mrs. Shamburger is?'

'It's only seven-thirty-five. She's invariably tardy.' Very odd diction for a student.

Melvyn turned. 'Not always, surely?' he said, smiling up at them.

Ashley, a young white woman 'of generous proportions',

even by Delta standards, turned the puce colour of the velveteen pyjamas she was wearing.

'Sorry, professor. I didn't know you was listening.' Her hillbilly accent and grammar distressed Melvyn's delicate New England nerves.

'I couldn't help it,' he said. The other girl—*woman*—was slim, not that he was supposed to notice their bodies, but in that dress, which clung to her athletic frame like the drapery of the Nike of Samothrace, how could he not? Her face was as blank as a phone screen. As a man, he knew he *must* not pay attention to what a woman looked like, and as a writer with a postmodern training, he knew that to describe a face, even to notice one, was bourgeois and old-fashioned: We are all faceless now. Or meant to be. But as he caught her eye, and the fixed, intense stare behind her glasses, another worry troubled him. Should he repress his urge to look? Was feminism turning him into a eunuch? Was that what women wanted? He had a moment of defiance: he *would* look if he had the urge to. Hell, yeah. But who was this girl or woman? Ashley was in one of his classes. Was her friend a Creative Writing major too? He tried a teasing tone: 'I heard you calling my wife *Mrs.* Shamburger. Hasn't she managed to expunge that term from you all's vocabulary?' *You all:* ten years in the South had turned him into a hick. He would have to curb that tendency.

'Yeah, she's like, it's sexist,' said Ashley, 'but I reckon she's just into being called *Doctor*. Or *Doctor Mrs.*'

He chuckled. Frida was indeed a pompous ass. Would he ever escape her?

The slim girl crossed her legs with the languor of a film star. Her dress was so short that he glimpsed red panties. *You are practically upskirting!* his inner Frida berated him.

'Is it true she took your name when you guys got married?' the girl asked.

You guys, not *you all.* Upper-middle class, then, if she was even from the South. Her accent gave no clues. He hoped she came from a more civilised state than this one. Might she even be a cultured New Englander, like himself? 'Yes, it is true,' he said.

'I'm lovin' it,' Ashley said, with a child's delight at her own wit.

Melvyn had endured thousands of jokes about hamburgers, and groaned.

'But why?' said Ms. Red Panties. 'I heard she's a radical feminist.'

'She sure is.' His gaze kept slipping towards her long, marble-white legs. 'I guess Shamburger sounds hysterical to you. But imagine if your maiden name was Gorgonzola.'

'Gorgonzola?' gasped Ashley, suppressing a chortle.

'Yep, like the cheese. It's a name from northern Italy. She's Italian-American.'

'Like Don de Lillo or Camille Paglia,' said the other one, whose legs were bare, in fact naked, nude, oh boy. 'But what about Frida? We heard that isn't her real name either.'

'It is now,' Melvyn said, impressed she knew the novelist and the scholar. 'Man, but that's a secret. How'd *you guys* hear about it?' *Show Ms. Smarty-Panties you're no hick.*

'She re-invented herself, then?' she said. 'Inspired by Frida Kahlo, I presume?'

'Right,' Melvyn admitted, impressed again. But how unoriginal it was of Frida.

'Cool,' said Ashley, making it two syllables. 'So what's her real first name?'

Frida had not forbidden him to reveal it, but he guessed she would be displeased if he did. And yet to make up for his shame at being married to Frida, he wanted to confide in these girls, or women. Especially the smart, stylish one with the glasses. 'Gladys,' he said.

Ashley's jaw fell open, pantomiming amazement. 'Woah, dude!'

'Gladys Gorgonzola,' Red Panties said. 'No surprise she changed her name.'

Yes, the girl or woman had breeding, class, intellect. Could he dare to hope she might like him?

'But where can Frida be?' he said, scanning the hall.

The Xenophon Fullerton Auditorium had curved banks of blackish benches and desks rising steeply from the lecturer's dais. Wainscoting and brass Victorian lamps gave the hall a warm, golden glow. Students loved the Hogwarts atmosphere. Most had draped their massive bodies in shapeless tee-shirts and jeans, though a few females—the slimmer ones—wore short skirts, and makeup. How many were here for extra credit? Half at least, probably. A wave of murmurs broke as Huw arrived with Miranda.

'Woah,' Ashley whispered. 'Get out of here! Professor Lloyd-Jones' wife is *hot.*'

'Indeed,' agreed Nike. 'Imagine making love with her.'

She was a lesbian, then. Damn! But how she spoke—almost quaintly, for a student.

'She's *way* younger than he is,' Ashley said. 'That's gross, right?'

'Not at all, he's devastatingly attractive too,' her friend purred. 'That *accent.* Those grey sideburns. He's like a sexy vampire. I'd make love with him too. Or both together.'

In fact then she was bisexual, or pansexual, or polyamorous—whatever the hell that meant. Melvyn's initial disappointment turned into relief, then jealousy, and finally resignation. Grow up, he told himself. She's a kid. Why would she find *you* hot? As for Huw being *sexy*, to Melvyn the Welshman looked typically British—just scruffy, with bad teeth. Neither tall nor athletic. *Sexy? Give me a goddamn break. I'm way sexier than he is.*

But at that moment Frida stamped into the auditorium, in a billowing black evening gown, sleeveless—revealing the dragon tattoos Melvyn had begged her not to get. The audience gasped, probably not at Frida's appalling taste, which he doubted they noticed, but at the tall, dreadlocked white woman whose cowboy boots clopped behind her.

Savanna B. Manley swaggered in like a victorious Olympian. Several girls or women—there were adults in attendance, at least people of adult age—broke into a high-pitched howling, whooping and yipping. Ululations. He had underestimated the reputation of the writer of *Bloody Blades,* the graphic novel-in-verse about a teenager's battle with cutting herself. The idol threw off her white leather jacket with a rock-star flourish, flinging it over the back of a chair, and sat with her long legs wide apart, just like a guy—a very sexist perception, he recognised and scolded himself for. Ms. Manley smiled with simmering triumph. Melvyn braced himself for the usual narcissism and stupidity, and ogled Miranda…

… Who was in a summer dress, short *and* low-cut. She reminded him of a cheerleader with her permed blonde hair and all that lipstick and mascara. Southern belle, for sure, sadly. Christ, she was hot, though. Huw turned towards him at that inopportune moment, saw Melvyn leering at his wife, and gave him a queer little smile. What exactly did it mean? *I'm on to you? I see you lusting after Miranda, but she's mine, you hypocrite, you slug?* Or maybe he was just being friendly as usual. What *did* a Welshman think? The Brits were darned hard to figure out. Enigmatic, inscrutable. Once Huw had called himself a Druid, tongue-in-cheek probably, but there was something in it. He was Oxford-educated. Smart. Mystical. Maybe just weird. Not sexy at all. Melvyn slumped lower, trying to disappear.

Frida poked the microphone, which popped, then peered over the lectern as if she were struggling to keep her head above water, clutching it hard. But by degrees, her face took on the familiar frightening smile, lips curling first, eyes crinkling next. Like a motivational speaker's, it didn't indicate joy or amusement. No, an uplifting speech was coming. Why did everyone do such sappy, cloying introductions nowadays? Virtue-signalling, of course.

Melvyn *despised* virtue-signalling—although to be fair he did it all the time himself.

'Thank you all *so* much for coming,' Frida warbled, in the unctuous voice she used to convey sisterliness and sanctity. 'I'm so happy to see all you young, creative women here.' A cue for an outbreak of whooping. 'And guys of course,' she added.

'I believe you young women will save the world,' she continued, her eyes brimming with tears. Could she be sincere? Even for Melvyn, it was hard to tell. She said stupid shit like that even at home, and yet she had never convinced him that her feminism was a true faith so much as a convenient creed that furthered her career. She had not been so fanatical when they met. All through grad school she had allowed him to support her with his trust fund money. Still, he had to admit that she was capable of working herself into a lather, as she was doing now—to masterful effect, judging by the squeals. But what about the guys in the hall? Didn't they feel a bit left out? Couldn't a few of them help save the world too?

Frida thanked the Dean and the College of Liberal Arts for supporting the Writers in Diversity series, her newly-shorn head bobbing respectfully towards the elderly Dr Jorgen Jorgenson in his bowtie and pinstripe suit, who sat beside his much younger husband, Timothy. In the spotlight her reddish bristles glinted. She reminded Melvyn of Van Gogh in his lunatic phase as her voice rose in ecstatic awe:

'And it's my great honour and pleasure to introduce to you someone *Saloon* magazine has described as 'a literary genius worthy of the Nobel Prize'.'

Melvyn smirked: Frida had written that hagiographic appraisal.

The audience was in ferment, barely reining in its desire to holler, shout and scream. Frida's voice blared like a trombone at the Pride parades they attended as allies, with traces of her childhood East Boston vowels, though she strove to speak like a Boston Brahmin: 'She has defied genre boundaries, mixing graphic novel and verse. She has fearlessly advocated for the outsider, the teenager who is transgender, anorexic, addicted, who self-harms…'

Or all of the above, Melvyn thought, having been forced to read Savanna B. Manley's 'slim volumes of prophetic power' by his wife. If they were not so woke in theme and tone, would they ever have been published? Doubtful.

'Her first novel, *Shemale,* sold 200,000 copies and *Library Magazine* hailed it as 'compulsory reading for diverse YA English classes'. The sequel, *Bloody Blades,* was an international bestseller and the movie will star Tinker Quick.' Frida paused for a collective gasp. 'Elsa has interviewed her twice, and her latest novel, *Switchbitch,* was featured on Obadiah's Book Club. She has been the recipient of a National Legacy for the Arts grant, as well as a MacAlfred 'Genius' grant, and the American Transgender Association has honoured her as a hero. *Tempo* Magazine named her one of the most influential one hundred women alive. Our last First Lady, the cool one we all love, called her 'a visionary'. In verse of breath-taking originality and power, our guest has transformed the literary landscape of the United States. I am beyond thrilled to introduce you to … Savanna B. Manley!'

Beyond thrilled? Hyperbole. But Frida had always resorted to clichés.

A tsunami of applause thundered. Amid screams of joy, the percussion of stamping feet and the snare-drum rolls of clapping, amid whistles and ecstatic howls, students brandished phones, snapped photos. Spotty cheeks and chubby cheeks shone with tears. Huw glanced around, a supercilious look on his Welsh face. He dared to smirk. Melvyn could not imagine how any professor could be so reckless.

Might Manley be the Real Thing, though? Graphic novels in verse were not really Melvyn's thing, but like all his colleagues, except Huw, he accepted that every form of art was equally valid. You couldn't cling to elitist, patriarchal notions. Pop culture was just as deep and complex as the highbrow stuff. All the cool leftist critics agreed. You only had to consider the genius raps of Mustwe East, or the inspiring auto-fictional songs of Tinker Quick. *Game of Crowns* was as universal as Shakespeare. Like obviously. Melvyn's own idol was DFW—he had slogged his way through *Infinite Jest* in a mere two years without understanding much—actually, anything—but, hell, it sounded smart. The lanky granny did not look as intellectual or as cool as DFW, but authors could not be judged by appearances. Writers were a repulsive tribe on the whole. Except the latest young women writers, of course, who were all smoking hot. Publishing houses sure knew who was marketable.

Melvyn's heart and ears were open, he told himself, suppressing a fantasy of the newest literary genius, the simpering Charlotte Silk, whose fiction was barely at his freshmen's level, though boy oh boy, she had the looks and bod of a goddamn supermodel.

Bow-legged in her cowboy boots, Savanna B. stomped to the lectern. Frida waddled to the seat beside Melvyn, gazing on Manley with operatic veneration, hand on her chest.

'Good Goddess,' Savanna said, 'thank you *so much* for that, Frida. It's totally freaking awesome to be here with you all at Oxbow State University. What a cool audience you are. You don't know how buzzed I am to see so many young women writers in front of me. Girls, you are *gorgeous*.' More yips, yowls, and squeals.

'Girls?' Melvyn whispered to his wife. 'Are you still allowed to say that?'

Frida clucked with irritation. 'Of course you can, if you're a woman.'

Huw hissed, 'Clichés,' at his wife then turned around to Melvyn and Frida and said, 'Aren't there any bloody blokes in here?'

Frida frowned. Ms. Manley—could that be a pseudonym?—began to tell her life story, in a folksy way. Sell it in fact, like an expert saleswoman.

'I gotta tell you women,' Manley said, her dreads forming

a flying halo as she shook them like a stoned reggae singer, 'you are *way* cooler than I was at your age. Trust me. I was a total nerd. All I did was read books, real serious literature,' (she pronounced it *litera-chew-er*). 'Louisa May Alcott. Alice Walker, Maya Angelou.' She let the weight of those immortal names sink in. 'I had mental health problems, too, like Prince Harry, they ran in the family, and my daddy couldn't keep his hands off me. That's right, sisters, I write what I know. So maybe it wasn't surprising that I started doing drugs, tons of damn drugs, pot, acid, cocaine, heroin, the whole nine yards, I was a real hippie. And I was cutting myself too.' She slipped that in artfully.

'She's got them eating out of her hand,' Frida murmured with admiration.

Huw shot Melvyn a *mocking* glance. Could anyone be so politically incorrect, so insensitive, so unwoke—so reckless? Melvyn pulled an inscrutable face in reply. Looking around the auditorium at all the worshipful faces, he wondered that Huw dared show his irreverence. The Maenads would tear a man limb from limb if he slighted their goddess. With a shudder, Melvyn imagined these plus-size Americans in fawn-skins, snakes coiled around their arms and thyrsi in their fists. That Manley suffered from mental illness he had already divined from her books, and her daughters had suffered from the same tragic problems, the writer was testifying now, breaking into sobs, arms and dreadlocks flailing.

'That was when I found Jesus,' she proclaimed in an exalted nasal whine, 'and the mission he had gave me. He commanded me to write poetry, and promised me that he personally would inspire me, to teach noble young women like you that whatever you've been through, you will prevail, as long as you trust in Him.'

She paused, apparently seeing that these words puzzled many. *He? Him?* What was Manley thinking? Ms. Smarty-Panties said, 'Patriarchal' aloud.

Undeterred, Savanna raised her voice: 'Or Her, like obvs.'

She bit off the end of the word. 'God or Goddess, who cares, right?' She suppressed a murmur of dissent by yelling: 'I tell you this, sisters. You trust your innate beauty, whatever you look like. It don't matter if your figure is different from a model's. You own your bodies, 24/7. You're goddesses. Am I right, or what?'

Rodeo squeals, shouts, stamping, whooping, whistling and yipping.

With a jubilant grin, Huw sibilated: 'The glorification of victimhood.'

Miranda poked him with her elbow. Melvyn pictured that host of ample Maenads descending on Huw in a frenzy, ripping his flesh with their teeth and nails.

Melvyn held up an index finger. 'Don't judge her till you've heard her read.'

She opened a book—crimson as gore in a horror flick—and began to recite, in the sententious tone favoured by so many American poets. Pitched higher than her speaking voice, which was masculine, indeed manly, (hence her sobriquet?) she read mawkishly, without punctuation or pauses. Her verse was not just blank, without any rhymes, but had no meter either, or even any real content. It was indeed blank. Cliché followed cliché without rhythm or euphony; the images were obvious or stilted; nouns and verbs were tangled in webs of qualifiers; and the plot—what there was of it—was sophomoric and derivative.

In short, it was shit.

Not just common-or-garden commercial shit, either, the work of an insipid mind—Melvyn was inured to that after years teaching creative writing—but devious shit, meant to manipulate and exploit the vulnerable, the troubled, the pathetic. So he supposed. If she were sincere, the woman was as batty as a barrel of squirrels.

And yet at the end, having read in her Messianic voice, Manley bathed in applause, the women weeping and keening like Arab matrons at a funeral. They were in paroxysms; they were moved. Well, wasn't that the purpose of literature? Crying colossi stamped down the stairs, clutching their sacred books, storming the table where Manley was enthroned, ready to sign her masterworks.

Huw and Miranda were already perusing the piles of novels—that is, Miranda was reading with a solemn, sultry expression—Melvyn had to loosen his collar—while Huw was examining *Bloody Blades* as if it were spattered with snot. The guy was actually wincing.

But he sniggered as he turned the pages. Like a goddamned teenager.

'You find it funny?' Melvyn asked.

'Immensely,' the Welshman replied. 'Pretentious and portentous. I wondered if her writing might improve without that nasal, whining delivery. But no. Look at the line-breaks. Quite random. An orang-utan might have done as well.'

Miranda frowned at her husband. Oh boy, what a babe.

And then Frida appeared, her face flushed with exaltation. Was the emotion manufactured? Actors managed it through self-hypnosis. And in these hysterical times, academics had to be 'passionate', too, especially in the liberal arts. Melvyn skulked behind her, hands in his pockets, dreading what she might come out with.

'She's so incredibly human, right, Huw?' Frida said.

Melvyn cringed. Knowing Huw, he would say something withering.

Huw looked down on her with that insufferable British air of superiority and sarcasm. Lofty as George the fucking Third. 'I wouldn't go *that* far,' he said.

'Sweetie,' Miranda warned him. Melvyn repressed a smile.

Frida's gold nose ring twitched and trembled.

'Are you being enigmatic again? I can never tell when you're joking,' she said. 'You must have been impressed, though? Don't you think she's a genius?'

Huw glanced with glee at Miranda, who was immersed in

Shemale. She nodded, encouraging—no, warning. Warning, dude! Melvyn leaned in, eager to hear every word.

'Fuck me, Frida,' Huw said, 'do I think she's a genius? About as much as I think Tinker Quick is a genius, or Mustwe East. The woman's a talentless halfwit.'

Frida's nose-ring shuddered, her forehead creasing, her scalp scarlet beneath the copper brush of bristles. She wheezed, pure East Boston now: 'Unbelievable. You insult me to my face when we're surrounded by students.'

Huw rolled his kingfisher blue eyes. 'I didn't insult you, Frida, I insulted that fraudulent excuse for a writer.'

'Who *I* invited here,' said Frida, raising her fleshy arms and flexing her muscles in a weird way, so that her blue dragons convulsed.

Miranda telegraphed a reproach to Huw, who smiled back. Have I gone a bit too far? his smile meant. Not that he cared, plainly enough. She nodded at him to leave. Melvyn had a sudden inspiration: could he use Huw as a lightning rod for Frida's ire? She might spare him, then. Seldom had he had such a brilliant idea. It took possession of him at once.

He followed them out, while Frida blundered through the herd of students, scattering them, to appear at Manley's side with an apostolic smile on her face.

'That was brave of you,' Miranda said to Huw as they left the auditorium.

'Foolhardy, you mean. Unwise. Reckless. Impetuous.'

'You need that promotion, honey, and she *is* the director of your program.'

'I know. I'm sorry.'

'You don't really sound it. You sound half-contrite, half-proud.'

You go, girl, Melvyn mentally urged her. *You mean he's a patronising prick.*

'Do you always have to be so brutal?' Miranda asked.

'It's my hot Celtic blood,' he said.

'Well I guess you'll just have to write a bestseller if you lose your job.'

Huw reeled—unless it was an illusion of the mauve sunset. Neither he nor Miranda had noticed Melvyn, as far he could tell. They were passing the peristyle of the fountain, an arcade of slim columns. Students slumped on the benches, captivated by glowing screens. Some looked stoned and doubtless were. Traffic grumbled by on Connelly Street. Melvyn addressed Miranda as he caught up with them: 'Hey, so what did *you* think of the reading?'

She stopped abruptly. Underwater lights came on, illuminating the jets of water, which arched behind her, framing her dramatically. She had blue breasts.

'I found it moving,' she said, her breasts flashing like police car lights.

'Me too,' Melvyn said. 'Deeply moving. Manley is quite the genius, right?'

'Really?' To Melvyn, Huw sounded like Richard Burton or Anthony Hopkins. His voice had that sonorous Welsh cadence, but also a touch of brutality.

'But maybe I'm as half-witted as *you* think Savanna B. Manley is,' Miranda said. 'Do you think all women are sentimental? Men can be so goddamn arrogant.'

'Of course I don't think that. But tell me what you found moving in it. I couldn't see anything in it,' Huw said, not even looking at Melvyn.

'Naturally you wouldn't,' Miranda said. Melvyn's heart beat harder.

Huw watched her walking away from him—as lightly as a ballet dancer, Melvyn thought, as lightly as Frida had once walked—before hurrying after her.

'Perhaps I was wrong,' Huw said humbly.

'Won't you tell me?'

'Not now,' Melvyn heard. Miranda's tone was as final as Frida's. It would be indiscreet to tag them further, although he wished he could. Huw *was* arrogant: Miranda had nailed it. With joy, Melvyn took out his note-book and scrawled:

Oxbow State is entering an electrifying phase. Oh boy oh boy!

THREE

The Song of the Sea-Monsters

As flies to wanton boys are we to the gods, Gloucester says in *Lear*. They kill us for their sport. The Bard was right about that. They seldom even give us a warning.

The next evening, Huw was sitting on the swing-seat on the porch, sipping tea, slipping into a trance. The garden was lushly green, aflame with blossom; after a brief thunderstorm, the wisteria and azalea bushes were dripping. Scraps of poetry in English and Welsh skipped across his mind. But musical tempests were also menacing, cellos hurrying for shelter, violins squealing, frantic with fear, when Miranda drove up to the kerb in her hybrid, and again he recalled the choir's command, to leave the academy and write. He had told Miranda about the angels with their trumpets, the cherubim on the clouds, the patriarchal deity, the whole vision, but she had not taken it seriously. How can you consider leaving your job when we need the money? she had said. Was she worrying about that now? For ages after turning the engine off she sat tight, hands on the wheel. He had not mentioned the choir's other pronouncement, that she did not love him. How could he? To articulate such an idea might make it happen. When she finally emerged from the carbon-grey carapace of the vehicle, looking like the actress she was often mistaken for, one famous for a role as a dancer, her face made-up, hair curled, in a chalk-stripe trouser-suit, she tripped past him, ignoring his greeting and his wave. Had she seen him? She was never rude. All Huw's doubts and fears of the past few days returned with redoubled force. Just what was the matter with her?

He followed her indoors and found her in the kitchen, at the table in an alcove festooned with potted plants. In one hand she had a glass; in the other, a bottle of port, which she clutched by the neck, upside down, like a German stick grenade.

'I need to get drunk,' she said. 'Do you mind?'

'Owen will be home soon, you know,' he said, adding in an attempt at humour, 'Please don't lob that bottle at me. It's not like you to get drunk.'

'Can't I let myself go sometimes?' Her features belied her annoyance, or strove to: her face froze in an expression of crazed beauty-queen happiness. Preternaturally bright eyes, TV presenter smile. Huw's worry that his best work was behind him, and teaching had riddled his mind with woodworm, was forgotten. A catastrophe was approaching. Just a couple of days ago Miranda had told him that she would only stay with him as long as he made her happy. Had he failed her? If he had, would she give him a chance to make amends?

He took a small glass of port to accompany her. 'It's funny,' he said, to remind her of their luck. 'People say passion doesn't last, but mine is undiminished. After six years of marriage. I know how fortunate I am to have found love so late in my life.'

She swigged the port, traces of her glassy grin remaining on her face. Huw reached across the white-painted pine planks of the table and laid his hand on Miranda's right arm, which held the glass. On any other day she would have placed her free hand over his, pressed her palm against his chest, responded somehow. But tonight she did nothing but guzzle, giving no sign that she was aware he had touched her.

'Can I get drunk, then?' she asked, looking towards but not at him.

'Be my guest,' Huw said, with a trace of sarcasm.

'Sourpuss. You're so… I don't know, so damn *American*, sometimes.'

'*American*? Me?' He wished she would look him in the eyes.

'Bible Belt Baptist. Sensible. Self-righteous. You've been here too long, Huw.'

How long had he been in the States? Seven years or so, starting with the Master's in Creative Writing at Iowa University, where he had met and married her, followed by the three-year teaching appointment in Oman, and then the return to Miranda's home state in the Deep South. Had it been too long? Was he turning into a Southern prig? The fear that he might be informed the vehemence of his denial: 'Jesus Christ, Miranda. I'm from Wales. I come from a noble line of tipplers, topers, sots, soaks, boozers, carousers, and dipsomaniacs. I'm damned if I'll let you blacken my name with an insult like 'Bible Belt Baptist.' I'm as much of a sinner as you are, so help me God.'

She smiled without mirth or tenderness. 'Let's both get drunk then.'

'What is it?' Huw asked her. 'What's going on? Tell me, love.'

'I've got to get drunk first.'

He heard the dogged resolve in her voice. 'Shall I get the dinner?' he said.

'I'm not going to eat.'

'I'll have to get something for Owen. He'll be home soon.'

'Go ahead.'

Huw cracked some eggs and beat them with a fork. 'This isn't about me resigning, is it?' No answer. 'You haven't you lost *your* job, have you, love?'

'God, no. The Department of Psychiatry couldn't function without me.'

'Car accident? Mass shooting? Not another war?'

She shook her head. Her eyes glittered like ice crystals.

'I wish you wouldn't drink so fast,' he said. 'You know it makes you ill.'

'I want to be sick. I want to puke my goddamn guts up.'

'Has someone in the family got cancer or something?'

'Nothing like that. But it is something to do with the family.'

'Won't you tell me what it is?'

'I've got to get plastered first.'

Owen sailed past the window on his bike, arms crossed, headphones on. A minute later he was in the kitchen, grunting a greeting, his eyes not meeting Huw's.

'What's for dinner?' he said, in a mid-Atlantic accent.

'Omelette, I'm afraid,' Huw said.

'Again?'

Huw nodded discreetly at Miranda.

Seldom perplexed, Owen raised his brows in interrogation.

Huw nodded back, barely perceptibly. 'I'll call you when it's ready.'

Owen left the room, all bones and long limbs. Miranda was drinking. She did not look at Huw. He observed her, though: her face was pale—or was that just the make-up?—and her eyes were remote, glazed. Her posture, usually perfect, if a little rigid, was different. She crouched over her glass, encircling it with her arms as if afraid he would snatch it away.

'Don't you want to take your jacket off?' he asked her.

'No.' The monosyllable was a body blow.

Was she working up the courage to tell him she was leaving him? Might she be having an affair? He could not imagine it. Her behaviour had not altered in the past weeks, and he had been just as loving and attentive. But he remembered her saying she had been moved by Manley's work. Perhaps he should have given that more thought. To him it was an odd confession—like admitting you enjoyed the music of Mustwe East or Tinker Quick. Was it possible to love someone who valued such twaddle? Of course it was. He put a plate over the omelette, held it in place, then turned it over and glanced at Miranda. He reproved himself for his arrogance—that was what she had accused him of. Hubris. Pride comes before a fall.

'What did you find so moving at that reading?' he said, trying again. He glanced over his shoulder as he stood at the stove. She materialised from her underworld, and visibly *collected* herself. She was in pieces, in fragments.

'I identified with her. The teenage girl.'

'But you've never cut yourself, have you?'

'Not yet.'

'*Not yet?*'

She clucked. 'I want to. It's me or my mom.'

'What?'

He gaped at her. She did not reply. He smelled burning.

'Oh Christ, the sodding omelette.' He took the pan off the burner. The omelette was seared but still edible. Or so he hoped. He started hurling together a salad. Did other people have crises while cooking for their teenage sons? In fiction a dramatic scene was never interrupted, but in reality the drama often had to wait.

'Dinner!' he called up the stairs. He hoped Owen would not notice how sloshed Miranda already was. Fortunately, he focussed at once on the food when he came down. He sat and scrutinised his plate. 'Aren't you two eating?'

'We'll eat later,' Huw said. 'Probably. How was school?'

Owen nodded rhythmically at the music in his earbuds—metal, by the sounds of the crunching guitars. 'Tastes like shit,' he muttered. 'You incinerated it.'

'Sorry,' Huw said. 'Bad day so far. And about to get worse, I fear.'

Owen glanced at his stepmother. 'Yeah, right. Chicks are all the same, dude.'

Huw expected an exasperated hiss at the sexist language, but Miranda was either not listening or did not care. She poured another glass—her fourth or fifth. Then, unsteady on her feet, she headed for the cutlery drawer, from which she took a Rambo-sized carving knife. With a dazed expression, she pondered its blade and stumbled out of the kitchen.

Huw caught up with her in the living-room, where she swayed beside the sofa. 'Drunk as a skunk,' she said, prolonging the syrupy Southern vowels. 'I just need to cut my face. Is that OK with you?'

He took the knife from her and put it down. He held her arms. She did not resist.

'Of course it's not OK with me. Why?'

'You really want to know? My mom hurt me.'

Huw knew his wife was not fond of her, but they were always courteous with one another, and he had never suspected anything sinister of his mother-in-law. 'What do you mean? Today? What's she done?'

'Nasty things,' Miranda said, in the awestruck voice of a child. She looked oddly girlish. Trusting. 'That's why I need to hurt myself. If you'll just let me slash my cheeks or stab my eyes, I'm sure I'll feel better.'

He suppressed the urge to weep. 'I won't let you harm yourself, darling. You know that.' He hoped Owen could not hear. Let him be oblivious.

'Would you cut me then? You could chop off a finger for me. This one.' She held up the little finger of the left hand. 'I'll give it to you as a present.'

'Of course I can't do that, my darling. Are you serious?'

'I've been thinking about it all week. I was sure you'd like to have one of my fingers. I was planning to cut one off and send it to you in a letter.'

Huw had never seen her drunk, let alone heard her talk about childhood abuse or such sick impulses. Horrors stampeded through his brain. It was not, could not, be happening. If she were nuts, life would be unthinkable. He would not let her be insane. If he pretended everything was all right, maybe it would be. Once again she reminded him of the Hollywood actress with the enamelled smile. He hoped to God that Owen had heard nothing. With luck, if his music were loud enough, he would not have. Right then Owen loped past them, eyeing the carving-knife in his father's hands with concern. Then, to Huw's relief, he was gone.

'When did your mother do these nasty things to you?' Huw said.

'I've had a bad day. Will you bear with me? Let's go back to the kitchen. I bet I could drink you under the table.'

He led her by the arm. She stumbled, but was not as unsteady as he had feared.

'Is it OK if I have waking nightmares tonight?' she said when she sat down.

'What do you mean? You're worrying me. What's the matter?'

'That's the question, isn't it? Everyone thinks I'm sooooo sane.'

'You are. Probably the sanest person I know.' Until tonight she had been, anyway. That was partly why he had married her, for her balance and serenity.

She gulped the port like a child gulping cola; it dribbled down her chin. 'Oh I'm fucking sane, all right. I'm the best administrator Garson has ever known, she says. Do you know why?'

He dabbed her chin with a tea-towel. 'No. Tell me why.'

'Because I can hear the monsters breathing in the sea.'

'We're hundreds of miles from the sea, you know. I wish I knew what was troubling you. I feel so powerless. I don't see any monsters.'

'I don't see them either. But I hear them.' She chugged her port. 'Gasping for air, sucking it in, sighing. Splashing, struggling to stay afloat. They get tired of swimming all the while, thrashing their tails and bellowing. They tread water.'

'I don't get it. What's that got to do with you being a great administrator?'

'Can't you see? The monsters send me messages. They're real smart.'

'What do the monsters say, Miranda? Do they speak English?'

'Don't patronise me, Huw. I know you think this is crazy. It is crazy. But what if it's true, too? Obviously they don't speak in words. They make high-pitched squeals, like whales or dolphins or submarines. What do they call that, radar?'

'Sonar.'

'Sonar, right, thank you, professor. It's a sort of language. You don't decode it with your mind, the way you do with words; you decode it with your heart. It's like music. An emotional language. I understand the monsters. I'm pretty smart too.'

'I know that. But let's get this straight. You're saying that mythical beasts in the ocean advise you how to run government mental health programmes, and a department at a Medical School. They communicate in submarine squeals, which you understand?'

'You got it.'

'Are you pulling my leg, Miranda? Tell me this is all a joke.'

'Hey, do I ever fuck with you?' Her lips tensed.

'You've got to admit, it's a stretch. Are you trying to tell me that you base multimillion-dollar decisions on what monsters squeal at you in sonar? And if so, how long has this been going on? You know what your therapist would say about these monsters, don't you?'

'That they're projections. That is what he says, you're right.'

'Well, what do you think of that?'

'I know they're projections, but they're real to me. So yeah, I do base my decisions on how I feel when I listen to their songs. It's been going on about four years now, since we lived by the Indian Ocean in Muscat. Remember those days?'

'Of course—they were among the happiest of my life.' In his mind they retained a fairy tale quality. He tried to picture what she had seen at that time as she gazed through the carved lattice-work of the window-screen at the sea. It was silver and black and effervescent. Sailing dhows rode their anchors in the bay, rocking, writhing, plunging and rearing, twisting and turning, anxious to break free from their moorings. On a cliff to the right, the floodlit Portuguese fort had overlooked Mutrah harbour. A full moon blinked like a blind eye as a cloud closed over it and uncovered it again. From behind their two-hundred-year-old house, from the entrails of the city, came the lovestruck cry of the muezzin, atop his minaret. Huw smelled fish, seaweed, spices, baked mud bricks, salt. He did not hear the monsters.

'All right,' he said. 'Let's say the sea-monsters are real. You still haven't told me what happened to you today. Can you? How did your mother hurt you?'

'Oh, that wasn't today. It was a long time ago, in days of yore.' She smiled at the quaint phrase. 'I just remembered today.'

Slowly, painfully, as she drained the bottle, it came out. Her mother had hit her very hard when she was a child; once she had choked her. She had entered the shower when Miranda was bathing, and pulled her pudenda, telling her that one day it would all be loose and ugly. Huw asked if she was sure; Miranda said she was. He wondered why she had never mentioned any of this, how it was possible she had only just remembered. She answered that the memories had been there, but confused, like half-remembered dreams. She had not wanted to think about them. In that case, he asked her, how could she be certain that she was recalling them accurately? She just could, she said. It was up to him whether he believed her.

He did, he told himself, of course he did. He allowed her to finish the bottle, thinking it might soothe her, help her sleep. He escorted her into the bedroom and undressed her. He decided to stay awake and watch over her. To his surprise she fell asleep almost at once, and slept as peacefully as an infant. For hours he gazed at her. But at some point he must have dropped off; he was startled awake by her shuffling back into the bedroom. 'I've just taken a bottle of sleeping pills,' she slurred. 'I'm fine, though. Please let me die.'

And yet she submitted passively to him wrapping her in a dressing-gown and driving her to the hospital. The doctor on duty in Emergencies reminded Huw of a figure in a Persian miniature. Miranda answered her questions like a child. Lunesta, whole bottle. Benzodiazepines. Ten, twenty? Some port wine. Half a bottle.

'Why did you do this?' the doctor asked her gently.

'I'm tired of being sensible,' Miranda said. 'I want to be bonkers now.'

'*In love with lunacy, I'm sick of wisdom and reason*,' the doctor murmured, in English, with a slight accent—but that was Rumi, Huw remembered. They would have to pump Miranda's stomach, she told Huw. Go home and sleep. The doctor's eyes were grave, black, beautiful, and it was shameful of him to notice them, but he could not help it.

'How can I?' he said. 'Can't I stay with her? Why did you do this, Miranda?'

His wife did not respond, but looked up at the doctor, expecting her to answer for her, which she did, in verse again: '*Every storm the Beloved unfurls, allows the sea to scatter pearls*.' She spoke in English, half to herself, half to Miranda.

But when Huw said, 'Rumi again—are you Persian?' the doctor threw him a keen glance. Curious or contemptuous? Was she reproving him for being distracted?

'Go home,' she said with calm authority. 'You may return in the morning.'

He kissed Miranda's forehead, embarrassed, and trudged out.

As he drove home, Tocqueville, with its centuries-old oaks and ashes, its bushes in blossom, and its Craftsman houses, might have represented an American idyll. And yet there was something sinister, something of *The Truman Show* about it—and Miranda, too. He had once overheard Broome loudly describing Miranda to another student, and clearly meaning him to hear, as 'Your typical little Barbie doll.' Was it too much of a strain, keeping up the glossy Instagram image of perfection?

Was this the fatal flaw of American life?

He remembered a summer's day a couple of years ago,

when he and Miranda had climbed Cader Idris back home. She had been solemn and somber, as she often was, but also calm, collected. He pictured her on the crest of the great cliff, the highest and steepest in Wales, without makeup, her face clear and sane. Even then, though, she must have been hearing her sea-monsters. Other odd recollections came to him: that she had confided that when driving an urge to swerve into the path of an oncoming car often nearly overpowered her—he had dismissed it as a joke—and that she had persuaded him to move their bedroom from the upper storey to the lower because upstairs she always had an impulse to hurl herself from the window. Evidently he was married to a madwoman. Could he cope with that? Was that a selfish concern? It was. He would just have to learn to cope with it.

The words that came into his mind were Rumi's. *In love with lunacy, I'm sick of wisdom and reason.* What a relief that might be, to abandon yourself to madness. These days, nearly everyone had surrendered their reason. Half-blind with tears, he wept as he drove. But who was he weeping for—Miranda, or himself? His self-pity disgusted him. *Every storm the Beloved unfurls, allows the sea to scatter pearls.* That was what the doctor said. Had she spoken to console Miranda, or him? But he could not think any further.

His car had made its way back to the blue house, with its covered porch and square white columns. They had bought it because it looked like a writer's house. But now it struck Huw that terrifying things happened in picturesque old houses: witches plotted to murder the innocent, impostors took the place of true brides, stepmothers treated children cruelly, and the hero had to leave home and brave terrible trials. Huw had hoped he would die in this house. Now, as dawn broke and he got out of the car, he knew it was just a temporary refuge.

FOUR

Capital Thought Crimes

In his book-lined study, seated on a buckwheat *zafu* cushion, Melvyn was meditating. Make that trying to meditate. From the lounge came the usual torrent of television din. He was a mild man, but for once peevishness had got the better of him. He had fantasies of yelling curses, switching off the TV, or better still, taking it out with a swift kick. Stifling the negativity—*Remember, the superior man controls his emotions*—he arose from his kneeling posture, took a deep breath, and imagining himself a Zen monk treading on tatami mats, glided—*No*, he edited himself, *prowled*—towards the roaring television. The sitting-room door was open. Of *course* it was. Enthroned on her colossal black leather recliner was Frida, laptop open on her hams, while *Upton Abbey* blasted from the flat screen TV.

'Sup?' said Melvyn, proud as ever of his resonant bass-baritone.

Frida was stabbing the keys in a frenzy, a Nazi wireless operator in an old movie. Caps, exclamation marks. Outrage or feminine solidarity? Both, knowing her.

'Just grading papers. And working on my novel of course.'

She was on Facebook too. 'Of course you are. How silly of me. I wondered if you might be watching television. As the volume is so high, you know.'

She cast an irate glance over her shoulder. 'Hey, *my* gender can multi-task.'

In his gentlest voice he said, 'Psychologists disagree with you there.'

'Yeah, but what do those jerks know?'

Melvyn held his tongue: *The superior man does not speak on impulse.*

Should he politely ask her to look at him? He foresaw her answer: *Can't you just walk around the couch?* He did so, negotiating the obstacle course—a fetid paper bucket of brown sludge from Sundoes, a ziggurat of paperbacks on the pedagogy of Creative Writing, a dog-eared pile of essays or stories, and the even more dog-eared dog, Darcy, unsuitably named, considering his obvious lack of pedigree, asleep at Frida's slippered feet, and nearly as dishevelled as she was. Onscreen, English aristocrats chaffed each other in refined tones, and Melvyn looked down on his wife. Literally. *I guess I shouldn't look down on her,* he told himself, *but I can't help it, after all.*

'Still in PJs, I see,' he said, glancing at his watch. 'At half-past eleven.'

'Don't guilt-trip me, Melvyn. What's the point of being a writer if I can't work in my pyjamas? Huh?'

Striped flannel PJs, bought in London during the mythical epoch of their honeymoon. They were baggy then, and stylish, in an old-school way, on her still-slender body. Now the frayed pant legs were filled like pork sausages. At that unkind simile, bells shrilled in Melvyn's mind. To compare his wife to … that unlucky animal—he repressed its name—was not merely unacceptable, but *unthinkable.* And yet the more thoughts he hacked off, the more grew back, like Hydra heads. Now the image of Napoleon in *Animal Farm* superimposed itself on Frida's face.

People said you could get used to anything, but the disastrous deterioration of his wife's figure still amazed and distressed Melvyn. Traumatised him.

How superficial, he admonished himself, hearing Frida's voice in his head. What about her noble mind, her talent, her idealism? Wasn't that the real her? Again he heard her hectoring inner voice. Maybe he should love her for her personality, but goddamn, her personality sucked too, big time. Besides, there was just *so much* of her body—it was hard to ignore. It billowed and barged and bullied its way into all his thoughts, even the ones he kept covered up in the corners. All righty, then. Be fair. Be *kind,* as Frida might say.

Her hair was no longer a cascade of Jane Austen-inspired curls but shorn, indeed shaven like a storm-trooper's. All the same, her face did retain traces of its former charm. The same low brow and startled, slightly hysterical eyes; the upturned nose, once cute, but now, with the thick gold ring piercing the columella, undeniably, inescapably porcine. His internal editor cut in again: *porcine* was not a word a man could use to describe a woman these days. *Ev*errr! Alternatives? Piggy? Worse. Swinish? *Much* worse. What if you moderated it with an adverb? Sweetly swinish? Prettily piggy? Forget it. He half-expected her to snort. Well, he did. Her lips were pursed. Was she concentrating or just ticked off? Ticked off, of course. He felt like grinning that he had achieved that.

'I've been wondering,' he began. She did not so much as glance up. He took a deep breath. 'Whether you—I mean *we*—shouldn't maybe, uh, start exercising regularly.'

She did snort. Loudly and hoggishly. *Oops. There you go again.*

'You already do. Karate, Tai Chi. You mean me, don't you? But I go to the gym *all the time* too. Last week I went like twice. Well, once, anyway.'

Yes, and dawdled on a treadmill at 1.6 miles an hour, while reading *The New Yorker* and watching Obadiah, he thought, but had the sense not to say aloud.

'We could stand to lose a little weight,' he ventured. 'Don't you think?'

With a great shuddering movement, she turned her pink face towards him.

'You're thin as a stick. You're fat-shaming me. That's misogynistic, Melvyn. Chauvinistic. Toxic. Just fucking say it. You mean I'm fat, right?'

Melvyn was not so dumb as to fall into that trap. No woman was *ever* fat: he knew that. Everyone knew that. 'Of course—not. I'm just talking about our health.'

'Bullshit,' Frida boomed, pitching her powerful contralto even lower. A pity she did not emulate those mellifluous feminine British voices. 'You're talking about our sex life. I'm not dense. You just see me as a sex object.'

You wish, Melvyn told her mentally—a capital thought crime. Unsayable.

'What matters,' Frida declared, 'is not a woman's body but her mind.'

'I've never fully understood that. I mean, I get it that you inherit the genes for your body, so you're not to blame if it sucks, and neither do you deserve praise if you get an athletic one.' *Like mine,* he thought, proud of his awesome, ripped physique. 'But what about your mind? Isn't that just the product of your genes and upbringing too? If you're smart, do you deserve any more admiration than if you have an athletic body? Besides, just how deep are most minds? Aren't they usually kind of superficial too?'

'Maybe *yours* is, Melvyn. So now you're saying I'm superficial?'

She was deflecting again, not answering his main question. Melvyn could not win this argument. He had done his best to admire his wife's mind, but had long ago reached the conclusion that it was unoriginal, lazy, and tribal. Like many academics, she had done her doctorate to convince herself that she was an intellectual. And she clung to the belief that she was one. Clung *fiercely,* she would have said, cliché-monger as she was. She *was* superficial.

'You know I'm not saying that,' he said. *Coward,* he hissed internally.

Frida's meaty elbows poised on the padded armrests. Melvyn feared she was about to lever herself up and lurch at him. But his words mollified her: she sank back into the soft leather with a sigh. 'Anyway, it's all a matter of perspective. I mean our idea of the beautiful. It's just fashion. Look at Rubens' nudes.'

Melvyn called to mind *The Three Graces.* They were statuesque; she was—not.

'Do you know what Rocky said to me yesterday at the reading?' she said.

'Yes, I do.' He recalled Roquette Rathhaus's obsequious Southern face, seething with insincerity, as she came up to Frida. She had hugged Frida with quasi-sexual enthusiasm. 'She said you looked fabulous in that sexy violet velvet dress. She admired the way it revealed your voluptuous curves. I believe that's how she expressed it.'

'Yeah, right. Well?'

Was she inviting him to corroborate Rocky's opinion? *Sure, your curves would appeal as voluptuous—to the guy who carved the Venus of Willendorf.* Yet another thought he had to censor. When did that start, having to police his own mind?

'I see that.' Man, he was a fake, even to himself. 'Sure, it depends on context.'

'I *own* my body,' Frida said, thrusting out her lower jaw like Mussolini.

Her grandfather was an Italian Fascist before he emigrated to Boston, Melvyn remembered. Pencil moustache, mean, thin lips: he had seen the photos. He had killed Abyssinians. She must have inherited her pugnacious expression from the black-shirt bastard.

'*I* think I'm sexy,' Frida went on. 'Besides, I'm American. I'm average here.'

More's the pity, Melvyn was unable to say. Why couldn't she model herself on those slim, fey English ladies on the screen? Why hadn't he married one of them?

'But *you* don't find me sexy anymore, do you?' she said, her voice curdling with menace. The red bristles on her scalp glistened. Her nose ring trembled.

Now he was on treacherous ground. Panic surged in his throat. How might he respond? *I try, God knows, but despite my efforts, those mounds of quivering flesh overwhelm any desire I feel.* No, there was only one acceptable answer: *Of course I find you sexy, darling.* But he couldn't bring himself to lie so shamefully. Instead he hung his head like a naughty boy, hoping she would not press him.

'You only do it in the dark these days, don't you?' Frida insisted. '*Drunk.*'

He sensed that his best course was to maintain silence. But his insurgent thoughts would not be stilled. Why was he yoked to—to this 'female of repellent aspect', as Oscar Wilde might have described her? Because of the girls? They were grown-up now. *Women.* Because of the job? He had tenure. Of course it would be awkward if he and his wife got divorced but remained in the same department. Get to the point, he chided himself. Confront her. Force her to admit her fault. Be a *man.* Be like Bruce Willis. Bruce Lee. Or Clint.

'That's not true,' he mumbled. *Liar, liar, pants on fire!* 'Anyway, I came in to ask you to lower the volume a tad. Surely you could? I am trying to meditate.'

'Meditate or daydream?'

'I do meditate, you know. When I'm allowed to.'

'Geez, why don't you just shut your goddamn door?'

'Mine was shut. Why isn't yours? Ever?' A hellhound awoke in his belly, stretched, stiffened, its hackles rising. It bared its teeth. But he still had it tethered. 'Why must the whole house revolve around you, Frida?'

The scummy brown ponds glimpsed through her granny

glasses got murkier. 'Isn't that obvious?' she said, leaning forward and swamping her laptop with her belly.

It was a pivotal moment. Things were about to be said that would change his life forever. Frida was on the verge of unleashing words she had long yearned to utter, annihilating words. She would not shout. But he knew from the crimson flush on her cheeks, and the quivering nose-ring, that she would be merciless. He remembered a department meeting when a rhetorician she pretended to be friends with had dared to suggest that Frida had undeserved release time. Frida had routed the upstart with murderous invective—in fact the woman had died months later, of a sudden and mysterious illness. Death by rhetoric!

'I have no idea what you mean,' he said.

'What do you actually *do*, Melvyn? Apart from sitting on your ass all day and daydreaming? Huh?' She wobbled, threatening to upset her chair. 'How long have you been writing that so-called novel? When did you last publish anything?'

The hellhound strained at the chain, snarling. 'I might ask you the same question. I have published a collection of poetry and a book of flash fiction, at least.'

'You asshole. You think flash fiction counts? How many articles and essays have I published? How many books? I'm an *authority* on the pedagogy of Creative Riding.'

The hell-hound slavered and lunged. It wanted to bite and rip. Still, he spoke softly. 'Some might say that's a fraudulent subject.'

Her brow burned, bright red. 'Creative Riding is fraudulent?'

'The *pedagogy* of Creative Writing. What do you have to say about it? Be honest: nothing but platitudes. Those who can, do; those who can't, teach.' This was great fun.

Her nose-ring shook. 'I guess that's why you became a professor, then,' she sneered.

'Maybe—but for damn sure it's why *you* became one.'

Her trotters swung off the table on which they had been reposing, and she swept the computer off her lap. She lumbered to her feet, knocking over the foul-smelling coffee, flanks heaving, and lowered her snout—she was about to charge, surely. She was the Empress of Blandings, Lord Emsworth's prized possession in the Wodehouse stories, the stoutest pig in Shropshire. Oh man, if she could read his mind! He would be dead meat.

'All right, you asked for it, wise guy,' she said. 'Why does the house revolve around me? Try this: because *I'm* the director of the Programme. *I'm* the one with the international reputation. *I'm* the full professor. You came into Oxbow State on my coat-tails, and you're tolerated because of me. You're my sidekick. My lackey. My puppet. Have you ever dared vote against me in a meeting, Melvyn, even once?'

He hung his head again, whipped. *Pussy*-whipped. He had not.

'*I'm* in charge,' she said, 'in the department and at home. *I wear the pants.*'

The hellhound wanted to howl, but the chain choked him. All Melvyn could do was nod ruefully. 'You really get off on the power, don't you?'

'Why the hell shouldn't I? Men enjoy it, right? Why shouldn't a woman?'

'Surely it's unseemly to enjoy it for its own sake, whatever sex you are.'

'*Gender*, puh-lease.'

'Whatever. The *I Ching* says Power should be exercised for the good of a community. The superior man does not seek to gratify himself, but benefit others.'

'The superior *man*. Like you, Melvyn? When are you going to get over your dumbass patriarchal hang-ups? What about the superior *woman*?'

'What about her?'

'You just don't get it,' she said with a nasty laugh. 'You're looking at her.'

The words stung like a slap. 'Jesus Christ.' The person

before him was not merely his middle-aged, portly wife, red and vibrating with rage, but also, as she had made him see, a potentate. A petty, narcissistic one, sure—yet a potentate all the same, who wielded real power, in the university and in the heart of his own home. And he had fed this monster.

What could the wounded dog do? Snarl, flail with fangs and claws, maim and murder? How typical of a man that would be, to behave like a beast or a savage.

Whine scathing, sarcastic words, then? They would be harmless, empty. For she had spoken the truth. She had made herself his mistress, or master—whatever—and he had submitted to his thraldom. Because he believed in equality, he had always told himself: now he understood he had deceived himself. He had just been weak. And if there was one quality no woman could stand, however much she protested otherwise, it was weakness in a man. Very well. He would change. Was that possible? According to conventional wisdom, no. The leopard's spots and all that. According to the sacred laws of literary fiction, though, characters could change—*round* characters could, proclaimed E.M. Forster. But could he, Melvyn, behave like a hero in a novel? Could he find strength in himself, redeem his life?

He dared hope so. But what did he want? That was the question he asked in every workshop, of every character. Of course he wanted to leave her. He had longed to for ages but had stayed for the girls' sake. Yes, it went without saying that he would have to go. But underneath that longing was another, darker desire. He would show her who was in charge. Exact his revenge. His wrath would be terrible.

Wagner rumbled in the dark, icy caverns of his mind. He would exult in her utter humiliation. He remembered reading about a study on the cannibals of New Guinea. None of them ever expressed remorse for killing an enemy. On the contrary, years later, they recalled their murders with pride and delight. Melvyn had that primitive streak too. Not that he would slaughter and eat her, of course, heh-heh. But what about that superior man of the *I Ching?* Which was he? Savage or sage?

Darcy stirred and gazed at him with doleful eyes—in commiseration. Darcy knew a whipped dog when he saw one. But even Darcy's pity did not last long: within moments, he was licking his genitals.

Melvyn bared his own teeth in a canine grin. 'Sure, you're the Superior Woman.'

That placated Frida. She turned back to Facebook.

She was scowling and hissing about Huw, some blog post of his. All at once an idea came to Melvyn, devious, delicious, and simple. This was how he could wreak his revenge.

'Enjoying Huw's essay?' he said, his inner cannibal coming to the fore.

Frida spoke through her teeth. 'It's about novelists of genius. All male, of course. Dead *white* fucking males. The goddamn patriarchy. That English asshole.'

'Welsh.' *Twist the blade. Needle her. Make her hate him.*

'Whatever,' she snapped. 'A Welshman is basically a kind of Englishman, right?'

'I guess you're right. Those Limeys are pretty darn smug and snobby.'

'The hoity-toity way he called Savanna a talentless halfwit.' The lurid greens and blues flickering over her face turned her into a troll. 'I could tell he meant me, too.'

Inside Melvyn a joyful fire burned. 'Yeah, maybe. You've always had great intuition, Frida.' That was a lie but the rest was not: 'I have a feeling you'd like to destroy him. You *could*, you know.'

Frida gaped up at him, taken aback: 'Oh yeah, I know.'

Melvyn gloated. 'Will you?' he whispered. Now he knew what Iago felt like.

Frida's eyes were unfocussed: presumably she was imagining future deeds. The fleshy face with its skull-cap of red bristles trembled; the gold-nose ring quivered. 'I just might,' she said, hoarse with desire.

'I bet you could have him fired by Christmas,' he hissed over her shoulder.

Her fingers stubbed her keys. *What about WOMEN?* she wrote, a ghastly operatic grin on her green and blue face. 'I could, but you know what? That's too good for Huw.'

His mouth watered. The slavering of his chops flummoxed and thrilled him in equal measure. Where was the Superior Man now? Who cared? 'Oh yeah?' he said.

'He deserves to be humiliated, humbled, brought to his knees. I can think of ways of tormenting him, of prolonging an excruciating torture.'

Horror and excitement battled in Melvyn's mind. 'I bet. You're *so* creative.'

'Yeah, I am,' Frida said, punching 'Enter'. 'This is going to be so fucking cool.'

Melvyn practically snapped his jaws. He smelled blood. He savoured the tearing of flesh. He would be in at the kill. But for now, he must bide his time.

Softly, like a Buddhist monk gliding on tatami mats, or like Garfield, on his cushioned paws, he padded back to his den. To meditate. The Superior Man knows the meaning of the time. He *would* achieve enlightenment. But not yet, he prayed, please.

FIVE

The Marvels of Modern Science

No one would have dreamed that Miranda had tried to kill herself just days earlier. Of course, she was heavily medicated. Even so, as she sat on a Gustav Stickley settee, wedged between their hosts, Dr Matthew McBane and his wife NeAmber, much too intimately to Huw's mind, Miranda might have been a *Vogue* model. With her hair in a topknot, her pearls—natural ones from her first 'starter' marriage to a dotcom millionaire—and her creamy bosom half disclosed by the décolleté of her velvet cocktail dress, with her white stockings and stilettos, she was flawless, the epitome of the *lady*—an archaic term, but right for the Grace Kelly type, who inspires awe as much as desire. Huw put her on a pedestal, she sometimes complained, which was true. He had always laughed at that, but now he wondered why it bothered her. Was he Pygmalion? Did he adore her simply as an ivory statue of his own creation? If so, he was not wholly responsible. She had once welcomed his adoration—but perhaps no longer. He tried to think of something else.

Huw buzzed about in the McBanes' Prairie style living-room,

sipping Sauvignon Blanc and surveying the oak bookshelves. The complete works of Freud and Jung in black leather, but also Adler, Reich, Rogers, Klein, Neumann and Fromm. The fiction ranged from the Western canon to contemporary North American eminences. There were lots of black women novelists. Dr Matthew was literate or wished to appear so. As was Miranda's other boss, Dr Garson Gneiss, pronounced 'Nice', as she had told him with a hearty laugh. She had come with an effervescent blonde poet named Isabella DiMarzio who unlike Huw was ferreting through the shelves, making fierce, lightning jabs at books that delighted her: verse by Audre Lorde, Sharon Olds and Carolyn Kizer. A triumphant squeal accompanied each strike. But Garson's attention was diverted from her paramour. NeAmber, a woman with the muscular figure of a tennis champion and an indelible grin, had just asked her, in a voice dripping with insincere solicitude, whether Garson's tumour had been analysed yet.

'Oh sure.' Garson sat on a low Mission ottoman. To Huw she looked like Queen Victoria in her later, jowly years. 'It was malignant, all right.'

'I'm *so* sorry.' NeAmber crossed her long mahogany legs with a coquettish glance at Huw, clearly checking that he was watching. He was. She reminded him of a femme fatale in a noir movie. 'So are you going to have surgery?' she said.

Isabella DiMarzio tossed her plaited blonde mane and neighed. McBane snickered, but did not smile. He never smiled. Flat affect? Or just a serious bloke? Miranda gazed at Garson with the veneration of a peasant adoring a statue of the Virgin. Did she always behave like that with her boss, or was it the drugs? And why didn't anyone answer the question?

'What the hell?' NeAmber said. 'You guys know something I don't?'

'Apparently,' her husband said. 'Garson has already had her surgery.'

'That was PDQ,' NeAmber said, her lips contorting almost into a snarl.

The others exchanged smug, knowing looks. Music percolated from the speakers. Classical guitar, carefully curated. Lily Afshar's *Hemispheres*.

Dr Gneiss twirled the stem of her wineglass. 'The surgery wasn't performed by a human doctor,' she said.

'Do you mean the doctors used AI?' Huw said. 'Some kind of robot?'

'No,' said Dr Gneiss. 'The surgeon was alive, but not from our world.'

NeAmber shot a look at Huw. 'What the actual holy fuck?'

'Garson had it done,' said Isabella, pirouetting in her thigh-high boots, her spun-gold hair and lipstick shimmering, and flinging out her arms like a Cossack dancer, 'by an extra-terrestrial surgeon.' A flourish of trumpets seemed to accompany her words.

'You're shitting me,' NeAmber said. 'Huw? What do you know about this?'

'Nothing.' Despite his shock over Miranda's suicide attempt, which had left him emotionally drained, he had to fight the urge to burst out laughing.

In contrast to her voluptuous girlfriend, Garson sat with her knees apart, a squat, rectangular figure, oddly asexual like a pre-Colombian stone goddess, stolid and majestic. 'I've been in touch with extra-terrestrials for years,' she explained. 'I communicate with them telepathically. They have outstanding skills. They're *way* smarter than any human doctors. We have tons to learn from them.'

NeAmber's mouth gaped, pantomiming astonishment, but retained the unnatural grin. 'I'm sorry, but you shrinks fucking slay me,' she said. 'So what did you do, Garson? Call the ET dude on your cell-phone and make an appointment? Where did he carry out the surgery? In a spaceship? A planet in another galaxy? A supernova?'

Garson spoke patiently. '*She*. No, she was able to perform it at my home. And I didn't need to use my phone. I told you already, I communicate with them telepathically.'

'What about nurses?' Huw said. 'Instruments? Anaesthetists?' So dazed was he from watching over Miranda that he doubted he had understood her. Was it an elaborate leg-pull?

'You don't understand,' Isabella said, leaping into the air with her hands above her head. She was in her late thirties, a bit old for such antics. 'She didn't need nurses or anaesthetists, let alone instruments. She could see inside Garson's skull, and she operated by probing with her fingers.' She curled and uncurled hers, a pantomime witch working magic.

'Extra-terrestrials have fingers, then?' NeAmber was clearly enjoying all this.

'Sure they do,' Isabella said, with a talent show smile. 'But she wasn't using them in a corporeal sense. She wasn't there in body.'

'No?' said NeAmber. 'Just, like, in spirit or something?'

'The doctor visited in her astral body,' Dr Gneiss said. 'She used the energy emanations of her fingers, like X-rays or micro-waves. They can penetrate flesh.'

Miranda nodded as if it all made perfect sense. NeAmber shook her head. 'Sometimes I wonder if y'all…' she began. Instead of saying 'are cuckoo' or something, she did not finish, seeing her husband nodding. McBane, with his flaxen curls, puffy pink cheeks and astounded, round eyes, reminded Huw of a gigantic new-born. A cartoon caricature of a baby.

'Did you see her too, then, Isabella?' Huw said. 'The extra-terrestrial surgeon?'

She hesitated too long before replying. 'Sure I did.'

'What did she look like?' NeAmber said. 'Green, four arms and all?'

Isabella glanced at Garson, who replied for her:

'It's impossible to describe an extra-terrestrial,' she said gravely. 'What you do notice is their brilliance. It's like looking at the filament of a light bulb. You can hardly see the wire. We can't properly perceive their physical bodies, if they even have them. They're just a blaze of light to us. Humans have very poor eyesight.'

'What colour are these extra-terrestrials?' Huw said.

'It depends. Blue, mauve, green. At times crimson or orange.'

NeAmber giggled. Huw imagined a psychedelic figure, faceless, a whorl of lurid hues. 'Did it hurt?' he said. 'Having surgery without anaesthesia, I mean?'

'Not at all. You don't need anaesthesia for brain surgery. The brain feels no pain.'

'Amazing,' NeAmber said, stretching and admiring her magnificent legs, which gleamed as if they had been oiled. 'I would never have guessed.'

'Nor I,' said Huw. 'The marvels of modern science.'

Garson's glance was sharp, but finding his face blank—years of dodging fights in Welsh pubs had given him that skill—she relaxed and smiled at Isabella.

'What's really amazing,' the poet said, prowling and sashaying like a model on the catwalk, 'is that the tumour has totally vanished, according to the CT scan.'

'The ET had a CT scanner? A virtual one?' NeAmber said. 'Awesome.'

'Not the ET,' Garson said. 'I had the scan performed at the hospital. On a regular machine. It confirmed that the surgery was completely successful.'

She had either imagined her tumour, Huw supposed, in which case of course there was no trace of it now, or else had really had one but had been operated on by a human, and had convinced herself and the credulous Isabella, that the doctor had been an extra-terrestrial. Huw guessed that Garson would not tell a calculated lie, but she might work herself into a hysterical state. She was *suggestible*, as the lovely Elise had speculated he was himself.

NeAmber had not fallen for a word of it. To her, it was just a hoot. What about Miranda? Her face gave nothing away. *Your typical Barbie Doll,* Broome had described her. Flawless, she meant, empty of emotion or thought. Was that true? Was there a person inside? Of course there was. The poor thing was drugged to the gills. Barely conscious. But was it possible to stay sane when loonies like this surrounded you? Had they infected her?

McBane rose, announcing dinner, offering his arm to Miranda, an antiquated gesture which Huw expected her to reject—yet she stood and took his arm without demur, while NeAmber towered over her on the other side, gloating, bloody gloating—or was Huw so worn out that he was delusional? And if Miranda were just a Barbie doll, a male fantasy, what did that say about *him*? Was he that shallow? Did he love *her*, or had he just been projecting all along? He had to set aside these questions as he was waved to the head of the table, while Garson and Isabella sat side by side to his left, and McBane, Miranda and NeAmber sat in a row to his right. McBane wanted to keep Miranda sheltered, or perhaps imprisoned, between himself and his wife. That must be it: he did not trust Huw too near her. Huw considered making a joke but knew it would fall flat. Americans seldom had much sense of humour, and McBane—like Miranda—had none at all. If Huw protested, he would come across as petulant, and someone would riposte with a jibe about him being lovesick or possessive. All right, he was. Was that so terrible?

They had catered sushi for starters, with a crisp California Pinot Grigio and Paco de Lucía replacing Lily Afshar on the stereo. *Entre dos* Águas, the rumba soundtrack of *Vicky Cristina Barcelona*—chosen to evoke the painter's desires for two women? Matthew quizzed Isabella about current poetry, casting titbits on trendy contemporary fiction to Huw with equal aplomb. NeAmber simmered beside Miranda, speaking sotto voce. Huw had murky inklings. NeAmber's murmurs were conspiratorial, improper—sexual, surely? He picked at the stale sushi with distaste.

McBane asked if Huw had been to Mexico—he had

not—and supposed that he must admire the country's writers, particularly Carlos Fuentes and Juan Rulfo. He did, but it struck Huw as an insidious turn to the conversation. Only last night, Miranda had suggested they visit the country, a proposal Huw had rejected at once.

'Miranda longs to go to the Yucatán,' Matthew said, stressing the first syllable of the province, as Americans usually did. 'I guess you'll be going with her, Huw?'

Annoyed that she had broached the subject with her boss already, Huw said, 'I doubt it. With the wars between the drug cartels, it's far too dangerous.'

Matthew forked sushi into his rubbery infant mouth. 'I disagree. But what a pity. I was hoping you would come with us.'

Mines detonated in Huw's brain. He turned to Miranda. 'What? You're going without me? With *them*? When was all this decided?' She avoided his gaze and did not reply.

'Miranda invited us a couple of days ago,' Matthew said. 'It'll be good for her. Therapeutic. Mayan culture is so rich.'

A couple of days ago? Before she had spoken to him? 'I see,' Huw said. 'I didn't know the plans were so advanced. It would have been nice to have been told. May I ask exactly who's going, Miranda?'

She turned her eyes on him and opened her mouth. But words failed her. Was she unable or unwilling to speak? Or not allowed to? NeAmber spoke up for her:

'Just Matthew and I.' Her eyes sizzled with excitement. Why? Huw's mind did a back-flip. 'Of course Miranda invited Garson and Isabella too.'

'Did she?' Huw said. Miranda had to be quite insensitive—or else devious.

'Yeah, but sadly we can't go,' Isabella said.

'More extra-terrestrial surgery coming up?' Huw said.

Garson glowered. 'Actually, no. Isabella's new book is coming out.'

'*Sappho's Saffron Threads*,' Isabella said with a glittery grin.

'So she'll be going on tour,' Garson said.

'What about you, Garson?' Huw said. He hoped she might go and protect Miranda from the McBanes.

'No, I can't, either. Someone has to run the department with an iron fist. Besides, Mercury will be retrograde next month. I can't risk a trip to a foreign land.'

Now Huw remembered Miranda saying that Garson would only decide on critical issues, like launching new public health campaigns, or writing major grants, after casting a horoscope. He had supposed they did it for fun. Now he suspected that Miranda's sea-monsters and the stars were responsible for all key decisions in the Psychiatry Department.

'Hang on—you're going next *month*?' he said. 'Surely that's a bit rushed?'

'The summer holidays are coming up,' Matthew explained.

'But will Miranda be fit to travel? So soon after her… '

'I can look after her if she needs professional help,' McBane said.

That was what Huw was afraid of. Babyish as McBane looked, there was something sinister about him. The psychiatrist had designs on Miranda—but what kind of designs? NeAmber cleared their plates away, with the help of Isabella, who flitted and pranced, with dance-like gestures, like a fifth century Greek *haetera* on an Attic vase.

'Miranda has suffered a big shock,' Garson told Huw, 'and will need *everyone's* understanding and support.' From the look she gave him, it was clear she meant him.

'I realise that of course,' Huw said, hurt. 'I just wish she'd included me in her plans.'

'She did,' Garson said. 'She invited you, didn't she?'

'I suppose so.'

'I'm sure you could still go with her.'

But Huw was not sure. Nor did he want to. In any case the conversation was cut short when NeAmber and Isabella brought in the second course, kimchee, which looked like tripe and smelled like hot, wet, unwashed socks, although everyone sighed and inhaled its aroma with delight. Meanwhile Paco furiously chastised his guitar, slapping its sides, knocking the top with his knuckles and fingernails, while gypsy women stamped their heels and clicked castanets, and men clapped and shouted in harsh, primitive voices. While Huw tried to eat the revolting kimchee, tears rose to his eyes. Despite his embarrassment, he did not brush them away. To make matters worse, McBane displayed no tact on seeing his distress.

'Are you all right?' he said with professional distance.

'I'm fine.'

'Are you sure? You look like you may be upset by something.'

'I'll be fine.'

'I could give you a Valium,' McBane said.

'No, thanks.' Huw flung a glance at Miranda, hoping she would come to his aid. But she was oblivious of his misery, or indifferent to it. She was talking to NeAmber in low, intimate, happy tones. Huw thought of teenage girls, discussing their dates, or the dresses and shoes they planned to wear for a party.

She had not spoken a word to him since they arrived.

On the stereo a tenor shouted out his pain, while Paco fanned and thrummed and struck the strings and a hail of notes spat at Huw and ricocheted off him.

Those hailstones stabbed his cheeks and stung like hell. *¡Ay, ay, ay, ay!*

SIX

You're So Far Above Me

Thank God, the knock on Melvyn's office door was not the peremptory, pork-knuckled one of his wife—when she bothered to knock at all—but a timid, tentative tapping. Hesitant. Arrhythmic. *Ergo*, a student; a female student, he guessed.

'Come in,' he carolled. He kept the door unlocked but shut to discourage faculty and students who simply wanted to shoot the breeze. Nothing happened. With a sigh, he rose from the deep leather armchair he had bought to impress visitors, and opened the door. Just as he had imagined. Long, straight, mousey hair, parted in the middle, and glasses. She was taller than Melvyn, although he was above middle height. Large-framed, the Kate Winslet type, but not overweight, she shrank apologetically, touchingly, inside her gabardine raincoat, which glittered with raindrops. Familiar somehow. He raised his eyebrows in enquiry.

'Excuse me sir,' she said, not quite meeting his eyes. 'Are you busy?'

'I am,' he said, consciously professorial, 'but this is one of my office hours.' That sounded a tad priggish to him, so he added, 'So of course you may interrupt me.'

'You are so kind,' she simpered, with a flat facial expression that triggered a recent memory. Her voice was familiar too: unusually educated for an OSU student, with the ringing cadence of old money. When he was at Dartmouth as an undergrad, all the co-eds had spoken like that. Still, he could not place her.

'You're not one of my advisees, are you?' he said, barring the doorway.

'No, sir. But I would like to come in. If I'm not bothering you too much.'

He fled behind the barricade of his huge desk and sank into his seat, without holding the door open for her. She shut it after herself.

'Please open that,' he told her. He smelled a delicate, costly perfume.

'Oh, is that a rule?'

'Not exactly. But it is what we call 'best practice.' Male professors keep their doors open to protect themselves from charges of sexual harassment.' *Quite apart from the greater risk of protecting yourself from your jealous wife.*

'Oh, I'm not going to sexually harass you. Not yet, anyway.'

Oh boy, she was dangerous. Weird too: her words were flirty but her expression was not. His laughter came out high-pitched, jumpy. 'Still, I would like you to open that door.'

A vertical crease appeared between her eyes, but she did go back and crack it. Two inches or so. But for sure this chick was too shy to throw herself at him, so he let it go.

'You don't remember me at all?' she said, standing before his one oil painting.

He searched his memory again. 'No, should I?'

'I met you at that reading last week. I sensed that we connected.'

Of course! Now he remembered—not her face, frankly, but

her voice, her manner, and dammit, if he had to fess up, her body. She was the Nike. Those legs. The *red panties*.

'Oh yeah, sure. So um, what did you think of Manley's work?'

'*Work*?' She spoke with the scorn of a Susan Sontag, a true bluestocking—whoops, like co-ed, that was another banned word. 'I found her trite and vulgar. As you must have.'

'Naturally,' he said, flattered. Boy, she was smart. He would have recognised her if she had been showing more of her body, he realised, but as soon as that evil idea struck, Frida's face intruded in his brain, a caricature cartoon, red with rage, bristles on her scalp erect, nose-ring trembling, her nostrils belching steam. He hoped she wasn't monitoring his mind again. Even so, oh boy was he curious to see what lay beneath the student's raincoat.

'You're wet,' he said, at once wishing he had not used such a suggestive word. 'Won't you take off your coat?' Did he sound like he was hitting on her?

'Oh no, I'm fine,' she said, not taking the hint. She gazed at his pictures with the attention of a museum visitor: the reproduction of Waterhouse's 'The Lady of Shallot' above his desk, and the portrait in oils of a lady with an Edwardian chignon, in a gilt Art Nouveau frame—his wedding present for Frida, which she had detested on sight.

'I love to see pictures of women on a man's walls.' Her tone was not flirtatious—or was it? 'I adore the Pre-Raphaelites.'

An undergrad who knew the pre-Raphaelites? 'Thank you.'

'Who is she?' she asked, indicating the portrait with her longish nose.

Embarrassed, he blurted, 'My wife,' although that was stretching the truth.

'Is that so?' she said. She inspected the picture. 'I can't see the resemblance.'

'Well, I bought it because she looked like my wife. Back then. To me, anyway.'

'You must be so in love with her.' Was her tone accusatory? Ironic? Just polite?

In *love* with her? How preposterous! 'She doesn't look like that now,' he said.

'No, she looks very different. How tactless of me, I apologise. Still, as Shakespeare says, '*Love is not love which alters when it alteration finds.*'

'You like Shakespeare?'

'Who doesn't?' She spoke like Sontag again.

'Most OSU students. I can't get my daughters to read him. Or even my wife.'

'Anyone with *intelligence* appreciates Shakespeare.'

Once more, hardly tactful—but he liked her forthrightness.

'He is a Dead White Male, though,' Melvyn said.

'Only a fool would fail to read him for that reason,' she said.

'That would include half of our English Department.'

'Certainly. But I think for myself.'

'So I see. But that's so rare in a university these days. Won't you take a seat?' He waved at the pair of chairs on the other side of his desk. 'And tell me what I can do for you.'

At last she sat, not provocatively—she was wearing jeans, flat pumps, and beneath the raincoat, a cashmere sweater, like the Sloane Rangers of London he had heard about on a TV documentary. *Ladylike*, if that was still a permissible word.

'I have a copy of *Flasher*,' she said. 'I hoped you might sign it for me.'

Although the collection had been published over a year ago, she was the first student—actually the first person—who had appeared in his office with such a request.

'Sure,' he said, with the debonair, dimpling smile he often practised in the mirror, for when he eventually became famous. 'I'd be delighted.'

She carried a briefcase but did not open it. Instead she spoke: 'I think you're brilliant. The equal of the greatest writers.'

Spot-on! The girl was brilliant herself. 'You're a Creative Writing major then?'

'No, sir. A Psychology major.'

That figured: they were always eccentric. 'How did you hear about my book?'

'I have a friend in one of your classes. They told me about it.'

'They? Male or female? Or are they obsolete categories now? You mean Ashley?'

'I'd prefer not to say, sir.'

Her caginess was weird. 'You don't need to keep calling me sir.'

'I'd prefer to. I can't imagine calling you anything else, ever.'

'I do have a name. It's Melvyn.' But what did she mean by that 'ever'? Was she anticipating a lifelong relationship? Planning one?

'I know that, sir. But you are so far above me…' She blushed. 'I feel I can only address you with deference, and to be frank, with awe.'

What a discerning girl she was! 'You are a mysterious young woman,' he said. And a tad nutty? Or was it only the quaint formality that was drilled into Southerners? 'You won't tell me your friend's name, or call me by mine, and yet you want to chat with me, I still have no idea about what. It's all quite intriguing.'

'I'm thrilled I'm intriguing you. I want to talk about *Flasher*. And everything.'

He coughed noisily. 'Let's start with the book. What did you like about it?'

'I loved the sex scenes,' she said, looking him straight in the eye at last. 'They're so graphic and detailed, so insightful. You understand exactly how a woman feels in bed. What she wants. That scene where the vicar and the au pair have sex standing up, and she puts her foot on a chair. I was practically gasping at that one. I found it deeply erotic.'

'It's not meant to be.' What if Frida were to burst in on them now? 'The sex scenes are disturbing, right? There's rape, sadism, manipulation. They're far from porn.' He hated his demure tone. *I'm like Mr Collins in Pride and Prejudice. Prim: priggish. A professorial prick.* 'The sex is there to illustrate how people, especially men, abuse their power.'

'I see that, naturally, that's part of its brilliance. I love the way you are able to analyse a relationship through sex.' She paused. 'I'm going to be a sex therapist.'

The panic button in his brain shrieked. 'Are you kidding?' He gulped, hoping she would not notice his Adam's apple bobbing, out of control.

'I am deeply interested in sex. It's the fundamental human interaction. I feel certain you agree with me, sir.'

'I guess I do…' What the hell was he saying? A *sex* therapist? Could she be on the level? If so, was this an emergency—or the miracle he had been longing for?

Her mouth twitched into a smile, or a facsimile of one. He remembered Olimpia, the beautiful automaton of Hoffman's *The Sandman.* No, she was disconcerting, but maybe just forward. Of course she was gauche. It was not unusual for students to ask intimate questions. Probably her intentions were quite innocent.

'I'd like to be your friend,' she said. Or maybe not innocent at all.

He fidgeted with a pen, unable to answer.

'Could we have coffee some time?' she said.

Are you out of your mind? he thought. 'Sure, why not?' he said.

'You are still married, then,' she said, glancing at the painting, 'to her?'

Surely she knew? Everyone knew the Shamburgers. 'The woman who looked like her, you mean. Frida. Yes, we are still married. For the time being.'

She smiled without showing her teeth. 'Our lives are always in flux,' she said, adding in her haughty New England tones, 'She must have been beautiful. Back in the day.'

'Kind of.' *Cute rather than beautiful. And summer's lease hath all too short a date.*

'You deserve a beautiful woman who can make you happy.'

Absolutely! 'Heh-heh, I guess I do. You're so—'

Sensitive, shrewd and smart? Or deranged, ditzy and dicey? She was not like the usual coquettes angling for higher grades, with their languid smiles and drooping eyelids, but she was definitely suggesting… something. Or was he just being paranoid? Probably the girl was just awestruck that he had published a book. How many authors could she have met? He reminded himself that she had asked for his autograph, that was all.

'Yes?' she prompted him. 'You were saying? I'm …'

'You remind me of the Nike of Samothrace. You want me to sign that book?'

She fished it out of her briefcase. 'Thank you so much, I *adore* that statue.'

Wow, she actually knew Greek culture too. 'I wish you wouldn't call me sir.'

'Sorry, sir.' The cover photo was of a woman, shot from behind, wearing a raincoat, which she held open, flashing someone. Did that explain *her* raincoat?

He turned to the title page and crossed out *Melvyn Shamburger III*. 'Who shall I make it out to? What's your name?'

'You mean my real name?'

His pen hovered like a fly above the page. 'Don't tell me you have aliases?'

'Sure. I despise the real one. And maybe it's better for you not to know it.'

Oh boy, she was trouble, all right. 'I guess it's up to you which name you go by.'

'Call me Jezebel. Guess whether it's the real one or not.'

'I imagine it's not,' he chuckled.

To Jezebel, my mysterious, appreciative reader, he wrote. *I am glad you found these stories*—he considered 'enjoyable' or 'interesting' but rejected both and settled on '*stirring*'. With a further hint of flirtatiousness, he ended: *Good luck in your future career! Yours,* and signed with a squiggle resembling Arabic calligraphy, and many dots and flourishes.

'Will that do?' he said, handing the book to her, open at the inscription.

'Oh yes, sir, thank you, that's wonderful.' She held the book to her chest as if she treasured it. But then, unfortunately, still far away, but approaching fast, came the foghorn blasts of Frida's voice. Melvyn went into lockdown mode.

'I better get back to work,' he said. *And get the timebomb out of here.*

'Yes, sir. Can I email you about having coffee?'

Better make an excuse: it was near the end of term, he was busy, maybe not a great idea, on reflection. Anything. Avoid any compromising situations.

'Sure,' he said. The blasts of the klaxon were close—when had Frida started to shout all the damn time? He stood and flailed, off balance. Jezebel stood too and held out her hand for him to shake. Irreproachable. She was not gorgeous, but statuesque. Not that he found her hot. Not at all. Not a bit. As she left, he cringed behind his desk, awaiting the collision.

A final blare presaged the crashing of the door into the wall, and cracked plaster, and there stood the Empress of Blandings, bristling, steaming, her snout lowered to charge:

'Who the hell was *that*, Melvyn?'

Oh no—she only used that snorty tone when she was suspicious or angry. 'Just a student,' he said, hunkering behind his desktop screen.

Frida's grunted: 'I smell cheap, vulgar scent. Sheesh!'

Keep your head. Don't contradict. Distract, divert, deflect. Be a politician. Sidetrack. Stir her up. He stammered, 'Uh, seen Huw yet today?'

Frida's low brow crinkled and darkened. 'Him! You'll never guess what he's been up to! I am going to nail him so good!' Smoke smouldered around her nostrils.

Melvyn fought back a snicker. *Whew, that was a close call. Well done, guy!*

SEVEN

The Phallocentric Canon

Huw always pedalled his racer like Geraint Thomas chasing the yellow jersey in the Tour de France—but since Miranda had set terms on their relationship, had her breakdown, attempted suicide, and arranged to go to Mexico with the McBanes—since his life had begun to unravel a couple of weeks ago, he had been sprinting on his bike yet more swiftly, trying to overtake his grief and anxiety. Skimming the smooth black roads of Tocqueville, brushing the white and pink blossom that overhung them, phrases curled and leapt beside him, inside him, beneath and above him, hissing, thundering. All he had to do was hold on, keep his balance, his mind clear and empty, and ride the wave. Sentences sizzled as he surfed through another tunnel of trees. Once again the power was upon him, the sacred power of the bardic tongue and the earthier one of the invaders, intertwined. They seized his heart and spirit, turned the world into a glorious blur, and Huw knew his writer's block was broken.

Then a camouflaged pick-up flicked past, nearly clipping him, with its horn blowing and mad, male shouts. Out of the windows hung naked torsos, and tattooed arms, shaking fists and beer cans. A moment of terror turned into fury. Huw yelled a Welsh curse and tore after them. But he could not hope to catch them, and what if he did? They were four, he was one; they were in their twenties, he was nearly fifty.

Besides, the swirling waves of Welsh and English had retreated, and he was on dry land again, approaching the university. Could he remember that passage vouchsafed him, straight from the teeming tongues of his ancestors? Thank Christ, he could. He began reciting as he rode, to memorise it, in a loud, exultant chant.

But disaster struck again. As a saloon car passed, a woman leaned out of the front passenger window. 'Get a fucking car!' she roared. A *woman*! He flipped her off—the indispensable gesture in American traffic. Millennials were tolerant, supposedly, and yet it was white youths who always mobbed and menaced him on his bike. What was more, the car was an Audi, driven by the lovely Elise, he saw, as it turned into the car park. Worse still, rack his brains as he might, the miraculous passage he had been reciting had quite vanished. Not a wisp, not a word, was left. Cursing in Anglo-Saxon terms now, he dismounted by the pedestrian crossing. Even so, he had to jump aside to a swerving SUV. The driver was Frida and she was texting. No one was paying attention to anything that mattered.

When he reached the classroom after leaving his bicycle in the empty rack, he found his students not chatting as students had done in his day, but scrolling through social media or texting on their smart phones. They leaned against walls, lolled against pillars, or sprawled on the floor. Elise sat on this far from spotless surface in one of her fetching mini-kilts, fingers jabbing phone keys, knees drawn together in a concession to modesty, although her ankle-length suede boots were wide apart. Her posture offered a splendid view of her legs to anyone lounging nearby on the floor, and yet not a single guy, some of whom must have been straight—surely?—nor the lesbians, Jordan in her denims, and her girlfriend Nutmeg, in her short shorts, or the transgender student, Trudy—no, Truman, Truman, he reminded himself—was flirting with her. Or even noticed her. What the bloody hell was wrong with them?

'Good morning,' he said. As usual, no one replied. Not even Elise.

The only student who made eye contact with him was Walt, the podgy boy with the piping voice and supercilious smile. 'They're like *ants*,' he said.

His tone invited a sardonic smile or a mordant comment. Huw winced: let the lad interpret that how he would.

Nonetheless, Walt's classmates were less comatose than they appeared. Charleston glanced up from his tablet and snapped:

'As a matter of fact, boy wonder, I'm working for the downfall of your class.'

Walt shot a bittersweet, patrician smile at Huw. *You see?*

'And I'm writing a piece for *The Siren* on the LGBTQIA+ community,' murmured Jordan. 'Maybe I could interview you?'

Walt disdained to reply. He was indeed gay, Huw suspected, but not out.

'Me, I'm researching organic farms in the state for a project,' said Nutmeg.

Huw unlocked the door. Elise sprang to her feet in a single, fluid movement.

'I was checking how many likes I got for my new profile picture,' she said.

'I rest my case,' Walt said, with a jubilant glance at Huw.

'Eight hundred ninety-three,' Elise said. 'Damn, I can do way better than that.'

'Let me see,' said Truman, flushing violet. 'Gosh, Elise, you look gorgeous.'

Hear, hear, Huw mentally congratulated Truman—although she, or rather he, he, he, had not dared look the President's daughter in the eye.

Once seated, after the customary complaints about

rearranging the seats—Huw insisted on a half-circle, while they preferred rows—the students crumpled in their chairs.

'You all look so eager to discuss literature today,' Huw said.

'We don't *mind* talking about novellas,' Jordan said. 'Like, we don't hate it.'

'But we prefer to watch the movie versions,' said the tall, curly boy who had just sauntered in and whose name Huw could never recall, Frank or Hank.

'What we don't get,' Jordan said, 'is why there are no women on your syllabus.'

'Surely it's not all dudes?' said Truman. 'I'm so done with the patriarchy.'

Huw crouched behind the enormous monitor on his desk. 'I'm surprised that this question is only coming up now,' he said. 'Didn't you read the syllabus earlier?'

'Hell no,' Hank or Frank said. 'No one reads shit like that.'

'If you don't,' said Huw, 'then surely you don't have the right to object?'

'We have read it now,' said Jordan. 'Leastways, I have. Could you just answer the question, please? Why aren't there any women on the syllabus?'

'I had two criteria when I chose the texts. First, they had to be under fifteen dollars. I couldn't find any novella collections by women at that price.'

'There's nothing by African-American authors either,' Charleston said.

Huw said, 'True. But not all the authors are white. There's an Asian and a Latin-American. And García Márquez did have some African ancestry.'

'They all had penises, though,' Jordan said.

'Presumably,' Huw said. 'Though I was under the impression that one's genitalia is no longer considered a useful criterion for determining gender? Isn't it a social construct?'

Everyone glanced at Truman, who flushed purple. 'Sure, right,' he said.

'Are you trying to tell us some of those dudes identified as women, or were gender-fluid?' Jordan asked Huw.

'Of course not. Look, there are excellent novellas by African-Americans and women, and by African-American women. I could give you a reading list. I will.' He hesitated, aware that the words he planned to say were potentially explosive. 'But my second criterion was that the novellas had to reach the very highest standard—be worthy of the canon. That's why I chose collections by Tolstoy, Chekhov, Mann, García Márquez and Kawabata.'

Jordan's sigh sounded like a punctured tyre. 'That's cool beans that you considered the cost. Most profs could care less. And I dig it that these dudes are all awesome writers—except maybe that one Japanese guy, who's super creepy…'

'*Eeew,*' said Elise. 'Totally.'

'But,' Jordan went on, lying back, legs spread, with the confidence of someone who knew she was the most gifted student poet, 'the canon is phallocentric. And very white.'

'Cultural imperialism,' Charleston intoned. 'Colonialism. White oppression.'

Huw was about to object that García Márquez and Kawabata could hardly be accused of that, but Jordan forestalled him: 'The tyrannical patriarchy,' she said.

'I just wish you would have included at least one woman,' said Broome.

'And a black dude,' said Charleston.

'And like a lesbian,' said Nutmeg.

'Or a gay guy,' said Walt helpfully. 'Or someone who self-harms.'

'What about a pedo?' said Frank or Hank, smirking. 'Or a trannie?'

'We don't say that word!' Jordan said. 'And you know it.'

'I don't give a damn,' Frank or Hank said. 'Well? Would you like to see transsexual—excuse me, trans*gender*—writers represented, Trudy?'

'*Truman*,' Jordan hissed. 'Asshole.'

Truman turned a rich shade of mauve. 'I would like that, yeah.'

'Do you see my predicament?' Huw said. 'Must I include every minority? And in direct proportion to their percentage in the US population? If so, how many Chicanos must I include? How many women Chicanos? How many lesbian, bisexual, or trans Chicanos? And the same with native Americans, Jews, Islanders.'

'We don't expect perfect proportional representation,' Jordan said.

Huw stood up, suspected his flies were open, and fell back into his chair behind the desk so he could check. No, they were done up. He stood again, wished he were taller, nearly sat down once more, but instead left the shelter of his desk to strut in front of the class, in the manner of an officer giving a briefing. Except that he was under fire. Friendly fire.

'I have a question for you,' he said. 'Dr Roquette Rathaus teaches a course in which all the poets are women. Does anyone object to that?'

The students were silent and their faces blank—all except for Frank or Hank, who cackled. 'Yeah, anyone pissed at that? And what's-his-face, the prof who wears Hawaiian shirts. The dude with the ponytail and the man-boobs.'

'Luke?' Walt said. 'That's fat-shaming.'

'Yeah, Lucky Luke. All the writers in that dude's creative nonfiction workshop are fags, dykes, or trannies. No kidding, man. Not one normal dude.'

The students emitted groans, grunts, growls, snarls and hisses.

'You may not approve of the bigoted vocabulary,' Huw said, 'But I notice no one denies the substance of his claim. And yet when I draw up a single syllabus featuring only male writers, there's practically an insurrection.'

'Say what?' Elise susurrated.

'Rebellion,' Jordan explained. 'But that's different,' she went on in a tone that reminded Huw of ministers in Welsh chapels. Sanctimonious. 'Luke and Rocky are redressing centuries of repression by the patriarchy. Whereas you are just reinforcing it.'

'I don't accept that. My intention wasn't political. I just wanted you to read the best novellas available.' Surely he had won the argument now? The disgruntled faces and body language—crossed arms and legs, torsos turned away, eyes averted—suggested otherwise.

'All right,' he said. 'You win. What if we add a woman to the syllabus?'

'*One*?' Broome boomed as if she were copying Frida.

'Unless you're willing to buy several new textbooks.'

'I just don't want to do any extra work,' Elise said.

'We could drop *House of Sleeping Beauties*, if you all find Kawabata creepy?'

'Gross,' said Nutmeg. 'But who would we read instead?'

'How about Muriel Spark? *The Prime of Miss Jean Brodie.*'

'Where's she from?' said Walt.

'Scotland.'

'White, obviously?' Charleston said.

'Not all Scots are white, Charleston, but I'm afraid Muriel Spark was.'

Charleston scowled—playfully, though. The lad had a sense of humour.

'Many Scots consider themselves oppressed,' Huw said. 'Like the Welsh.'

'Give me a break, man,' Charleston said.

'Our languages were banned,' Huw said. 'The Irish were starved.'

'Yeah, but not enslaved,' Charleston said.

'Actually, many Irishmen were sent to the Carolinas as indentured servants, practically slaves,' Huw said. 'But certainly it was worse for Africans.'

'Why don't we read a novella by an African-American woman?' Jordan said.

'How about Nella Larsen's *Passing*?' Huw said. 'It's about light-skinned women who manage to pass for white during the Harlem Renaissance. What do you think?'

The entire class voted to replace Kawabata with Larsen, except for Walt, who complained about the extra cost, and Elise, who had already read Kawabata and did not want her work to go to waste, and Frank or Hank, who did not explain, but sneered eloquently.

'Good,' Huw said. 'And now I hope we can leave identity politics behind and talk about literature and writing for a change.'

The novella up for discussion was *Death in Venice,* which he had picked for its imagery and symbolism, its flawless structure, and masterly use of exposition—and also, admittedly, because its subject matter was a homoerotic obsession, which he expected would please the LGBT members of the class. But he was wrong. Although Jordan said she dug it, Walt demurred, objecting to the portrayal of Aschenbach as a 'pedo'. Nutmeg said he was a Kevin Spacey type guy, and he disgusted Broome because he was not in control of himself. Huw pointed out Mann's philosophical underpinning in Nietzsche and Schopenhauer, but the students were unable to grasp the concept of determinism. Elise said it was just an old-school story about snooty Europeans, and like, who cared? Charleston jumped in: You could read it as a critique of bourgeois decadence, not as Marxist as García Márquez's *No-one Writes to the Colonel,* but clearly influenced by Weber. Huw pressed him for more.

'Give me a break, dude,' Frank or Hank said, 'it's just a story about *faggots.*'

'Homosexuals, puh-lease,' Walt said.

'I object to that term,' Truman said. 'It's homogender. The patriarchy just perpetuates the concept of biological sex to keep women and the other genders in subjection.'

Frank or Hank bellowed. 'How many are there? I thought there were two.'

'At least a hundred,' said Truman. '*Hello?* Everyone knows that.'

'That why you decided to buy a dick at the clinic and become a dude, then?'

'Let's focus on commenting on what she said,' Huw said, but although Frank or Hank's face wore a malignant grin, silence fell like a hard frost over the class. Jordan crossed her arms and glared at him. 'What?' Huw said.

'You said *she*,' Jordan said. 'Truman wants us to use male pronouns.'

Huw flushed. 'Did I say that? I'm sorry, Truman. It wasn't deliberate. It's just that for the last two years we were all calling you *she*, and sometimes I forget.' The apology fell on deaf ears. Jordan continued glaring, and Truman had a blank, autistic stare. The class was back treading the well-worn paths of identity politics, patriarchal oppression, and victimisation. Outrage at Huw's insensitivity ran high. His attempts to steer the discussion back to language and literature proved fruitless. Still, he consoled himself as the class collapsed, he had defused the unrest over the preponderance of male authors on the syllabus. The inclusion of Nella Larsen guaranteed that, surely?

While he reminded the students of their homework, Broome, the 'mature student' and former model, rushed out like someone fleeing a crime scene, in spite of her size, knocking Jordan and Nutmeg aside as if they were bowling pins. Elise advanced with a bold air. When she reached his desk she stood there with an expectant look. He had to speak first.

'I hope you're not upset about the paucity of women writers on the syllabus.'

'I'm not sure what that means. Something about women writers in poor cities? No, it's all good. I don't really give a shit, you know? I mean, sure, if Jordan and Nutmeg and the rest make a fuss I'll join in, because of feminine solidarity and all. But it's no biggie, right?'

'What is a big deal to you, Elise?'

She gave him a long look, which might have been a come-on. 'You know, fashion, lifestyle. Making it. Becoming someone. I got my own YouTube channel, you know.'

'Good for you,' he said, but it sounded condescending.

'Thanks, I've got twelve thousand followers. I was wondering if you've reconsidered my offer to read your fortune' Her gaze was deep, unflinching. Did she mean to tempt him?

The last of the students had trooped out. Huw wavered, flattered. And worn out from stress—the indignation over the 'phallocentric' syllabus, the thugs threatening him from the pick-up, and that woman screeching at him. She had been in Elise's car, he remembered.

'Who was that girl who screamed at me as you passed me in your car this morning, Elise? Women don't usually do that. That was you driving, wasn't it?'

'Yeah, sorry. Sorority sister. It was lame. She's a hick, you know? I'm real sorry.'

'I don't understand why it infuriates Americans so much to see me cycling.'

'I guess they think you look like a pussy.'

He laughed. 'Hardly a politically correct term, is it? All right. I don't believe in it, but you can tell my fortune. How do you do it? With cards?'

Her steady look almost *smouldered.* 'No. Give me your right hand.'

After a second's hesitation, he did so. She took his hand firmly, and with her index finger traced the lines, hollows and mounds of his palm. Huw hoped she would be brief.

'I've never seen a hand like this before. A *very* prominent Mount of Venus, criss-crossed by dozens of lines. Hundreds, oh man. You are a totally awesome lover. You have a strong tendency to promiscuity, a need for instant gratification. Right?'

'I *was* a bit of a womaniser, once, a long time ago.'

'Your heart line is very long, and curvy. You express your feelings easily and are happy with your love life.'

'I am.' Was that still true, though? And should he have admitted it?

'Your headline is deep and long; you think clearly and logically. But it's also curved. You're super creative.'

'If I weren't, I'd be in the wrong profession, wouldn't I?'

'Your lifeline is long, deep and curved too. You're full of vitality.' She looked up at him, meaningfully. 'On the other hand, your fate line isn't so strong. You've controlled your life pretty much, up to now. Maybe too much.'

'What do you mean? Surely being in control is a good thing?'

'You shouldn't plan so much. Sometimes you have to let things happen. Your hand is square, the fingers short: that shows impulsiveness, creativity. You're impatient and *very* highly-sexed.'

'My sexual appetites seem to feature rather prominently in this reading.'

Instead of making a flirty rejoinder, she said, 'Just a moment. Let me look at your lifeline again. I don't like to say this, Huw, but I see several catastrophic events.'

She had called him by his first name. Not only did her insight ring true—but if it were all a game, why would she reveal anything unpleasant? Didn't fortune tellers usually say what people wanted to hear? Unsettled, Huw began to believe her, although he was conscious of his inconsistency: only last night, at the McBanes', he had felt that the astrology and other esoteric practices of Miranda and Doctor Gneiss were absurd.

'Catastrophic events?' he said.

Elise's lips twitched. 'You know, divorce, losing your home or your job, life-threatening illness, that sort of thing. Shit, maybe all of those. Yeah. I'm sorry.'

He tried to smile, but queasiness overcame him. She stroked his palm with her index finger. 'And when will these catastrophes befall me?'

'I can't say exactly. But in mid-life. Oh, man. Right about now, actually.'

At that moment in the corridor came a ponderous, elephantine thumping. Stertorous breathing, an indrawn whistling wheeze, followed by a grumbling moan. Then a snare-drum crack, as the door smashed into the wall. They both froze.

There, filling the doorframe, and jammed in it with the biggest and fullest tote bag he had ever seen, was a crimson humanoid, scalp bristling, fleshy bare arms juddering, dragons flapping their scaly wings, her mouth open in shock and horror and the thick golden ring in the snout quivering with indignation. She smelled of steam, smoke, and stale coffee.

'Morning, Frida,' Huw said, his hand still clamped in Elise's. 'How are you?'

Frida forced herself through the doorway, snatching at the bag, snorting and panting.

'How am I?' she began, with a dangerous Diamondback rattle in her throat. 'I'm fine. What I want to know is how *you* are, and what you imagine you're doing.'

Huw prised his hand out of Elise's. 'Elise was just reading my palm,' he said.

Elise nodded. 'Right, Dr Mrs. Shamburger. I have awesome psychic abilities.'

'Is that so?' Frida said, turning to Huw: 'Don't you think it's a tad indiscreet, holding hands with a student here, when anyone might happen along?'

'It was innocent, Dr Mrs. Shamburger,' Elise offered, with the self-assurance of being the President's daughter.

'I'm sure it was, Elise. *On your side.* Thanks, you can go now.'

Elise flounced out, tossing her hair over her shoulder, offended. How dare Frida dismiss her like that?

'As for *you*…' Frida began.

'Give me a break. I was just—'

'I know exactly what you were doing. Teaching male authors.

Male, *cis*gender, *heteronormative* authors. Aren't you ashamed? Not one single woman!'

How could she have heard so quickly? Then Huw remembered Broome barging her way out of the classroom a few minutes ago.

'You have a spy in my class.'

Frida did not answer. Huw insisted: 'Do you deny it? Who is it, Broome?'

'I can't tell you who told me. She just told me what's going on. As the director of the program, I have a right to know what's taught in the classrooms. You told them there were no women who have written good novellas.'

'I did not. I told them there are excellent novellas by women. Broome is a liar.'

'Or *you* are. Anyway, there are tons of women you could be teaching.'

'*Tons*?' he said, but she failed to catch his sardonic tone.

'Yeah, tons who are as good as the white males in the canon. Better.'

'I don't only have white men on my syllabus. But OK, who do you suggest?'

'Sandra Cisneros, *The House on Mango Street*.'

'Not a bad book, but surely it's a collection of linked stories?'

'All right then. Marguerite Duras,' (she said, 'Margaret Dure-ass') '*The Lover*.'

'Hardly up to the standard of *The Death of Ivan Ilyich*, is it, or *Death in Venice*?'

Frida lurched at him. 'That's your opinion.'

'Obviously it's my opinion,' he said, stepping away from her. 'What a fatuous thing to say. Who else's would it be? Perhaps you expect me to express your opinions?'

She bent one of her legs, which were encased in leggings, and pawed at the floor. She lowered her head. Huw braced himself for a clumsy charge. Her bare, full-sleeve tattoo arms rose higher and higher. Would she wallop him with those massive hams?

Beads of sweat glistened on her brow. Her tiny pondwater-brown eyes were bloodshot.

'I expect you to teach people who represent our students,' she said with a grunt. 'It's our responsibility to teach authors they can identify with.'

'Then I should be teaching a majority of immature, poorly-educated authors who spend their time playing video games, sexting, and smoking marijuana. And since virtually all our students are white and middle-class, presumably our syllabi should reflect that too? As yours does, in fact. Doesn't it?'

She snorted and her nose-ring quivered. 'You've been looking at *my* syllabi?'

'For instruction, naturally. You teach nearly all white, middle-class American women writers, don't you? Authors of a similar background to your own, in fact.'

'I don't believe it. Are you daring to criticise me?'

'I'm pointing out a fact. But you are daring to criticise me. And spy on me.'

'How dare you say *dare*. I'm the frigging director of this programme.'

'And I'm a tenured professor. So I have complete autonomy over the content of my syllabi, provided I teach the course content. And I prioritise quality of writing over identity issues and social justice. I happen to think that's more important for creative writing students. I know that's not fashionable. But it's my prerogative.'

Frida lowered her head again, apparently on the brink of charging.

He went on: 'What's more, I respond to student complaints and suggestions. I have just added a woman writer to the syllabus. Did your spy tell you that?'

'No,' Frida said, but realised her mistake at once. 'She's not a spy. Who?'

'Nella Larsen,' Huw said. Frida looked blank. 'Do you know her?'

Frida frowned. 'Of course. I mean, not in depth. Isn't she from Minnesota?'

'She was black. Or rather of mixed ethnicity: Danish father, black mother. From Curaçao. How many African-Americans do you teach, Frida?'

Frida's neck folds juddered, but she did not answer.

'Do you teach any at all, Frida? How about Latin Americans? Asians?'

'Fuck you, Huw,' she said as she stomped towards the door.

When Huw got up to the third floor and passed Melvyn's vast corner office, a girl in a dripping wet raincoat was slipping out of it. Furtively. Huw entered his own office, fell into his chair, wishing he had not been so abrasive with Frida, ignited his desktop computer—and saw hundreds of emails awaiting him, many marked 'urgent'. But one howled for attention. Its subject line, all in caps, and terminating in a thicket of ejaculatory spears, read:

ALLSTRAIGHTMALESONYOURSYLLA-BUS!!!!!WHY????!!!!!!

Frida had dashed that off before clomping down the stairs. Beneath was one from Miranda, also bellowing:

PSYCHOTIC SPELLS MAY BE HOME LATE DON'T WAIT UP.

He took a deep breath to calm himself. On his desk was a framed photograph of Miranda, her hair pulled into a topknot, her face powdered, white as chalk, her lips red as strawberries, her neck and shoulders bare, vulnerable—in the same pose, maybe consciously, as the actress in the poster for *White Swans*, and with the same deranged air. Were those blue lines on her forehead blood-vessels, or cracks in the china? *Pull yourself together*, he told himself. *For her sake and Owen's. Can't afford to lose your job now. Will she keep hers? Just read the bloody thing.* Outside a chopper's rotors churned, flattening the treetops. He had the sensation that some figure in the ether was watching him. Was he under surveillance?

Having hallucinations, sea-monsters paddling in muck in my office. Psychiatrist recommends committing myself. I'd prefer not to. Garson thinks I should. Matthew doesn't think I need to. Invited me to his house tonight for dinner. Sweet of him. Sea-monsters told me to accept. One of them has a beard and reminds me of my dad. So I guess I'm going. - Andamir

No salutation, no 'love', and the odd, misspelled name. A mistake, or some kind of joke or puzzle? It was an anagram, so maybe the latter. What did she mean? That her identity was confused, back-to-front? An internet search came up with nothing. More troubling was the news that she was hallucinating again, and that her psychiatrist and Garson, admittedly not the sanest mental health professional herself, recommended urgent in-patient treatment, which would mean heavy sedation. Equally troubling was the news that Matthew had invited Miranda to his house—just her, apparently. And she had accepted. Hadn't she considered his feelings at all? Just weeks ago he was happy. *Cachu hwych*, he said. It was all fucked now.

He wanted to roar, strap on armour, hack McBane and Frida to pieces. *Coc y gath*[1].

1 Lit. 'The cat's prick'. An expression of dismay similar to 'Fucking hell.'

EIGHT

It is the Young Fool Who Seeks Me

Melvyn stood on the doorstep, unable to ring the bell. Jezebel's house was a McMansion with proliferating gables and roofs, windows of all shapes and sizes, disproportionately colossal porch columns, and a round tower with a witch-hat roof—but its tackiness was not the reason for his hesitation. Although Jezebel had promised her father would be out, now that he was here, Melvyn lacked the courage. Or did he have a genuine conscience? What would the Superior Man do in this situation?

He clutched his cell phone like a talisman. He pulled up an *I Ching* app, typed in the question, Should I enter? and came up with the fourth hexagram, Immaturity, Youthful Folly. *It is not I who seek the young fool. It is the young fool who seeks me. At first, I inform him with clear answers; but if he importunes, I tell him nothing. He must persevere to succeed.* The young fool had to be Jezebel, making allowances for the misogyny of the ancient Chinese sages. Not him. Obvs. He had one moving line, the third one. *Like a foolish girl, throwing herself away, a weak, immature man…* That could not mean him either. *As a girl owes it to herself to wait until she is wooed, so also it is undignified to offer oneself. Nor does any good come of accepting such an offer.* This was a tad confusing. Was the *I Ching* counselling him to desist? He consulted the second hexagram indicated by the changing line. Number 18, Removing Corruption. The Condition read, *Guilt is implied.* The Judgement added, *Inner weakness, irresolute drifting, combined with outer inaction, inertia and rigidity, lead to spoiling.* Jeez, couldn't those mandarins have been a bit less ambiguous? On the one hand, they told him not to offer himself; on the other, they said inaction led to corruption and guilt. So what was he to do? He stood paralysed, aware that anyone in a car might recognise him and have suspicions about a man loitering outside a McMansion, on a school day.

He had an itch to relieve himself so overpowering that he considered unzipping and letting go, right there on the doorstep. *Be a man*, he told himself. He raised his hand and made a martial arts fist. He could totally punch a hole through the front door, splinter it, smash it to smithereens. Or simply knock it. He let out a high-pitched, ferocious scream. His fist did not move. The damn thing just stuck there, frozen. *I'm a cartoon character, a jerk. I'm Mr Magoo.* His arm wilted, like… like—well, it was better not to think about what it wilted like. Defeated, he turned to go.

At that very moment, the door opened.

'Yes?' asked a woman's voice—but not Jezebel's. He swung round to face her. It was a real, honest-to-God adult woman, forty or so, in totally bodacious shape, yet old enough to be Jezebel's mother. Oh, my God. *Was* she her goddamn mother?

'I'm here,' he began, but stopped abruptly. How could he explain that Jezebel had invited him? Not only was it 'inappropriate', but also, he realised now, he did not even know her real name! 'I'm here… ' he repeated, stalling again.

'Yes, I can see you're here,' the woman said, eyeing him with amusement. 'I heard the blood-curdling scream. Like Kung Fu fighters make in those old movies, you know? Are you all right? You haven't injured yourself?'

'Oh no,' Melvyn said hurriedly. 'I just uh, stubbed my toe on the uh, step.'

'That sucks. Maybe you've broken it. Want me to examine it? I'm a nurse.'

'You're a nurse?' She looked like a *Playboy* playmate.

'Sure, why shouldn't I be?'

'Are you—' *Jezebel's mother,* he wanted to say, but could not without giving the game away. He started again. 'I'll be OK. You see, I was invited here, by, by—'

'My sister,' the woman said, smiling broadly.

'Your sister? You're her *sister*?' Cool it, he told himself. Like the Fonz.

'Sure, why shouldn't I be? Oh, do I look too old to be her sister?'

'No, of course not. But she never told me she had one.' Unsurprising, really—even though Jezebel was much younger, her sister was far prettier.

'You'd better come in. You're—I've forgotten your name. Is it McDonald? Something to do with hamburgers, right?'

'Shamburger,' Melvyn said testily, as always when anyone teased him about it. 'It's actually an ancient German name. Nothing wrong with it.'

'Of course not,' she said, holding out her hand like a man, and pumping his with masculine strength. 'Shamburgers are tasty. Once in a while. I'm Delilah.'

'*Delilah?*' His voice cracked with incredulity.

'Why shouldn't it be? You sure do repeat a bunch of things, Mr Shamburger.'

'*Dr* Shamburger,' Melvyn said, his amour-propre under attack also from the mounting pressure in his bladder. He was astonished as Delilah—could that be her real name?—led him through a vast, echoing atrium, high as a church nave, and then another hall of a room, destitute of furniture, carpets or curtains. Their footsteps echoed as though they were in a cavern. If only he could pee here, on the parquet floor!

'Have you just moved in?' he said in a strangled voice.

'No, we've been here a year. Oh right, the house is practically empty. That's our dad. He's into minimalism. Like the Japanese, you know?'

'But what's the point of having a huge house if there's nothing in the rooms? I'm sorry, I don't mean to be rude.' Melvyn clenched his teeth. *Hold it in, hold it in.*

'No problem. Hell, I don't know. It's his money. He lets me live here for free so I don't complain.'

They reached an immense kitchen with granite counters, an island with stainless steel stools high enough for giants, distressed 'rustic' beams, and a stained glass window, depicting a half-naked woman with a defiant expression—a reproduction of Aubrey Beardsley's *Salomé.* On the island stood a bottle of red wine, glasses, crackers and a blue-veined, crumbly cheese: *Gorgonzola.* Deliberate? Sure, it was.

'I get the feeling there's a theme going on here,' Melvyn said. When Delilah looked at him questioningly, he went on: 'I mean Salomé there, and you, Delilah, and, uh—' he trailed off, hoping she would supply Jezebel's real name.

But she did not take the hint. 'Oh the Biblical names. Right. All names of *femmes fatales* too, right?'

He nodded, frustrated he could not winkle the name out of her. She poured two glasses of Châteauneuf-du-Pape, and cut a few crumbly slices of the cheese.

'Gorgonzola?' he said.

'In your honour,' she said. So it *was* a good-humoured if sly dig at his wife's name. 'My sister asked me to entertain you for a while. Do you mind?'

Actually, it was damn embarrassing. But it was a rhetorical question. What the heck was Jezebel, or whatever her goddamn name was, up to? Keeping him on tenterhooks, augmenting the suspense? Or just inconsiderately late? He had to admit that Delilah was attractive, built like an aerobics instructor, as tall as her sister, but more willowy. Curves in all the right places. Could he flirt with her? Should he? Was that the idea? But how could he, knowing that Jezebel might appear at any moment?

'Take a seat,' Delilah said, handing him a wine-glass. Waterford crystal.

Drinking would be excruciating. He crossed his legs. 'No thanks, Delilah.'

'You're too funny,' she said, rubbing her hands, which had some cheese stuck to them, and then sailing over to the sink. Oh no—she was going to turn the faucet on! Melvyn gritted his teeth. Could he resist wetting himself? The water gushed out of the tap, in an unstoppable flood, powerful, invincible.

'Are you all right? With your face screwed up like that you must be in agony.'

He opened his eyes and uncrossed his legs. 'I am. May I use your…?'

'Sure.' She laughed with the malice of a Disney witch. 'Right over there.'

He began to sprint for it but two realisations arrested him: first, that he looked an utter dick, running for the john like a toddler; and second, that the violence of the movement might unleash the mighty torrent. Stiffly, he slogged his way across the colossal kitchen, slamming the door behind him, unzipping with frantic haste, and then, eyes shut, blissfully letting go. Oh what joy! When he came out of his quasi-orgasmic trance, his beatific face smiled at him in the mirror. And he saw what he had barely registered as he burst into the bathroom and tore at his flies: a number of framed monochrome photographs, 'Extremely *inappropriate* photos,' said his internal Frida. Of naked or nearly naked young women, clearly pornography, but 'tasteful' compared to the porn of our age. These Victorian models did not have the pneumatic figures of modern porn models and actresses, nor did they look tall. They had rounded bellies, as in old paintings. And full bushes of pubic hair. Who decided that porn models should have shaven pudenda? When? Sometime in the nineties? And why? Someone found it sexier. Because they wanted women to look like little girls? Wasn't that a tad pervy? Melvyn found the women sexy, in spite of their homeliness. They leered at him knowingly. *We know what you want, Melvyn. Sure we do. Come here. Would you like to touch me? Would you like me to touch you? Here? Or maybe here?* As he zipped up, he wondered why antique porn adorned the walls of a family bathroom. *Must be an unusual family*. But what was normal? Who decided? (Frida, in their family.) Whose values were right? Whose were more feminist? Maybe those Biedermeier pictures, with the women's black stockings and long, elaborate hair, turned on the members of the household. Aroused them. Or they just were not hung up about sex. *Imagine that.*

'Feeling better?' Delilah said as Melvyn came out beaming.

She had a hell of a nerve to tease to him like that, but he did not take offence. 'Goddamn right,' he said.

'What's your name?' Delilah said, proffering a glass again. This time he took it. 'I mean, your Christian name.'

'My Christian name?' No one said that anymore. When had Christian names become reactionary? 'Melvyn,' he said, gulping wine and wolfing the Gorgonzola.

Delilah drank too, leaning against the counter, which pushed her pelvis and hips towards him. Was that a provocative pose? She wore a tee-shirt dress, split to above the knee. *Hot* damn. Sure it was provocative. 'Melvyn,' she murmured. 'That's right, I remember.'

Melvyn hoisted himself onto a stool as high as a stepladder. 'I wonder how long your sister will be. And if your parents might worry, I mean, you know.'

'About her seeing an older man? Don't worry about that. Our mom was shot dead by an eight-year old at the shooting range. With an AR-15. An accident. I see that shocks you. It's fine, it was a long time ago. We're over it now.'

'I'm so very sorry,' he said with conscious gravitas. 'And your dad?'

'He's broad-minded, don't worry. I'm sure she told him she's seeing you.'

'I'm not exactly *seeing* her,' he said.

'You're wondering about my relationship with her, right? Since I'm so much older. No worries, I don't mind. She's a grownup. We're free. We're very liberal.'

'So I see,' he said, with an involuntary glance towards the bathroom.

'Did you like the pictures? Hapsburg Empire, 1890s I should think. Vintage porn. Taken in Vienna, Prague and Budapest. Pretty foxy ladies, weren't they?'

'They certainly were.' Once more he wondered if she were flirting with him, and if Jezebel might have brought him here to set him up with her sister, who was so much closer in age to him. But before he could develop those speculations, a door creaked and clicked shut. Someone was descending the stairs.

Jezebel entered the kitchen at a stately pace, unsmiling, in a full-length grey dress, cut low, with a high waist, right below the bosom. With her hair in a topknot, she had the air of a Jane Austen character. Her breasts were glowing white globes. She still wore her glasses.

'Hi, sis,' Delilah said.

'Thank you for looking after Dr Shamburger,' Jezebel said in a stilted tone. She held out her hand; Melvyn was forced to shake it.

'I'll leave you two alone, then,' Delilah said, with a flicker of a wink.

Melvyn had turned on his stool to greet Jezebel—rudely failing to rise, he realised, discomfited—and when he turned back, Delilah had already vanished.

'Bring your wine, sir,' Jezebel said. 'I'll show you my room.'

That was just what Melvyn was afraid of. 'Won't you have a glass?'

'I can't control myself after a glass of wine,' she deadpanned, taking one.

He climbed down from the precarious stool—how high was it, five foot?—and followed her. Even wearing ballet slippers, she was an inch or so taller than him. She moved noiselessly along bare, echoing corridors, up stairs, around corners, down steps, up more, through a picture gallery without pictures—there were hangers, and bright white rectangles where paintings had once hung, and empty, elaborate gilt frames—past numberless doors and dirty windows. He was in one of those impossible Escher houses.

'Delilah told me about your mother's tragic accident,' Melvyn said.

Over her shoulder, Jezebel said, 'I didn't shoot her on purpose. No one was to blame.'

She had killed her own mother! He did not know what to say. 'Not even the guy who let you use a semi-automatic weapon?'

'He was trying to teach his daughter to defend herself.'

In the Shamburger house, guns were anathema. 'I'm so very sorry,' he said.

She cast a sharp look over her shoulder at him, doubting his sincerity. She frowned. 'My bedroom, sir,' she said, opening a cheap, laminated door.

'At last,' he said. It was nothing like his daughters' rooms, with their posters of pop stars, clothes and shoes in heaps, teddy bears, Disney toys, photos, soccer boots, swimsuits, Harry Potter costumes, lacy pillows, and makeup. Jezebel's room was spartan: twin bed, dresser, and wardrobe, all white as teeth in toothpaste ads.

'You like it?' She sat on the white quilt, in a prim pose, hands on her lap.

'I wish my daughters would keep theirs as tidy.'

She stared, expecting him to do something. Her gaze was clinical, judgemental. He stood stricken, marooned on the parquet floor. The door behind him was still open. Should he shut it? Would she think he was making a pass at her? Did she want him to? Was he reading too much into her, or too little?

'Maybe this wasn't such a hot idea,' he said. 'You inviting me here.'

'Why not?'

'People could get the wrong idea. Your sister, my wife.'

'Does that matter? We're not that conventional, are we? What is the wrong idea, anyway? I'd like us to be…' she said, 'more intimate.'

'Geez, Jezebel, I still don't even know your real name.'

'Does that matter? What's in a name? As Juliet says.'

'It was awkward not to know what to call you when I met Delilah. If that's *her* real name. Is it?'

'She has other names too. Sometimes she calls herself Petronella.'

'Jesus, why? What was the idea of getting her to entertain me, anyways?'

'I thought you'd like to meet her, sir. And she you. We're close, although she's twenty years older. Would you like to sleep with her? Do you like her?'

'Sure I like her. But hell,' he lied, 'of *course* I don't want to sleep with her.'

'Why not? Don't you think she's hot? Most guys do.'

'Heh-heh, boy oh boy, you don't mince words. Sure, she's pretty…'

'So go for it. I bet you could sleep with her. I'll ask her if you like.'

'Oh man, what an unusual girl—woman—you are. No, please don't do that. I'm not sure I could—oh hell. You still haven't told me if Delilah is her real name.'

'Does it matter?' she said for the third time. 'Delilah, Petronella, who cares?'

'Geez, Jezebel, I guess so. I feel I've gone through the looking-glass.'

'Like Alice. Isn't that freeing—to go through the looking-glass?'

'I guess. But also kind of unsettling. We all fear the unknown.'

'I adore the unknown. I want to embrace mystery. Sit beside me, sir.'

He obeyed—at a safe distance. The door was still open. Where was Delilah?

'You are nervous, sir.'

'Damn right I'm nervous.' Why was that? She had practically offered to pimp Delilah to him, not exactly an unpleasant prospect, and he could probably have Jezebel as an appetizer. *Is this guilt?* he asked himself. *Or fear—of Frida—or what?*

'You're stiff too,' Jezebel said, 'if you don't mind me saying so. I promise you Delilah won't disturb us. You can say what you like. *Do* what you like, sir.'

Her words were unambiguous, yet her face and tone were flat; they did not rhyme with what she was saying. And her own posture was as rigid as his was. No doubt she was shy. Inexperienced. He was glad she was a bit nervous too.

It was nuts. A twenty-one-year-old *Jezebel* had manoeuvred him into her bedroom, with the intention of seducing him—and he was as limp as wilting cabbage. He blamed the tattooed, red-bristled ogre squatting in his brain.

'I wish you wouldn't keep calling me sir,' he said. Should he touch her, kiss her? That would spell the end of his marriage. Which would be fucking fantastic—but also scary as hell, dammit. 'I should be getting back to the university, Jezebel.'

'As you wish. I'm happy you came,' she said, although her face expressed neither joy nor disappointment. 'Come again. Will you think about what I said?'

'How could I forget? But—my conscience is troubling me, Jezebel.'

'Is that so? The Superego is overrated, sir. It's nothing but an internalisation of societal and parental values. You've done nothing wicked yet. But I trust you will.' She spoke without the slightest emotion. Melvyn couldn't make her out.

He gave her a lopsided smile, to which she did not respond, and stood up. She led him back through the cavernous house in silence. Only now did he start to feel the proverbial stirring in his loins. *Lousy* goddamn timing! He hoped she might embrace him at the door, but no, she only shook his hand, formal as a saleswoman.

Outside he gulped the air as if he had been holding his breath. He raced to his potent car in fear that someone might be watching—Jezebel or Delilah, from an unwashed window, or some student with a grudge. But it was none of these who saw him. Just as he unlocked the car, a pink convertible Corvette zoomed up. Like Barbie's. It was not Frida's car, thank Christ, but it was the second worst one in the world. In Tocqueville, anyhow. Rocky was gaping at him in disbelief. He waved her down, but she drove by, shaking her head.

He had become one of those guys in Greek tragedy. Yep, he was in *deep* shit.

NINE

Brutally Honest

In the small hours of the morning Huw was in his dressing-gown, on the porch-swing, waiting for Miranda to come home from the McBanes' house. The live oaks creaked, the cicadas shrilled, the tree frogs belched in a rhythmic chorus, and a bongo drum beat inside his chest. Slapping at mosquitoes, he murmured to Miranda: Are you coming home, love? What have I done wrong? Are you angry with me? His mobile showed she had still not replied to his message asking when she would be back. He called her and heard an ersatz Latina accent:

Hola, amigos! Leave a message, and I weel call you back, eef I feel like it. Adios!

He pictured NeAmber McBane saying that, the bimbo. Perhaps while wearing a Mexican hat. He tried to speak but could not. He sent a text instead. *I miss you, love.*

The azaleas that screened and perfumed the porch had a bluish tinge in the gloaming. Was that the hum of Miranda's hybrid? At last the Prius did appear, grey and ghostly. Equally spectral was Miranda, heels and slender legs emerging from the car first, glamorous and expressionless, in a skirt suit and pink silk blouse with a pussy bow, hair permed, immaculate. Too immaculate? Her heels ticked on the flagstones of the path. Would she explode? Would he? He stood. From the corner of her eye she registered movement, turned her head, and gave him a hollow stare. A mocking-bird burst into joyful song.

Come to me, he willed her. *Take me in your arms, tell me you love me.*

She climbed the three steps to the porch and halted, staring, silent, sullen.

If she came to him, she was still not lost. *Come to me, my darling.*

'What are you doing out here at six in the morning?' she said.

He could not answer. *Hold it in, boyo, hold it in. Bollocks to self-pity.*

Her straight-backed posture proclaimed confidence and power. Untouchably beautiful, the epitome of the American professional woman. He could not move towards her.

Her speech was staccato, each word a bullet: 'You guilt-tripping me, Huw?'

He shook his head and the unshed tears flew out. 'Not at all. Just happy you're home.'

'I'm going to bed,' she said, frowning. She walked in, not waiting for him, and he followed her sheepishly. He ascended the stairs behind her. In the electric light her legs in their nude tights gleamed like antique marble statuary. A few short weeks ago he would have slipped his hand up her skirt, laughing. Now he was at a loss.

Until they reached the library upstairs it did not occur to him that she was heading for their old bedroom, which they had moved out of because the height, and her urge to leap from the windows, terrified her. She paused and glanced at the filament of light under Owen's door. Was he already up? Or still up? Huw heard the clicking of a keyboard. *Still* up, dammit. But Miranda was already in their old room. A hopeful sign? In the dawn light the room was exactly as they had left it: cinnamon walls, wainscoting, the Victorian bed with the immense headboard, carved like the stern of a sailing ship. She undressed, dropping her clothes on the floor, not so much as glancing at him. The bed was made. She got in, and after a moment's hesitation, he discarded his dressing-gown and joined her.

The house held its breath. 'Are you going to work today?' he asked.

'Of course not.' She shut her eyes and opened them again. 'I guess we need to talk. About what's going on. Right now, what I need is space. You understand?'

Even *more* space? Huw knew they needed to talk, but right now he could not face the prospect of any changes. He stroked her hair and kissed her cheek.

He expected her to be unresponsive, but she turned towards him.

'I guess I have to let you have me first. Or I'll never be able to get a sensible word out of you, right?'

Was she teasing, flirting, or criticising, turning irony on him? Either way he did not halt his caresses, and she rolled towards him, less stiffly now.

'You only want me for my body.'

'Of course not, love,' he said, shocked.

'Sure you do. I'm just tits and ass to you.'

'Let's face it, they are superb,' he tried to joke.

She slapped his face, rather hard for playfulness, and then submitted to his advances. At first she did not respond, but then she did, and soon they fell into the Bossa Nova groove, in perfect time, and her accusation receded. Miranda came with her usual energy but less abandon, less tenderness. She did not gaze into his eyes. He kissed her; she did not respond.

'Feel better now?' Her tone was that of a nurse who had just given him medicine.

'Much better,' he said, hoping the sex had re-established their intimacy.

'Maybe we can discuss things, then. Now I've serviced you.'

Huw had been trying to get her to talk for weeks. 'For God's sake, don't put it like that. I'm not your client, am I? But we can talk. Aren't you sleepy, though?'

'I'm exhausted. But Matthew gave me some pills to keep me awake.'

'Whatever for? And pills, plural? He's not your therapist, is he?'

'No, but he is a psychiatrist. He can prescribe medication.'

'I know, but you're already taking medication, aren't you? Does he know that? Does your regular therapist know that McBane is medicating you as well?'

'Hey, don't freak out on me. Relax, dude. I can give you a pill if you like.'

'Jesus, Miranda, you want to medicate me now? How big is your supply?'

'Look, drop it, or I'm done. You want to talk or not?'

'Of course.'

'Good.' She sat up, ramrod-straight against the headboard. In the thin green light her torso was as white as ivory. With her breasts sticking out, taut, defiant, sculptural—and yes, wooden—she reminded him of a figurehead on the bows of a sailing ship. 'As I was saying,' she said, noticing the direction of his gaze, 'you just love my boobs.'

'You know that's not true.'

'Sure it is. If I were ugly, you wouldn't be with me.'

'I've never thought about it.' He did now. Would he? If he was frank, maybe not. The realisation shocked him: he had always believed he was in love with her soul.

'When my looks fade you'll leave me for a younger model.'

'No, I won't,' he said, meaning it, yet he heard the edge of doubt in his voice.

'Guys are all the same.'

'How sexist is that? Imagine if I said women are all the same.'

The figurehead gazed out to sea. 'You're too needy. You got

to give me more space. Right now I need to spend more time with Matthew and NeAmber. *They* understand me.'

'Are you saying I don't? Is that why you want to go to Mexico without me?'

'I never said that. I asked you to come. You still could.'

'The McBanes give me the creeps.'

'You think I belong to you. Get over that, Huw.'

'I'm not possessive,' he said, though as he spoke he knew it was untrue. But was belonging to someone a bad thing? 'I love you, that's all. Do you still love me?'

'Of course,' she said curtly. 'But our relationship has to change.'

The timbers of the old house creaked. The crickets chirped. 'How do you mean?'

'I told you, I need more space. Let me go out on my own. Have my own friends. Go on vacations without you. Do you love me enough to let me do that?'

Owen bumped about in his bedroom. Huw had no desire to have a holiday without *her*. 'I don't get it. Aren't you happy with me?'

She pulled on a pink velveteen pyjama top, a grandmother top. As he glanced down on her, she appeared to have a double-chin, and he imagined what she would look like when she was older. Not ugly but not alluring either. 'I never believed in the institution of marriage, the legality of it, the conformity, the restrictions. I agreed to marry you because it was the only way we could be together in Oman. Remember?'

He remembered, but had long believed she was as happy as he was. 'Are you saying you don't want to be married to me anymore?'

She took her time answering. 'I don't know yet. Does it matter?'

'Does it matter?' He heard a crash. A door slammed.

'I mean, what matters is love, right? Do we have to be married? Who cares? I'm not saying we can't be. I just need space, to breathe, to think. Let me have it, if you love me. Will you do that for me, for us?'

'Why do you want to go to Mexico so badly?'

'You know why. I want to see the Mayan ruins, and Frida's house.'

Frida Kahlo was the wrong model, with her self-absorption, her victim complex, her glorification of suffering, and her open marriage, but Huw knew Miranda would not like him saying that. Besides, he could not bear to lose her. 'All right,' he said grimly.

'Let me be free,' Miranda said. 'I need to put myself first. My diagnosis is serious. PTSD, bipolar disorder with schizoid tendencies, depression and anxiety.'

'Jesus Christ, when was this? So many conditions? Why didn't you tell me?'

'I didn't want to worry you. It's OK. I'm managing. I'm well-medicated.'

'I'll do whatever I can to support you. I promise. I love you.'

She nodded her thanks—but did not assure him of her love in return. 'Great. This weekend I want to go on a women's retreat. Is that OK with you?'

'What kind of retreat? Where?'

'In the country, up in the hills. The woman running it is a confidence guru. Her name's Petronella Pikestaff. NeAmber says she's the real deal. She kicks ass.'

'I'm not sure I want my arse kicked. And surely you of all people don't need more confidence, do you, love? I've never known anyone more confident.'

'Huw, you don't know me at all.'

No, he did not know her at all. He could see that now.

*

Later, Huw was stumbling about in the supermarket, alone as usual: Miranda no longer had the patience for shopping. She had stopped cooking and cleaning too—not that she had ever done much of either. Huw had left his glasses at home, so everything was a blur. Dawnesha Ceyonne sang a ballad over syrupy strings, dragging out single syllables over dozens of notes in mushy, meaningless flourishes. Supposedly *soulful.*

Huw used his trolley as a battering ram. 'Excuse me,' he called out to the sleepwalker blocking his way. He barged past him like Charlton Heston in a chariot race.

A tall, skinny shadow in a baggy tracksuit zoomed in on him. By the redolence of repellent scent and margaritas, he guessed it was a woman. By her air of focussed fury, a professional woman. By the Ozark screech— 'Heeugh! What's bitten you?' it had to be Rocky Rathaus. 'Oh, never mind. Guess what I saw this morning? Only Melvyn, coming out of one of those magnificent mansions on the west side of town.'

'Sorry, Rocky, I can't see,' Huw said. 'Why did the mansion upset you?'

'*Dude.* It was like eleven thirty in the morning. And he was so furtive. Tried to flag me down. Sneaky look on his face. Who do you think he coulda been visiting—on the *west* side of Tokeville, Heeugh?'

'How should I know? A friend? A colleague?'

'Heeugh, you are so naïve. So ingenious.'

'I think you mean *ingenuous.*'

'Uh? Oh, sure. But don't you see? We don't have colleagues on the west side. Those mansions are too pricey for professors. Except Business professors, of course.'

'I wouldn't live in one if you paid me. Nasty, kitschy things.'

'Heeugh—it was totally awesome. Heeuge, with gables and a kind of tower with one of those super cute roofs, like a fairy-tale, you know what I'm sayin'?'

'I suspected as much. Did it have columns too? Stained-glass windows?'

'Don't be so snarky, Heeugh. As a madder of fact it did. Anyways, what was Melvyn doing out there? It's so like weird. You think he's maybe having an affair?'

Good for you, Melvyn boyo, if you are. 'I wouldn't jump to conclusions.'

'I guess I godda tell Frida. I mean, it's my dooty, right?'

'If I were you I shouldn't meddle. If it's bothering you, why not just mention to Melvyn that you saw him? I'm sure he has an innocent explanation.'

'Of course, you would be on his side. As a man, I mean.'

'Not at all.' It was not so much that Melvyn was a *man*—to Huw he was a sort of superannuated adolescent, since he looked and behaved like one. 'No, I just feel sorry for any bloke who's…' *married to such a harridan*, he left unsaid.

'Who's what? And don't tell me I'm meddling. It's just solidarity with Frida.'

Frida Shamburger, Frida Kahlo. The monster in the Creative Writing Department, the monster of egocentrism, Miranda's sea-monsters. Melvyn's marriage, and Kahlo's, and his own. Too many tangles, weeds wrapped round his legs, trapping him. 'Ah, is that what it is?'

'Don't take that tone with me—that goddamn uppity Briddish tone.'

'I can hardly help being Welsh, Rocky.'

'Why not? How many years have you been here? Can't you talk like us?'

Usually he reined in his Welsh testiness. Now he did not. 'Well, I could. Let's see: I could reduce my vocabulary by eighty per cent, stop using compound sentences, mix up the collocations of my prepositions, insert meaningless phatic fillers into each phrase, and speak in strings of clichés. Yes, I daresay I could speak like you if I put my mind to it.'

'You are so *goddamn* condescending. How does Miranda put up with you?'

'She doesn't any more. Good-bye, Rocky.' He blundered off, and found himself at the checkouts. Dawnesha was still yodelling her overblown emotions. *I ee-ay, will always, love you—ooh-ooh-ooh-oohoo-ooh. I can't live if living is without you.* Why was such rubbish popular? Because we no longer have real emotions; we borrow them from movies and weepy songs. Or we do, but suppress them, because they reveal facets of ourselves we prefer to ignore. The manufactured sentimental versions are easier to deal with. Huw yodelled as he walked out. In Wales, someone might have joined in. Here people stared as if he were nuts. *Which I may be*, he thought. Maybe Miranda's madness was catching.

*

Arriving at his office after lunch, duly bespectacled, he found awaiting him a person with long, floppy hair, a suede jacket, white chinos and loafers, worn without socks. It was Timothy, *not* Tim, the much younger husband of Dr Jorgenson, the Dean of the College of Liberal Arts. Timothy had an infant's high forehead and bush baby eyes, big, blue and bulging, with purplish rings beneath them, which gave him the air of an inveterate Onanist. With those immense, doleful eyes, Timothy smiled, wistfully, and vainly. Definitely a wanker—in the literal sense. Huw would have put money on it.

'I'm *so* glad you're here, Huw,' Timothy droned, glancing ostentatiously at his watch. 'Like, finally. I need your help with this *insufferable* thesis. It's such *agony*.'

'Sorry I'm a bit late, Timothy. Just a moment.' His office was a disaster: cardboard boxes full of student work formed a Himalayan outline above his bookshelves, and his desk bore the marks of a recent Gestapo raid: open, ransacked drawers, torn papers, piles of trash.

Timothy sank with studied elegance into the armchair before it, crossing his legs as British men did, one knee over the other—which was considered effete here. A real man was supposed to sit with his legs apart. It was permissible to prop one leg up on another, but only the ankle could rest across the knee. Timothy touched his lips with his index finger, as if in deep contemplation, which knowing him was most implausible;

or urging secrecy, which was more likely; or signalling his sexual innocence, in a fey, disingenuous kind of way, which was more probable still. Huw told himself to be careful.

'I wonder if you've had a chance to read the latest section of my thesis,' Timothy drawled—not in the Southern manner, but more like a flamboyant boy Huw had known at Oxford, who had modelled himself on Oscar Wilde.

'Actually, I have.' What on earth could he say that would not traumatise the poor fellow? 'You did a good job of evoking the lives of yuppies in a Southern city. Their manners and mannerisms, their patterns of speech—even what they download to their smart phones to listen to in the gym, and what kind of latte they drink at Sundoes.'

Timothy's finger was back on his mouth. No, actually *in* his mouth. Would he suck it? He raised his eyebrows petulantly. *Is that all?* the expression meant.

'Mmm,' Huw hummed, praying for inspiration. 'Another thing you pull off well is…' (*Come on, think of something! Not Miranda and the McBanes or Frida and the prospect of losing wife and job and home.*) '… the gay scene in the state capital. The leather bars, the strip clubs, the parties. Very detailed, lots of specifics, very true-to-life. I can tell you're writing from personal knowledge.'

Timothy's bush baby eyes bulged wider. '*You* know that scene, Huw?'

'Well, no. I can't say I do.'

'You sure about that? You wouldn't be bi, Huw, but maybe chary of coming out?'

'Good Lord, no. Whatever gave you such an idea?'

'There *is* a rumour that you're gay, or bi. You must have heard it.'

'Not a whisper. How extraordinary.'

Timothy enunciated the syllables *ha, ha, ha*—less a laugh than a parody of one. 'No need to get defensive, Huw. It's not a trial. I'm not accusing you of a crime.'

'I just wonder why *anyone* would suppose I might be gay.'

Timothy tittered. 'Want to know my theory? They think you're so hot and handsome that you *must* be. They can't face the idea that you're not. They want to believe they have a chance with you, you see. My buddies have told me so.'

'Please tell them I'm straight. A hundred percent.'

'Everyone's a bit gay,' Timothy said.

'No, they're not. Never say that in a pub in Wales, boyo.'

'Oh, what a pity. My little friends will be *so* disappointed. What a heartbreaker you are, Huw.' Timothy grinned, delighted by Huw's discomfiture. 'But we're getting off track, aren't we? So what did you think of the plot developments in the novel? Terribly complex, aren't they? *Byzantine.*'

'Well, to be honest…' Huw began.

'Oh, no!' Timothy wailed, laying the back of his hand against the chalk cliff of his forehead in mock horror. 'Spare me your British honesty! Whenever you say that, I know you're going to say something just *brutal*.' He spoke with masochistic relish.

'My intention is never to wound. But if I'm not going to be sincere, why speak at all? Criticism is valueless unless it's truthful.'

'Sure, Huw, but you could be *kind*, no? That's what we all wish. Like— '

'Like who?'

'Well, like the Shamburgers, for instance. They're so *sweet*. Especially Frida. She *adores* our work. She says every single one of us is talented and special.'

'Do you really believe that?' Huw did not: Frida often lamented the banality and incompetence of student writing in private. 'Can everyone be talented?'

'Maybe it's a teeny bit of a white lie at times.'

'If she finds it all so wonderful, what do you learn from her?' Huw said.

'That's the problem, right? You're the only one we can trust. You're savage, but at least when you say something good about our work, you mean it. And when you tear our work to pieces, *unfortunately* you're usually right.'

Impatient with the affected talk, Huw had an urge to end it. 'So you want to know the truth about the novel? It's supposed to be a psychological thriller, but there's not enough action or suspense to make it thrilling, nor enough depth of character to make it literary. It's not even plausible. When the police interview Gavin, they believe his incoherent alibi. That makes me wonder how much you know about police procedure. And the crooks are Colombian drug-lords, from Medellín. A bit of a cliché, isn't it?'

'There *are* Colombian drug-lords. And some of them are from Medellín.'

'I daresay. But what do you know about them? Have you met any?'

'I've seen tons of them in movies.'

'Exactly. Your Colombian cocaine dealers conform to Hollywood stereotypes: they have ponytails and diamond ear-studs and they speak comical English. They have porn star girlfriends and they're savage sadists.'

'Do you suppose the real ones are kind and considerate?'

'No, but it's boring that they conform to our expectations. If you're going to describe them in depth they need to be complicated or surprising in some way.'

'Some people simply *are* stereotypes,' Timothy said. 'I am, for instance.'

'Absolutely.' Huw smiled to soften the barb, but Timothy looked hurt anyway. 'I know some people are stereotypes. But why put them in your novel? Who cares about stock figures? And talking of those, why does Gavin betray his husband in the first place?'

'He's so *old* and *fussy*. Gavin wants *adventure*.'

'And yet he has an affair with another old, fussy man. I wonder why.'

'I guess he's looking for a father-figure. Or he's just into older guys.' Timothy scrutinised Huw's face. Was he flirting? Christ, Huw hoped not.

Huw went on without mercy: 'Then Gavin agrees to meet Don Carlos in an empty meat warehouse—another cinematic cliché—and, incredibly enough for a young gay graphic artist, Gavin takes an automatic pistol with him.'

'You don't think gay men can use pistols? That's a tad homophobic, no?'

'I'm sure some of them can. But Gavin is such a soft and ineffectual person. He's often in tears. He can't even make up his mind about what to wear or how to comb his hair. Does he really think he's going to win a shootout with a drug-lord?'

'Sure he does, and he succeeds too,' Timothy said, pouting.

'Who's going to believe that? What are the odds?'

'It could happen. He could get lucky. Guns do jam.'

'They do in movies. But it's awfully lucky for Gavin.'

'Oh my God, you just *hate* my novel, don't you? Admit it. You think it stinks. You're telling me I'll never be a writer and I should give up, like this minute.'

How the bloody hell did Timothy guess that? 'I never said that. The novel does need work, though. Quite a bit, to be honest.'

'*To be honest*,' Timothy drawled. 'You're quite the piece of work, aren't you? So *judgemental*, so *English*.' He hissed the last word. '*Jorgen* says my work is brilliant.'

'He is your husband, Timothy. He might be a bit biased.'

'Melvyn says I'm gifted. Frida thinks I could be the next Brett Easton Ellis.'

And yet neither of them had wanted to admit Timothy to the program, Huw remembered. It was he and Luke who had argued for his admittance. Huw had discerned potential—which had not been fulfilled, since Timothy had been spoilt by his professors, all sycophants to Jorgenson. Apart from Huw, not one had dared to point out his work's faults. So naturally Timothy had assumed it was perfect.

'I'm not saying you're not gifted,' Huw said, ashamed of his hedging.

'You're not saying I *am*.' Timothy's voice wobbled on the verge of tears.

Huw sighed. How much praise did the boy need? 'You have potential. An ear for language, realistic dialogue.' Timothy still sulked. 'But a thriller must be plausible, and a literary thriller can't be full of clichés and stereotypes. You need more discipline.'

Timothy's face was flour-white. 'Thanks for your *honesty*,' he said, standing and flouncing out with the same insouciance as Elise did. Timothy flounced even more campily, swinging his hips and tossing his head like a male model on a runway. *You asshole,* that strut proclaimed. *I don't need* you *for anything!*

Huw sighed. In the past few days he had demonstrated his talent for antagonising people again and again. First Frida, then Rocky, and now Timothy. Would they all become enemies? On his desk, Miranda fixed him from her photograph frame with a glassy, incredulous, hurt look. Had he antagonised his wife too? *You asshole,* her expression proclaimed—didn't it? *I don't need* you *for anything either!*

Was he too honest? In Wales people expected honesty. At Oxford too. You mocked, ridiculed, took the piss. Blokes especially, and you gave as good as you got. It was fine to insult people to their face. Insults were not rude. You called your mates tossers, wankers, twats, prats, fairies, dickheads. Your *best* mates. In Britain blokes took it as a compliment if you insulted them or ragged them—it showed you regarded them as equals. You never did it to anyone less bright, or from a lower social class. That was bullying. And maybe the reason the Yanks were so touchy was that they had an inferiority complex. They believed Brits were brighter. And they were right. Unless the Brits were really snooty, arrogant bastards, that is.

Which some of them were. But Huw was not a snooty, arrogant bastard. Was he? *Was he?*

TEN

Is God a Guy?

A disembodied voice spoke over Melvyn. A blessing from heaven?

Thank you, Jesus, he murmured. Jezebel leaned back against the endless long pink hood of a Corvette, her eyes fixed on his, and with tantalising slowness lifted the hem of her dress to above her knees, to her thighs, to—OMFG!—to her—oh boy oh boy oh boy—right up to her goddamn *belly*button. But Melvyn directed his gaze lower.

No panties, not even those ephemeral V-string things from Vickie's Secret.

And by God, he was hard as a hammer. *Nothing* could stop him now.

He walked towards her, unzipping himself. She held out her arms to him.

Her voice croaked at him, loud and harsh. 'MELVYN! Get up already!'

He was on the brink of entering her when it cawed again:

'Melvyn, I won't tell you again. It's Sunday. Get up. Get ready for church.'

God or the Archangel Gabriel? Thunderheads filled the sky. Fork lightning flickered and crackled. Could God have that grating voice? Was He full of wrath? Melvyn lunged his lance at Jezebel, determined—but goddammit, she had vanished. Instead, *he* sprawled on the hood, arms waving, flies open, his proud Johnson exposed, vulnerable. And some stinky, slimy creature loomed over him, hissing, its scales scraping the concrete drive as it dragged itself towards him, foul smoke belching from its nostrils, jaws open, about to snap over his wilting member. He kicked at the vile monster with all his might.

'No!' he screamed, grabbing his privates with both hands. 'Leave me alone!'

'Melvyn, what the hell's wrong with you? Are you nuts? Wake up already!'

He opened his eyes and struggled to make sense of what he saw: a billowing purple pavilion, with wings sticking out of its sides, possibly vestigial, flabby, flappy, defaced by hideous pictures, yet furnished with claws, and a humanoid head sticking out of the top, a triple-chinned, blotchy head, with pink, pinpoint eyes, rust-red bristles on the scalp, a gold ring in its snout. It was no relief to find himself at Frida's mercy instead of the monster's.

'Hey, it's Sunday, right?' he groaned. 'Can't I lay in for once?' Or was it *lie in*?

'No you cannot lay in,' Frida tromboned. 'God, men are so slothful.'

You're calling *me* lazy? he nearly asked. You, who live on social media?

'On Sunday I go to church. Every goddamn Sunday,' Frida blared. 'And you accompany me. It's for our spiritual benefit, Melvyn. For the good of our souls.'

Have you even got a soul? Have I? Who cares? He just yearned to return to his dream and roger Jezebel on the hood of the

Corvette. Was that asking too much? He had been so darn close—on the point of entry. And Frida had kicked his ass out of the gates of paradise.

His loins throbbed painfully. If he couldn't bang Jezebel, surely he could at least go have a huge breakfast at Denny's, eggs and bacon and sausages and hash-browns, followed by pancakes with syrup and half a gallon of coffee? Then lounge about at home, maybe watch some football. The Patriots were playing. Pour himself a Brewski. Check out porn videos. That was his idea of a Sunday morning.

'I don't know why I have to go,' he said. 'Can't you go on your own for once?'

'Hey, I'm the goddamn subdeacon. What would the new vicar think?'

'Who cares? No one gives a flying fuck if I'm there. Actually no one gives a flying fuck about any of it. They're all just pretending to be Christians anyway.'

'Melvyn, how can you say that?' Frida tore the bedclothes off his body. Melvyn's Johnson poked out of his PJ flies. More like a garden worm than a king cobra, sadly. He covered himself, mortified.

'True, you rarely even pretend,' he said. 'Only when you put that dumbass purple surplice on. Then you think you're the Archbishop of fucking Canterbury.'

'Go fuck yourself,' Frida said quietly as she fumbled for something in her purse.

He stuck his lower lip out. He would not let her bully him. For once he would have his own way. Frida could not make him do anything. She was not his mother. Well hell, she kind of was. Anyhow, she was not his boss. Well damn, yes, in fact she was. She had no power over him. Shit, yes, she did have. Or very soon would have.

Frida had turned her purse nearly inside out. Melvyn glimpsed a black metal barrel.

'Was that a gun I saw just now?' he said.

'Oh yeah, I didn't tell you I bought one. A woman's got to be able to protect herself, right? This is the MeToo era. Broome showed me her Beretta and I thought it was cute.'

'Holy shit! You're packing heat now?' *This was bad news. Very bad news indeed.*

'Everyone has one now. Even Rocky does. We're already taking lessons.'

With a start he remembered Rocky seeing him scurrying out of Jezebel's McMansion. That was on Friday. Had she shopped him yet? He pictured her in a detective raincoat, like Jezebel's, spilling the beans, and Frida tapping a pencil as she listened. Rocky couldn't have betrayed him yet—if she had, Frida's fury would have fallen on him by now. But why not? Maybe she just had not had a chance. Or could her conscience be troubling her? He was sure Rocky did not have one. Her ethical development was at the level of an alligator's. Maybe a bit lower. Like Frida, all she wanted was power, position, and fame. And pleasing Frida was her strategy for getting it. So it was only a matter of time. When would she betray him? Of course, at church! Rocky was always there, fawning over Frida, having confidential little chats with her over coffee and cookies after the service. Could he forestall her? She wouldn't rat on him if he were standing beside her, would she? Stopping her was his only chance.

He leapt out of bed. 'I'll be ready in fifteen,' he said, heading for the shower.

Frida ballooned her cheeks, shook her head. Her tongue wagged like a bell clapper. Her jowls deflated. 'What a weirdo,' she muttered as he padded past her.

*

As far as Melvyn was concerned, the best thing about St. Michael and All Angels was that the hicks who filled the town's Southern Baptist churches and the Churches of Christ were absent. As Melvyn climbed down from the vast purple Shamburger armoured car in the parking lot, in his seersucker suit and loafers, he saw professors from Oxbow State or the liberal arts college, Prince, all dressed like civilised people from the North—which most of them were. Blazers, chinos, tweed jackets, linen suits. The women wore formless tents and jeans. No makeup. The downside, it struck him, as he opened the passenger door for Frida—she was a stickler for sexist, archaic courtesies—and cushioned her fall as she plummeted earthwards, was that no yuppie studs attended this church, which was known as an old liberal hangout. So Toqueville's babes, tanned, dressed to slay in spike heels and miniskirts and, and made-up like porn stars, were naturally absent too, and there was no eye-candy.

The second her Doc Martens hit the tarmac, Frida's face underwent its usual Sabbath transformation. Gone in an instant were the peevishness, the tight lips, narrowed eyes, flared nostrils, and wrinkled scalp. She smiled with the otherworldly expression of an apostle walking beside Jesus. She exuded serenity and saintliness. World-class acting.

'How do you do it?' he asked. 'I mean, walk that way. Like Princess Di.'

'Well done, Melvyn. Actually I do imagine I'm Princess Di. I *become* her.'

For Frida, that was an unusually frank admission. Even with Melvyn she liked to maintain her aura of sincerity and authenticity. Sometimes he wondered if her subterfuges and deceptions were so deeply ingrained that she came to believe them herself. But if you caught her off guard you might find a chink in the armour.

Melvyn was about to crow when he glimpsed Rocky and remembered he had to get to her before Frida did. Would Rocky rat on him? Had she already ratted? She would do anything to please Frida. Incredibly, several days after Rocky had caught him outside Jezebel's McMansion, Frida had still not mentioned the matter. Was she pointedly ignoring him? Or 'blissfully unaware'? Then he also glimpsed Jezebel, lurking like a detective. Oh no!

Please, God, he prayed, with more fervour than he had ever prayed in his life, *Please don't let that crazy girl make a scene. And please let me prevent Rocky talking to Frida in private. I'll give up beer and porn. I'll be good from now on, I swear. Thank you. Amen.*

'What are you smirking about, Melvyn Shamburger?' The voice was cultured, New England, reminiscent of Gore Vidal. Cooper, a Lit. professor with the etiolated, wincing smile of an elderly Somerset Maugham, a tall figure in a corduroy jacket, thin and bent as a pipe-cleaner. One of the few intellectuals on the faculty at Oxbow, he enjoyed teasing the creative writers.

'Hi Cooper, hi Burd,' Melvyn said, addressing Cooper's wife, a tiny woman with dyed blonde hair and intense, sparrow-like eyes. 'Just wondering why an inveterate atheist like you is always to be found here, Cooper.'

Cooper laughed silently but hard, his eyes closing. 'In a Southern city if you don't belong to a church, you have no social circle, so my lovely wife tells me.'

'What about you?' Burd's chuckle was razor-edged. 'Don't I recall seeing you two in the audience when Richard Dawkins came? And Christopher Hitchens?'

'We are believers,' Frida said, in bell-like Boston Brahmin tones, her face radiating beatitude. 'The concept of an after-life is comforting. Humans need it.'

'Even if it's untrue?' Burd said.

'Like fiction,' Melvyn mumbled. 'The kind of fiction Frida likes, anyway.' What the hell had gotten into him? For years he had been meek and submissive, and now all of a sudden, his impulses to rebel were breaking out, willy-nilly. It was scary, but exhilarating too. He saw from Frida's face that he had touched a sore spot.

'What's that supposed to mean? What kind of fiction do I like?' she said.

Cooper raised his eyebrows. He dyed his hair, but his eyebrows were grey.

'Let's face it, chick-lit. That *Scarf, Praise, Adore* woman. The one who wrote *The Private Life of Wasps*. Oh yeah—that other one too, the *Gaga Sorority*.'

Frida's brow darkened and furrowed. 'Chick-lit my ass,' she said, her accent reverting to East Boston. 'That's literature, but you're too prejudiced to see it.'

With that she stomped towards the imposing figure of the new vicar, who was welcoming the congregation at the door of the Victorian Gothic church.

'She likes that shit? Tonight you'll be sleeping on the couch,' Burd said.

'No sex in the foreseeable future,' Cooper added.

'I wish,' Melvyn muttered. Should he run after her? What if Rocky reached her before he did? Or, God forbid, Jezebel? To his relief, Frida was standing beside the new vicar, a woman of formidable height and build, in a purple chasuble, emblazoned with a lucent gold cross. She held her arms wide and beamed as she welcomed her lambs into the fold—with authority. Frida had resumed her gentle, beatific expression, but she was clutching a colossal silver-topped mace, which he feared she would brain him with. How had she gotten hold of that? Not only were her tats covered by the surplice, but also, as usual, she had removed the punky nose-ring. Why? Did the Episcopal God disapprove of tats and piercings? Melvyn bet he did too.

'You're smirking again,' Cooper said as the three of them edged past the vicar and Frida. 'What repression is going on in that devious mind of yours?'

'You must be the last Freudian critic alive,' Melvyn said, grateful that Frida had not cracked his skull open with that mace as they went by her.

'We're both Freudians,' Cooper said. 'Your fiction is strewn with phallic symbols. Just what are our deepest hidden urges? What are *yours*, Melvyn?'

'I hardly want to kill my father. He's already dead. And what other paternal authority figures would we like to murder?' Melvyn glanced at the mostly elderly crowd in the vestibule.

Their uniformly white faces were splashed with lozenges of bright colours from the stained windows. Jezebel, in her raincoat, stood alone beneath a panel depicting Mary Magdalene—a coincidence or conscious symbolism? The latter, knowing her. She peered at him from behind her glasses, staring in a creepy way. How did she know he attended St. Michael's? Or was she a member of the congregation that he had never noticed before? No, she was stalking him, for sure. What did she want? Hadn't he blown his chances with her? Then he noticed Timothy, a young fiction writer of negligible talent in the MFA programme, standing beside the dyed black hair and San Francisco moustache of Professor Jorgen Jorgenson, the Dean, who gazed at his husband with pride.

'I guess I wouldn't mind topping old Jorgenson,' Melvyn said.

Cooper laughed on the intake of his breath, like a Swede. 'That sounded very vehement, Melvyn. He's not that bad, is he? As Deans go, I mean.'

'He's an old bore. *The Faerie Queene*.'

'Homophobia, Melvyn? Surely not.' Cooper pulled an astringent face.

'I'm talking about Edmund Spenser. His research interest. You'd think there was nothing else of value in English Literature, to listen to him.'

'Oh that. I guess he is the best candidate for symbolic parricide. As for marrying our mothers…' he glanced around the vestibule, and located Burd, who had wandered off and was talking in assertive tones, 'We already have, no?' He laughed: wistfully, wheezing.

But Frida and the vicar were bearing down upon them, and Jezebel was still gawking at Melvyn, which he hoped his mother—or rather, his wife—had not noticed. Frida did have a condescending, suspicious smile on her face, and so did the vicar. But that was normal, of course. As a man in the Humanities, he expected women to treat him as though he had a mild mental retardation, plus sociopathic tendencies. So he wiped the impish smirk off his face. He had been a choirboy at his prep school and could look innocent at will.

'Hi, hi,' said the vicar, seizing each man's hand in turn and wringing it like an orange she wanted to drain of its juice. Melvyn nursed his crushed fingers afterwards, behind his back. 'I am the *Reverend* Crystal Nutt?' She emphasised the honorific in the same way that Frida emphasised 'Doctor' when she introduced herself. He had a hunch and misgiving that the pair would get on well.

'And what are we discussing here,' the Revd. Crystal Nutt asked with a falling intonation, as if it were not a question.

The patronising 'we' of the authority figure.

Cooper chuckled, with discomfiture. 'Just the usual Freudian stuff.'

Frida rolled her eyes. 'What else would *you two* be discussing?'

'Naughty boys,' the Revd. Crystal Nutt said, wagging the nightstick of her forefinger playfully at them. 'Well, we must run along, Frida. The Lord Awaiteth?'

As Cooper followed them into the nave, Melvyn gazed ahead like a blinkered horse, catching Jezebel out of the corner of his eye. Somehow she appeared at his side, in perilous proximity. 'Good morning, sir,' she said, unsmiling.

Melvyn affected surprise. 'Jezebel, I didn't see you. Are you Episcopalian?'

'Not exactly. My family belongs to a weird cult. But you are?'

'Not exactly, but my wife bullies me into coming here.'

Jezebel stood way too close and spoke into his ear. 'Oh no, how sad. Why?'

'She thinks it's good for her career. And it makes her feel important.'

'How inauthentic,' Jezebel said. 'Can't you rebel?'

Could he? Instead of replying, Melvyn asked: 'So what are you doing here?'

'I need to see you,' she said in an urgent whisper. Sweating,

Melvyn rubbernecked. Rocky was out of earshot. 'Could we talk after the service, sir?'

They had shuffled into the dimly-lit nave now. 'Can't it wait till tomorrow?'

'Tomorrow may be too late,' she said. 'It's now or never.'

Was she an Elvis fan? He pulled an ambiguous grimace of a face and fled, joining Cooper and Burd in a polished cherry pew. Nevertheless, moments later, Jezebel took a pew in front. She kept turning around to stare at him. Burd poked Melvyn's ribs:

'Who is that cute girl I saw talking to you? Does she have a crush on you?'

Luckily Melvyn did not have to gabble an emphatic denial because right then chanting began, and Frida came in, waving a censer from which frankincense poured, followed by the vicar in her purple, gold-edged robes, and a pair of acolytes. The congregation rose.

'Good morning,' said the vicar from the pulpit, with a crazed televangelist smile. 'And welcome to St. Michael's and *All* Angels? I'm the *Reverend* Crystal Nutt? It's my privilege to be your new vicar?' Her smug tone implied that the privilege was the congregation's. She spoke with the ultra-annoying upward lilt of the Valley Girl too.

'And now,' she said with the breathless excitement of a talk-show host, 'I'm going to ask *Doctor* Frida Shamburger to read the lesson for us?' Melvyn almost expected applause.

Frida stamped up to the lectern, a pure, apostolic expression on her face—who was she now, Melvyn wondered?—Joan of Arc in Ingres' portrait? Saint Theresa in Rubens'? She opened the Bible, and began to read the lesson, from Genesis, in flawless Boston Brahmin. A pity they could not have retained the noble English of the King James version, in an Episcopalian church. Instead he had to endure the flat phrases of some dopey modern translation. In a despairing moan, Frida rushed over Eve being created from Adam's rib, clearly to elide the episode, but her face glowed when she read with special emphasis that *both* man and woman had been made in God's own image. Melvyn had forgotten that bit. Her insinuation that God was transgender, or gender-fluid, made half the congregation sigh with delight. Now Melvyn pondered the matter, many of the faithful looked nonbinary themselves.

Still, he speculated, if dudes and chicks were both made in God's image, didn't that indicate that they looked pretty fit? He tried to imagine God as a squat, dumpy woman with sagging breasts. No way! On the other hand, as a supermodel, maybe without the usual sullen pout—hmm, that was *way* better. If God were female, surely she would be slender, like the naked Eves of the Renaissance, or Gisele Bundchen? He pictured a cross between a Brazilian underwear model and Botticelli's Venus. Face of the latter, body of the former. Oh boy oh boy oh boy. He could venerate *that.* Then he realised he was imagining her as white. *Racist!* hissed his inner Frida. Blushing, he remembered Jezebel, who met his gaze as he glanced at her. Hell, her body was spectacular too.

Unfortunately Frida's braying mangled his dreams. Still, his fantasies continued as she spoke. He pictured Eve strolling about in Paradise with a fig-leaf, and coming to the Tree of Knowledge, and the serpent. It reared up, like—let's face it, like an aroused prick, and no wonder, seeing that Eve, who had the figure and face of Jezebel, was on a shoot for the *Sports Illustrated Swimwear* issue. And she was in the raw, butt-naked, oh boy oh boy.

The erect reptile was hissing at her, Just taste this luscious fruit, Miss, just try it, and you shall be like God Himself. (Frida fudged the reflexive pronoun, making it indeterminate.) *Yeah, why not?* Melvyn could see Frida thinking. He read the emotions as they flickered over the screen of her face: anger that it was the woman who fell, sympathetic rebelliousness when she took the fruit, cunning when she offered it to her hapless mate, and indignation and outrage when Adam blamed her for it. But also a kind of perverse pride. After all, Eve *was* the agent of the Fall.

Woman had been far from submissive then! On the other hand, as God booted the couple out of Eden, he cursed Eve. 'To the woman He said, I will greatly multiply your pain in childbirth; in pain you will bring forth children; yet your desire will be for your husband, and he will rule over you.' Frida's knuckles whitened as she grasped the lectern and wailed those words. But her face was as purple as her robe, suffused with blood and resentment, and she ended with: 'And I will put enmity between you and the woman, and between your seed and her seed.' That was a notion Frida could get behind. She was all about enmity between man and woman.

The Revd. Crystal Nutt nodded with the approval of a teacher for a favourite pupil.

'Thank you so much, Dr Shamburger, for that impassioned reading? It was awesome, beyond beautiful? Sisters, and uh, brothers? And other genders, right? You just heard the Holy Writ on the Creation of humankind and the Fall? A neat story, right? But what I have in mind, if you'll indulge me for a while, is something I've been working on for my Doctor of Divinity degree: a feminist interpretation of the Creation story? Yes, you heard me right? The tyrannical patriarchy has misunderstood Genesis, *wilfully* misunderstood it? They emphasise the wrong parts: that God made man first, like that was a huge deal, and that woman was made from his rib, like she was just an afterthought? But think about it, guys?' the Revd. Nutt said, her amplified voice booming, and grinning with the mania of a motivational speaker: 'Adam was napping when God slipped his rib out? What does that mean. Why, the little guy was unconscious, of course, until a woman came along? And if you read without prejudice, Genesis proceeds along those lines? Adam is a dumb, obedient, dim-witted schmuck, you might say, while Eve is the inquisitive one, the intellectually curious one, the courageous one? The snake offers her the fruit of the Tree of Knowledge—and naturally she accepts it? What smart woman wouldn't. Only a man, always willing to submit to a dictator, would be content with his subordinate lot? Just notice: it's Eve who takes the fruit, of her own free will, and Eve who gets Adam to try it too? She's the pro-active one, the leader? What does Adam do. He denies responsibility? *She made me do it*, he says? *And you made her, God?* He's right there?' the Revd. Crystal Nutt said. 'God not only made Eve, but knew she would accept the fruit, and so—if God is omnipotent and wholly good—he or she wanted her to taste it? The prohibition was a trick, to whet her appetite even more? It's clear to me, sisters? Right from the start, God was trying to show us that women are smarter and braver than men? So we should be running things?'

Was the sermon satire? Stand-up? Melvyn glanced around at the congregation: most faces reflected astonishment, although many women, including Frida, were nodding in grave, passionate agreement. Melvyn remembered all the *I'm With Her* stickers during the last presidential election. Shit, even he had had one on his Hummer. What would Jezebel think of all this? She was rubber-necking again—*Ouch, horrible cliché that.* He looked away.

'But the ending's kind of a bummer, right,' said the vicar. 'God curses Eve, sentences her to the eternal tyranny of men? Sheesh. What do we make of that.'

She gloated over her flock. 'I tell you what, sisters? It was a palliative for the guys? Give them the illusion they're in charge, and they'll knuckle under? I gotta tell you, most of them are not so smart? Oh, sure, he or she might have planned a short spell, relatively speaking, of patriarchy? But make no mistake, sisters, she was already planning the matriarchy that would supplant it?'

Melvyn noticed the pronouns metamorphosising, and disquiet on the faces of Cooper and Burd, and derision on Jezebel's, unless that were wishful thinking. Yet also the unmistakable glow of triumph and vindication on Frida's.

'Now let us pray,' the Revd. Crystal Nutt said. 'I invite you to participate in a new, less toxic, less patriarchal version of the Lord's Prayer?. *Our Father* is so sexist, right. So unacceptable? How could we begin our petition instead. Hit me, sisters!'

'Our *Mother*!' yelled Rocky, squirming with excitement in her pew.

'You go, girl!' Frida stage whispered, wriggling too.

The Revd. Crystal Nutt beamed at Rocky. 'Thank you for that suggestion, Dr Rathaus? That's better than 'Father', for sure, but maybe it's like a tad exclusionary. What about our transgender friends. What about our friends who are questioning their gender, or determined to be indeterminate. We don't want to hurt their feelings, do we. I know you all agree with me?' Her face was stern. 'All righty. So I propose that we address our God as... '

'*Our Parent,*' Melvyn murmured audibly. Cooper smirked.

'Our Parent,' the vicar intoned, glaring at Melvyn, 'who art in heaven... '

'Our Parent who art in heaven,' the congregation echoed.

Melvyn wondered if Revd. Nutt would end the prayer with 'Amen'—or would it be 'Awomen', or 'Aparent'? But she stuck with Amen.

Even so, heathen though he was, he stumbled out of the church, as stunned as he would have been had he attended a torchlight Nuremberg Rally in 1936.

Burd cackled: 'Is your head reeling, Melvyn? Are you woke yet?'

He shook his head, nodded, then shook it again. 'I'm speechless.'

'A paradigm shift,' Cooper said. 'Our vicar is reinventing Christianity as a matriarchal cult.'

They had reached the vestibule, where the ritual of devouring chocolate chip cookies and swallowing brown water disguised as coffee took place. Rocky was already bounding like an overfed mastiff at Frida, who strode in with the self-assurance of a bishop, wielding the mace again. Melvyn rushed towards them, determined to reach Frida first.

He failed: Rocky assaulted Frida—that was hardly putting

it too strongly—and flung her furry arms around Frida's neck, tears streaming down her muzzle.

'Totally fuckin' *awesome* reading, Frida. Loved it!' Rocky said, swooning. Was she nonbinary? Melvyn wondered. She looked a bit nonbinary. Not butch exactly, but not feminine either. Maybe the new dogmas about gender were catching on because few educated men were masculine these days, and few of the women were feminine. The Revd. Crystal Nutt, who also looked nonbinary to Melvyn, was lolloping towards the two women, or gender-neutral people, and the maelstrom of their hug sucked her in too.

'Oh my gosh I'm sorry,' Rocky said, 'I shouldn't freaking curse like that.'

'That's totally fine?' the Revd. Crystal Nutt said. 'It's just enthusiasm? That means you have God inside you? Yes, she's inside you—inside all of us?'

Rocky wept. Excellent. Melvyn hoped she would forget about splitting on him.

'Your sermon was awesome,' said the poet, 'Beyond awesome. I have no words.'

Thank God for that. And how like her to have no words.

The Revd. Crystal Nutt and Frida wept too, but if Melvyn was not mistaken, at the same time they were squinting at him with condescension, or contempt. No one pulled *him* into the group hug. Why not? What did Genesis say? *Then the LORD saw that the wickedness of man was great on the earth, and that every intent of the thoughts of his heart was only evil continually.* Melvyn was pretty sure that meant him.

The three women loosened their grip on each other, but continued to move in a close, hypnotic circle, in a kind of dance. A pavane, perhaps. It was a sculptural composition, something like Rubens' *Three Graces,* indeed—harmonious in emotion, but chunkier than the Flemish painter's nudes. Thank God these modern American graces were draped, at least.

Cooper's eyebrows rose at acute angles; the two men

exchanged a glance of hilarity. Melvyn also intercepted a flirtatious glance from Timothy, which he ignored, and a questioning look—a summons, a call, an offer, an enticement, an invitation? —from Jezebel.

'The Holy Trinity,' said Burd. 'The Mother, the Daughter, the Holy Ghost.'

'Dr Roquette Rathaus is hardly ethereal, if she's the spirit,' Cooper said. 'As for the mother, if that's Frida—the Oedipal mother, Melvyn—beware her teeth.'

Melvyn could not grin back. The joke cut too close to the bone, and besides, Jezebel was within springing distance, her limbs tensed, her tail twitching.

He slipped away and joined her.

'Wow,' she said as he came up to her. 'And I thought the Tocqueville Church of Christ was unhinged. But these Episcopalians are insane. Truly batshit crazy.'

'I couldn't agree more,' Melvyn said.

'Aren't most of these people professors? They look like it.'

He nodded. 'I'm afraid the majority of them abandoned reason long ago.'

'I'm going to have to save you. Let's meet. Very soon.'

Oh boy oh boy. His head jerked in alarm. She took the gesture for assent.

'Great. Where? You weren't at ease at my place. Shall I visit you at yours?'

Are you out of your mind? he was about to say. Then he remembered—Frida would not be at home next weekend. She planned to attend some kind of radical feminist retreat in the mountains. And what's more, Thalia, who was still in high school, was flying to Boston as a birthday present, to stay with her sister, Clio, who was doing a BS in Journalism at Emerson with a Minor in Women's, Gender and Sexuality Studies. Having the house to himself would either be a miracle or the biggest mishap in his life, at least since his wedding.

'Shall I?' Jezebel insisted when he did not reply. 'Would you like me to, sir?'

Frida was approaching, with her deeply spiritual smile. Channelling Joan of Arc or St. Theresa. No immediate danger. Even so, he had to get rid of Jezebel fast.

'Let me think about that,' he said, fleeing.

Whew—not a moment too soon. The purple surplice flapped as it flew towards him. Hot air buffeted the fabric, which billowed about Frida's massive body. The bronze filings on her scalp glittered like a warrior's skull cap. She merely looked annoyed, not enraged.

Ergo, Rocky had kept quiet. He fell to his knees. Frida yanked him up by his elbow.

Thank you God, he mouthed. Good old Rocky had not ratted on him. Maybe she was not a servile shit after all. What was he thinking? Of course she was a servile shit.

'Melvyn, people are staring. Who the hell was that? Haven't I seen her before?'

'Oh her? Just a student,' he said, unaware that his *hamartia* was undoing him.

*

Why did therapists always have abstract prints on the walls? Did they think they calmed their clients? Or was the idea that like Rorschach tests, they would stimulate the imagination, liberate the subconscious? Nah, those tests were garbage anyway. Gauguin was Melvyn's idea of an artist, despite his penchant for young girls. Or because of his penchant for young girls? *If Frida could eavesdrop on my internal monologue, I'd be toast,* he said to himself.

'What do you really want, Melvyn?' Dr Pound was saying. 'That's what I'd like you to articulate. So far all I've heard is a litany of complaint about your wife. That's fine, but if you want to improve your life you have to set some goals. Why don't we work on that now?'

Melvyn regarded Dr Pound with respect, condescension, and consternation. Respect, because she was smart and literate, as she had proven in their counselling sessions; condescension because of her 'motherly' figure, since he could not eradicate his prejudice against overweight people; and consternation, because she had put him on the spot. He knew she was right, but that put the onus on him, and he had been hoping she would tell him what to do. Should he have a fling with Jezebel? That was what he wanted to know. He would never have a better opportunity. Should he leave Frida? He would never have a better opportunity.

'Gosh,' he said, with the smirk he had developed to signal his superior intellect, 'I guess we should start by defining what we mean by goals.'

'No need for that,' Dr Pound said sharply. 'You're smart enough to know what I mean. I'm asking you to state what you want out of life, what you'd like to achieve, what you'd like to do. Just be honest. Are you capable of that?'

'It's not so easy,' he said, eyeing her ginger hair with aversion. 'I mean, emotions are complex. I'm not a fourteen-year-old girl.'

'I see,' said Dr Pound, the blue lasers of her eyes boring into his. 'Yours are far more profound, more mature, and wiser, I imagine?'

Melvyn squirmed in his squeaky leather chair. She reminded him of Frida, that was the trouble, with that flabby figure and ginger hair. Not to mention her bullying tone.

'Well? Let me have it, Melvyn. Just talk. Let it fly.'

'I'd like to delete her. My wife, that is. Like an old, useless file.'

'What a curious way of putting it. Is that just a momentary wish or have you actually contemplated it as an action—by considering ways and means, for example?'

'At times I do feel like throttling her. To stop the ceaseless flow of inanities.'

'How interesting.' Dr Pound appeared to be enjoying herself.

'Anything else? Anything more gratuitous? Any forethought going into these murderous impulses?'

'A couple of times in the kitchen, when I was holding the carving knife, my fingers started tingling. With the impulse to stab her. Just to make a point, haha.'

She did not laugh. 'Was that unprovoked or did she say something to enrage you?'

His admission was unwilling. 'She said something to enrage me.'

'Can you tell me what it was?'

He laughed—*bitterly*, he thought, deploring the cliché. 'Always something belittling. Once she said I was *all right* in bed.'

Dr Pound made short, Frida-like snorting noises. 'Is that so devastating?'

'It was the way she said it. You know, like giving a student a C. Theoretically it means 'average' but everyone knows it's below par. 'All right' sucks, basically.'

Dr Pound sighed. 'So you feel she's not satisfied with you as a lover?'

Melvyn writhed in his chair again. 'How do I know? I guess she might not be.'

'You would like her to say you're fan-fucking-tastic in bed, then?' She was merciless. 'Have you told her *she's* fantastic in bed, Melvyn?'

'*God*, no,' he blurted, laughing. 'Are you crazy?'

'Let's hope not. Why haven't you told her she's great in bed, Melvyn?'

'Because she isn't,' he said, and then it all burst out. 'She's lousy. Just lays there, I mean *lies* there, like a beached whale. All that blubber, and those staring, pond-scum eyes. That red, raspy stubble on her scalp.' He shuddered.

Dr Pound glared at him. 'That's pachyphobia,' she hissed.

'No, Frida's not a Paki. Just an East Boston eyetie.'

'Pachyphobia means fear of overweight people. The last

acceptable prejudice. You despise fat people, don't you, Melvyn? They revolt you. Disgust you. Admit it.'

'No,' he said with all the indignation he could muster. 'That's not true. Like no.'

Dr Pound glanced at an onyx paperweight as if she had an urge to hurl it at him.

'Though I have to admit,' Melvyn went on, 'her fat turns me off. I can't help it.'

Dr Pound turned crimson, which made her hair look orange. 'You don't think your lousy sex life might be partly your fault?'

'Hell no. I never had complaints from anyone before. Jesus, I do what I can. Even with her. Last time we did it she wanted me to use a… a goddamn vibrator while we… '

'While you what, Melvyn? Go on. Are you afraid to say the word?'

Could he say *while we fucked*? No he could not. 'While we um, made love.'

Dr Pound's lips curled. 'I see. And you didn't like that, I take it. Using a vibrator?'

'It grossed me out. I had to use it while we were actually… you know.'

'Screwing? Why did that disgust you? Was it a blow to your amour-propre?'

'Well, I guess it was. I mean, can't she get off without a goddamn gadget?'

Dr Pound's face was as red as Frida's when she was furious. Redder, maybe. 'Tell me, have you ever used Viagra, Melvyn?'

'That's none of your business. Anyway, what's that got to do with anything?'

'You're getting angry. Great, that's the transference. You know what that is?'

He *was* angry. 'Don't patronise me, Dr Pound. I'm not some goddamn redneck.'

'So you know all about the Oedipus Complex? Sure you do.

I've read your flash fiction. Did you want to marry your mother, Melvyn? Did you marry her?'

She had him in a corner. 'I guess so. My mom was bossy too. Wish I hadn't.'

'*Have* you ever used Viagra, Melvyn?' She was a relentless interrogator.

Speak calmly. 'Of course I have. How else could I get it up with a goddamn inert whale like that? A skinhead whale with a goddamn ring through her nose like a prize pig.'

'You do hate her, don't you? And you're mixing your metaphors. But my point is this: if you need Viagra to get aroused, why shouldn't she need a vibrator?'

'You got me stumped there. But it's different, somehow.'

'It pisses me off when men are hypocrites like that,' said Dr Pound, glaring at him.

'Surely therapists aren't meant to get angry with clients?'

'We are human, too.'

'That never occurred to me. But it sounds like you're on her side. Are you?'

'No,' she said—lying, he was certain. 'I'm just pointing out inconsistencies. Trying to get you to think clearly and honestly. Let's go on. You'd like to kill her.'

'Only sometimes. Quite seldom, really. I mean, hardly ever. Haha.'

'Well, that's fine and dandy. You only have occasional murderous impulses. I think you'll agree you'd better not give way to them. So what's the alternative?'

'Divorce would be ideal. But I can't. Thalia would go to pieces.'

'Your younger daughter, right. How do you know that?'

'I asked her. She said she'd have a nervous breakdown, her grades would bomb and she'd start cutting herself again or doing heroin. Worse still, she threatened to start praying. To Jesus. God, I just couldn't handle that.'

Dr Pound smiled. 'She's already skilled at manipulating you, isn't she?'

'I resent that. She's a good kid. She adores me.'

'Another Oedipal complex? Or Electra complex?'

Fuck you, Melvyn wanted to say. 'Anyway, think what a nightmare it would be if we got divorced. I'd see Frida in meetings every day. And if I left Oxbow State, what chance would I have of getting another teaching job near here?'

Dr Pound tapped a pencil like a policewoman. 'So what else can you do?'

'I can't think of a goddamn thing.'

'What would you like to do? What do you dream of doing?'

'Getting my own back. Make her pay for all the humiliation I've had to endure.'

'Any ideas? Short of killing or maiming her, I mean.'

A sheepish grin crept across his face. 'Well, there's this girl.'

'Yes?'

'She's after me. I swear. She's the one that's making the moves. Not me.'

'One of your students, Melvyn? You could lose your job.'

'She's not a Creative Writing major. But she is a student at Oxbow State.'

'Really? What's her major?'

'Psychology, actually. Hot damn, I wonder if you know her?'

'She could've interned with me. I better not ask her name. How old is she?'

'Twenty-one, I believe. She's a senior.'

'So what's the problem?'

'What's the problem? You're kidding. She's Clio's age.'

'Is it that you'd feel guilty about betraying Frida? Is that the issue here?'

'Hell no. I'd feel *great* about that. It'd be like winning a Pulitzer. But surely you understand? Wouldn't it be vile to take advantage of such a young girl?'

'Woman,' Dr Pound said.

'Woman. Sorry.'

'We can't have it both ways. Either she's a woman once she's eighteen, as we keep insisting, in which case she's an autonomous adult with a right to her own sex life, or she's a child. At twenty-one. What do you think? Is she a virgin?'

'I doubt it. She says she wants to be a sex therapist.'

Dr Pound gave him a gleeful smile. 'You hit the jackpot, Melvyn. And she is twenty-one. *Way* past the age of consent. Even here in the States.'

'I can't believe my ears. You're telling me to go ahead?'

'I'm just asking you to think clearly. This is a grown woman, who can make decisions about her own sex life. If she wants to have sex with you, and you want to have sex with her, I don't see any impediment, unless you love your wife.'

'I'll be damned. I never expected to hear that from a woman. I told a couple of guys in the dojo,' he said, recalling locker-room talk. 'Of course they just told me to bone her.'

'That's not exactly how I would put it,' Dr Pound said with a sly smile.

And yet that was *exactly* what she meant. His therapist was giving him permission to have an affair. In fact she was instructing him to. Practically ordering him to. No doubt about it. Women were a mystery, and no mistake. He found himself laughing, unable to stop. It would be one in the eye for Frida. His joy was so intense, he nearly wet himself. But a doubt struck him: What would the Superior Man do? He would ask the *I Ching*. Then just go with the freaking flow.

ELEVEN

How to be a Badass Woman

For the past half an hour, whenever Huw tiptoed into the bedroom, he had found Miranda standing in front of the tilted cheval mirror, dabbing cosmetics on her face with the passion and perfectionism of Rembrandt working on a self-portrait. Not since a Stones concert they had been to, when she dressed for a fantasy date with Mick, had she taken so much trouble over her appearance. Knowing she would be late for her retreat, Huw tried one more time.

'Nearly ready?' he said.

'No,' she said. 'Go away and don't interrupt.'

Upstairs Owen was playing his drums, or destroying them, so Huw could not write either. Instead, he flipped through the glossy brochure on the table in the kitchen. On the front page, in Gothic lettering was the legend: *The Guild of Goddesses.* There was a coat of arms in comic book style: an escutcheon with the device of a helmeted goddess carrying a spear—Athene, presumably, in a garish coppery colour—supported by a leopard rampant and a lioness rampant. Beneath was a photo of a slim blonde in a pencil skirt with a slit and thigh-high boots with spike heels. Petronella Pikestaff, the caption read. Former model, burlesque artist and nurse. Founder of The Guild of Goddesses. Beside this was a quote from Obadiah: 'Petronella Pikestaff is a badass Southern woman who will transform your life and turn you into the goddess you've always been, deep down inside!'

Inside the brochure were photographs of Petronella being carried onto a stage by muscular black and brown men; of Petronella prancing, the men ranged behind her, dancing; of Petronella with her legs apart, a microphone held suggestively between them, an expression of orgasmic ecstasy on her face.

Huw chuckled. But the picture unsettled him too. What on earth was the purpose of this 'symposium'? Who was it for? A series of bullet points gave him the answers:

For women and woman-identifying persons
Learn the ancient lore of the priestesses of the forests
Become the sassy, badass woman you know you are
Unleash the goddess within
Find the power to demand what you want
Own yourself and the courage of your desire
Free yourself from pain and guilt
Discover your secret strength
Find your Inner Dominator
Learn to love your own unique Beauty

So far, so predictable. The usual self-help recipe of positive reinforcement, unrealistic promises, and compliments. Did anyone buy it?

Apparently so. There were numerous testimonials from Guild Members:

'Petronella is the real deal. She changed my life. I love you, Petronella!'

'A weekend with Petronella left me so pumped I'm ready for anything!'

'I learned to love myself and ask for more—and hell, I got it! Thanks forever, Petronella, Mother Goddess of the Guild! Women's lives will never be the same!'

If Miranda's breakdown had shaken her and left her needing a boost for her self-confidence, the symposium was probably harmless, at least. Or was it? Did he want his wife to become a sassy badass? And what about finding her Inner Dominator? The prospect of a sassy badass Inner Dominator in his life was not enticing. Just then, Miranda came in at last.

She strode into the kitchen as if she were Tinker Quick entering the stage at a stadium and taking possession of the crowd, her face grave, imperious, fully aware how superhuman she looked, her inner goddess unleashed. She was already badass; she had found her Inner Dominator. She fumbled at her side, perhaps for Tinker's riding crop. She looked as though she would like nothing better than to give him a couple of savage lashes across his face.

'You're not pissed off with me, are you, love?' he said, standing.

'For Chrissake, Huw. I'm late. You've got to get me there in half an hour.'

As they had to drive over seventy miles, that was impossible. But he neither told her so, nor pointed out that he had been waiting for two hours. She did look spectacular, he had to admit, even by her standards: the flawless face, as blank as the face of classical statuary; the voluptuous body, sheathed in tight black silk, her legs swishing in black stockings; the black nail-polish, the glittering blood-red lips. Old habits die hard: he reached for her.

'Don't touch me!' she said in chilling tones. 'Never touch me unless I tell you to!'

She's unwell, he told himself, hurt. *Fragile. Give her time. Let her get well again.*

As they walked outside he said, 'I was wondering what this seminar costs?'

'*Symposium.* What does it matter? I'm paying for it.'

'Still,' he said, as they reached the car, 'our finances are in common, aren't they? You often ask what I've paid for things. And sometimes you aren't happy. You've been known to persuade me not to buy something *I* wanted.'

'A thousand dollars. Hurry up and unlock the car, will you?'

He fumbled with the remote key. 'A thousand dollars? For a weekend?'

She seized the door herself, preventing him from opening it for her. 'Yeah, do you have a problem with that? You know how much money I make, right?'

'Quite a bit more than I do,' he said, getting in. 'As you often remind me.'

'Sheesh. Maybe we need to have separate finances. It's my life, Huw.'

And mine, he wanted to say, as he started the engine and drove away. But maybe it was not any longer—maybe he was wrong about that.

'Can't you go faster?' she said. 'We're late. Man, you're like driving at fifty.'

'That *is* the speed limit.'

'So what? Everyone speeds. You're so sensible sometimes, Huw, so goddamn British. So *boring.* No one drives under the limit, except really old people. Old ladies.'

'I do have a son, you know. And I love you. I'd rather not kill you.'

Miranda could not fume: her internal thermostat was set to freezing. Her face was impassive, white as frost.

'Anyways,' she said. 'It's not one weekend. It's two.'

'You mean you won't be home next weekend either?'

'You got it in one, Huw. And next weekend costs another grand.'

He put the Brandenburg Concertos in the stereo. Bach always consoled him.

'I can't stand violins,' she said, ejecting it. 'They're so miserable.'

She put another CD in the slot. Electric guitars, a country beat, a woman with a harsh voice and a Southern accent. It was a putdown song about a guy who didn't have a clue, didn't know where to put his hand, and couldn't even make the singer come. At least that wasn't Huw: he nearly always made Miranda come. All the same, the misandry depressed him. Near the end, the singer told her beau to fuck off.

'Jesus,' said Huw. 'Must we listen to this? You prefer this to Bach?'

'I do, yeah. I think she's great. She's taking control. Empowering herself.'

'Oh, is that what she's doing?' He suspected the singer was a lonely, bitter woman. The photograph on the CD case, of a middle-aged, angry person, confirmed his intuition.

'Just imagine if a man wrote a song about a woman failing to satisfy him sexually,' he said. 'What would women say about that? What would you say?'

'Men write sexist songs all the time. About how hot women look, how great they are in bed.'

'That may be superficial—but it's not exactly negative, is it? In this kind of song, the woman is taking no responsibility for the failure of the relationship. It's entirely the bloke's fault, and purely because he's a dud in bed. Is that fair?'

If Miranda was thinking of an answer, none came. The car climbed into the hills beyond the city. Trailer homes, gas stations, fast food franchises, and clapboard churches with witty homilies in metal letters on their white marquee boards: IF YOUR LIFE STINKS WE HAVE A PEW FOR YOU. BE THANKFUL YOUR (sic) STILL ABOVE GROUND. HOW TO HAVE A BETTER MARRIAGE EVERY THURS EVENING. *Maybe we should go to that one*, Huw thought, musing whether it was only possible to have a good marriage on Thursday evenings. Leaving the outskirts behind, they drove through an ancient forest, along curving roads, climbing then dipping, sheltered by the Romanesque arches of oaks and elms. Through the trees, he caught glimpses of mountains, round-backed, slumbering dragons. Reminded of the monsters again, he risked another question:

'You've been calmer recently. More stable.'

The country singer still snarled on the stereo. 'Maybe.'

'You haven't mentioned the sea-monsters for a while now.'

'Because I don't want to worry you. They still follow me.'

'Are they following us now?'

She nodded. 'Can't you hear them?'

'I'm afraid not. What are they saying?'

'It's hard to decipher. A lot of it's just noises: hissing and sighing and a kind of scraping sound, like they're scratching at their scales. A sort of swishing too. I think they must be rustling their tails and wings. You must hear that rustling noise.'

'That's the wind in the trees, Miranda. It's blowing hard.'

'No, it's the sea-monsters. They're skittering right along beside us.'

'And why do you think that is, Miranda?'

'It's obvious, isn't it? They have messages for me.'

'Can you understand what they're telling you?'

'Sure I can.'

'Will you tell me?'

'You won't like it.'

'Tell me anyway. I can take it.'

'I doubt it. They say I need to be on my own more. Maybe find my own apartment.'

He bit his trembling lip. 'Are you sure of that, Miranda?'

'It's a little indistinct, with the hissing and swishing, and the sound of the waves. And their voices are low. They croon, you know? Kind of like Frank Sinatra.'

'The sea-monsters sing like Frank Sinatra?'

'Something like that. Sorry. I know it must upset you.'

'Are you leaving me, Miranda? Are you telling me we're finished?'

'Oh no. I want us to stay together. I just need to be on my own for a while.'

'So you aren't divorcing me?'

She shook her head without looking at him.

'It does upset me,' he said. 'I'll be sad if we aren't living together anymore. I think Owen will find it a shock too. But what about you? Won't you be upset at all?'

'I might be, a bit. But it's what I need. And you can always visit me.'

'Great. Is this going to be temporary or permanent?'

'I don't know. Don't pressure me. You're always pressuring me.'

'I'm sorry. I try not to. So when might this happen?'

'See? Pressure, pressure. The sea-monsters advise the end of this month.'

'That's only ten days from now. Could you find a place that quickly?'

The angry, weary voice still sang. 'I already found one.'

'A done deal, then? Ten days. If you're spending next weekend at the retreat too, we won't even have a last weekend together. You do move fast.'

'Don't be snarky with me, Huw. That's why I got to move out, see?'

'Where is it then? The apartment?'

'A condominium. Just off Buzz Aldrin.'

'A long way. I can't walk there.'

'It's five minutes in the car. And no one walks anyhow.'

They drove on in silence, apart from the rising wail of the wind. For Miranda, doubtless, the hullaballoo persisted: the crooning voices, telling her things she wished to hear, and those hissing, swishing, scratching, flapping noises—what were they, the whisperings of her conscience? Or subconscious? Thank God she could not see her sea-monsters. But Huw fancied he saw swift shadows flitting beside them and above them, like immense clouds.

The mansion was a neo-Gothic extravaganza with towers and battlements and uplifting signs as they approached—BADASS WOMEN THIS WAY—YOUR TEMPLE, YOUR LIFE—PETRONELLA PIKESTAFF WELCOMES GORGEOUS GODDESSES TO THE PANTHEON—WOMEN WITH BALLS—DO WHAT YOU WILL—JUST ASK—YOU ARE HOLY! Huw sat in the car park, watching her legs snipping together like black scissors as she walked into the building, carrying a weekend bag. He could not face driving home yet.

He ejected the CD, got out of the car, and dropped the country singer into a trash bin. Then he walked towards the house, drawn by its weird architecture, and curiosity. He hoped Ms. Pikestaff would not implant men-hating ideas in Miranda's impressionable mind. As he approached the entrance, a woman came out to meet him. She was tall and statuesque, wearing a close-fitting grey dress, and glasses. She looked familiar. Had he seen her at the Savanna B. Manley reading, talking to Melvyn? In fact, hadn't he seen her coming out of Melvyn's office more than once lately? She was imposing, self-possessed for someone her age. Unsmiling, though—almost intimidating.

'Professor Lloyd-Jones,' she said, extending her hand as an older woman might. 'We haven't met but I know you from Oxbow State. I'm a student. My name is Jezebel. I've just welcomed your wife to the symposium. Are you a participant too? Do you identify as a woman? That was a joke,' she said, deadpan. 'I don't imagine you're one of Deli—I mean Petronella's dancers? You look fit and handsome enough to be one. But she prefers African-Americans or Latinos. My sister might be a little racially prejudiced, between ourselves.'

'Petronella is your sister, then, I take it?'

'Yes, my older sister. I'm here to facilitate the sessions and make a little pocket money. May I ask what you're doing—if you're not taking part?'

'Just dropping off my wife. I wonder what she will experience, what she hopes to find here. I don't know much about feminist retreats and life coaching. Is it terribly exciting?'

'It is for most of the women. Of course they aren't very smart. Oh, sorry. There may be exceptions. I find it all a bit silly, to be frank. I've seen it so many times now. But it makes them happy, and my sister's getting rich.'

'I like your directness. May I make a rather cheeky request? Could I watch the seminar for a while?'

'Not in the audience. It they discovered a male intruder, I dread to think what they might do. We have a security team, as well.'

'But the security team must be men, I suppose?'

'Yes and no. That is, it depends what you mean by 'men.' They *used to be* guys, but now they're transgender women. From Texas. Trans Bikers for Christ, they call themselves.'

'The mind boggles. Trans Bikers for Christ? From *Texas*?'

'Austin, obviously.' She gave him a wintry smile. 'Anyway—how could we pull this off? It might be fun. Do you mind taking a bit of a risk?'

'I'll take my chances with the transgender Christian bikers.'

'You wait till you see them—many of them are weightlifters. Real muscle men. I mean women, of course.' She flashed a brief Goneril-like smile.

He smiled back. 'Let's do it.'

'In case we meet any security women, do you mind wearing a disguise?'

'What kind? Would I have to dress up in drag?'

'No, just as a waiter. Petronella likes to have the ladies served by men. A reversal of the usual hierarchy, you see. Come along, this way. You can change here.'

She led him into a cloakroom, and instead of leaving, turned her back while he donned black trousers, a bowtie, and a white jacket.

'How do I look?' he said when he was ready. 'Do I pass muster?'

'You look Italian. Like Marcello Mastroianni in *La Dolce Vita.* Suave but also vulnerable. Perfect. Quick, this way. Your wife was late—they're already starting.'

He followed her down wainscoted corridors, through a room with hammer-beam vaulting and stuffed elk heads. Thickets of antlers. Loud thumping music was playing, with singing and rapping in Spanish.

'What on earth is that?' Huw asked.

'Reggaeton, to warm up the goddesses. Do you like it? Of course not.'

Jezebel opened a door and Huw found himself on a kind of gallery with her, overlooking what must once have been a ballroom, with a stage erected at one end, and rows of seats facing it. The seats were full, but he located Miranda, who was gazing expectantly at the stage. Not far from her were a number of Oxbow State students and faculty: Broome, Jordan and Nutmeg, as well as a transgender professor of Queer Studies called Marge, Rocky Rathaus, and Frida Shamburger, who was dressed like Toni Morrison, which is to say like the Queen at a State occasion, but with less taste, in a full-length ballgown, with a fur stole (could it be real?), a string of pearls, and a tiara. Had she concealed her full-sleeve tattoos, her buzzcut and nose-ring, she might have looked elegant. Well, maybe not, given her Hogarthian dimensions. She was talking to, or shouting at—the brazen blare was audible even above the nightclub beat—a massive woman with a butch haircut and clerical collar.

'Where exactly are we?' he asked. 'With these curtains we're nearly invisible.'

'I believe this was the musicians' gallery. This place was built for Xenophon Fullerton, the magnate who owned the mines. Convenient, sir, isn't it?'

Before he could answer, the music rose in volume. The bass and kick drum thwacked his chest, in a monotonous rhythm. The lights dimmed. A skirling of bagpipes began, and all the women leapt to their feet, shrieking, screaming, and howling.

Six dusky men came cavorting onto the stage, in skin-tight black singlets and leggings. The audience clapped. Miranda looked excited. The dancers darted offstage and returned, carrying a prostrate woman above their heads. They set her down on her feet and knelt before her, and the ovation reached a crescendo. 'Your Mother Goddess, Petronella Pikestaff!' boomed a deep DJ voice offstage. A single spot-light fell on her.

She wore a bolero jacket, a blouse with a pirate's ruff, over-the-knee boots, and a skirt so short that a broad band of stockinged thigh was visible. Her hair was a mass of gold curls. She was at least six feet tall.

'Impressed?' Jezebel shouted in Huw's ear.

He nodded. She stood unmoving in the centre of the stage, her legs wide apart, arms akimbo, smiling as the men made their obeisance, bending their powerful torsos before her, raising their arms. She surveyed the audience with the gaze of an empress. Then she flexed and cracked and struck, this way, that way, quick as a whip, sharp as a snake. The dancers leapt to their feet and capered behind her. The upturned female faces of the audience showed rapture—like Jordan, Nutmeg, and Rocky—or the transport of holy awe, like Frida, the female priest, and Miranda. They all swayed in rhythm. Shyly, joyfully they glanced at one another. Nutmeg grinned at Miranda, who smiled back.

The song, if it could be called that, must have gone on for ten minutes, though to Huw it felt far longer. The beat and the bass never faltered and nor did the dancing. Petronella had the poise and skill of a professional dancer—no, more, she led her troupe, and yet outshone them. She was better than a Bollywood star, slinkier than Tinker Quick. When the music halted, an acolyte handed her a cordless microphone, she made a Valkyrie screech, and the women whooped back.

'You're goddesses!' she yelled, her voice harsh. 'I love you all!'

Surely some of the women must storm out in disgust? Huw hoped Miranda would. But none did. Their gaze was reverent. Didn't they hear the insincerity in Petronella's voice?

'That was amazing, huh?' she bawled. 'Was it fun for you?'

The squeals and barks of the crowd were those of sea-lions showered with fish in an aquarium. Jezebel shot a sardonic glance at Huw. Beneath the epidermis of her dress, her body was taut, and yet her corporeality was the least essential part of her. Her mind informed her whole life—her clear, cold eyes showed him that. But what kind of mind was it?

Onstage, Petronella pranced and grinned. 'See, dancing releases nitric oxide in your blood. And pheromones. So you feel awesome—and *sexy*. Right? Who's feeling *hot?* Don't be shy, ladies. Come on, who's feeling *foxy?* I sure am.'

Arms went up: Rocky's, and Nutmeg's. The vicar's. Not Miranda's, thank goodness.

'Only about a third of you. That'll change, I promise ya. Trouble is, sisters, we're taught to *not* feel sexy, right? Didn't your momma teach you to be a *good* girl?'

Miranda nodded. 'And where'd that get ya? They praised you for ignoring your body, right? They praised you for being quiet, for accepting, doing what you're told. We gotta change that. We're not going to do what they tell us anymore. We're gonna do what *we* wanna do. We're gonna ask for what we want. *Demand* what we want. How about that?'

The barks and squeals of the sea-lion colony resounded.

'Beautiful, beautiful,' Petronella warbled. 'You can be sassy, see? You're all badass women, I can tell.' More squeals, yips and shouts. 'You're all goddesses. You're mistresses of your fate. Yeah, you are.' Was Miranda a goddess? Bodily, absolutely. Intellectually—she was bright, if a bit cracked, a bit potty. But was she in command of her emotions? Was there a spirit inside that perfect sculpture of flesh? She lacked the self-possession and serenity of Praxiteles' Aphrodite—but so did all these women. The essence had been left out. It was not so much that they were broken, as the old Emo song wailed, but incomplete. Despite her charisma, Huw thought, that went for Petronella too. Jezebel had a stillness and a spark—but she was an Artemis, a huntress, pitiless and cold. Welsh women often had that spark and fullness, and warmth too. So did South Americans. Unbidden, he recalled the Persian doctor in the hospital. She had that divine spirit also. But he forbade himself to think about her. Miranda was slipping away. If he wanted to keep her, he had to understand her. And change.

Petronella was summoning women to the stage, to declare something they wanted for themselves. The first was a mousey woman with poorly-cut hair and shapeless clothes who might have been a librarian.

'I wanna be a writer,' she said softly. 'I wanna be a legend.'

'Beautiful,' Petronella said. 'Put your hands together for her. What's your name, sister?'

'Delia.'

'Delia, fantastic, awesome. And what kind of writer do you wanna be?'

'A fantasy novelist. I've just been accepted on the MFA Program at Oxbow State.'

Frida and Rocky whooped frantically; Jordan, Nutmeg, and others joined in.

'That is so coo-ul. Wicked, awesome. I'm proud of you, sister Delia.'

Delia got an ovation as she strode off the stage—standing straighter than she had, and beaming like an actress on the red carpet.

Next Petronella pointed at Miranda, summoning her with a wave. Miranda shook her head. Petronella's hands flew to her hips, with a teasing smile. Nutmeg and Jordan pulled Miranda out of her seat. Everyone clapped.

When Miranda reached the stage, Petronella towered over her. 'My, you are *gor*geous,' Petronella said. Her voice had a hawkish, predatory edge to it.

'What's your name, darling?'

Her voice was tiny: 'Miranda.'

'Great, like Carmen Miranda, right? And what do you want, honey?'

A little louder now: 'I want to go to Mexico.'

'Tell us why, will ya?'

'I'm inspired by Frida Kahlo.'

'Woohoo!' shouted Frida.

'Sure, why is that, sugar?' Petronella said.

'Because she was strong. Fierce. She lived the way she wanted. She didn't even live with her husband—she just visited when *she* had the urge, when she wanted sex. And she didn't let her suffering define her. She transformed it into something beautiful, mythical.'

Petronella turned to the audience with the expression of theatrical wonderment that talk-show hosts like Obadiah and Elsa used to engage the crowd.

'Hey, this chick is the business, right? Strong, fierce—you hear that, sister goddesses? I see that strength, that fierceness in you, Miranda. Right, ladies?'

There was a howl and a roar. Huw noticed that like Delia's, Miranda's posture was already more confident—shoulders back, head held high.

'So tell me, babe, you gonna do it? You gonna make your dream come true?'

Miranda nodded with pride. 'I've bought the ticket already.' This was news to Huw.

'Woohoo!' yelled Frida. 'You go, girl!'

'You going alone?' Petronella asked Miranda.

'No, with friends. My husband didn't want to come.'

'Terrific, terrific. What do we need men for, sisters?'

'Nothing!' the gigantic vicar bellowed. A lot of women laughed.

'That's right,' Petronella said. 'I know some of you are into men. And that's okay. But you don't *need* 'em. Right? They need *us*, right? And we gotta teach 'em that—all of us goddesses. Show 'em who's boss. Right, ladies?'

Frida Shamburger roared. So did many others. From the podium Petronella produced a bullwhip, and handed it to Miranda.

'Take it, it won't bite you, honey.'

Don't take it, Huw pleaded. Miranda accepted it shyly.

'Crack it, sugar. Show him. Show us.'

'Sick,' Huw said.

'Oh, are you're into that?' Jezebel said. 'The kinky stuff?'

'Actually I meant the word in the archaic sense. Perverted. Depraved. Warped.'

Miranda's arm rose, hesitantly: then flashed out. The whip cracked.

Everyone screamed. Miranda walked offstage, clutching the whip, to another ovation, beaming as Delia had. Childish and absurd though it was, apparently the course worked. Huw wondered if he had never noticed a part of Miranda. He had considered himself a model husband. But what if he had not responded to all her needs? What if he had not nurtured her deepest desires? What if he had failed to draw her out, to listen to her when she spoke?

He spent another couple of hours in the gallery, in fascinated horror. More women came onto the stage and gave their testimonials. Then there was a period of 'quaking': women testified to their pain, howling and wailing while Petronella cradled them. Then more reggaeton, Daddy Yankee and Maluma, with wild dancing. When Petronella asked the audience who felt foxy again, almost all the hands shot up. Including Miranda's. She had been dancing with Jordan and Nutmeg, and exchanging smouldering glares with them. In the last session before lunch, a pompous-looking white man came on stage and sat behind a desk. He was middle-aged and bald, a portly figure in a business suit and tie.

One by one, women mounted the stage and asked him for things they wanted. To begin with all were hesitant. Petronella had to goad some into asking. Their initial demands were modest:

a kitten, a box of chocolates, a bunch of flowers. He shook his head irritably at each one. The women started laughing. Since he refused all their requests, it freed them to ask for more. One wanted a Porsche, another a black man with a huge dick. Many cheers. One shouted that she wanted multiple orgasms every single night. More cheers and whoops. The aspiring fantasy novelist wanted to be loved. The vicar asked to be an archbishop. Broome requested celebrity. Jordan asked if she could have a baby with Nutmeg. Nutmeg asked if she could be polyamorous. Rocky asked if she could be a full professor. Frida demanded the Pulitzer Prize—no, the Booker—no, the goddamn Nobel Prize. Miranda begged to see her sea-monsters. Then she asked if she could make another request. Petronella nodded. *I want my husband to see me as I am. Let me live my way. Can you do that for me?*

The man in the suit shook his head, without feeling. Was that how Miranda saw him, Huw, as a pompous old guy, denying her nature, scotching her desires and aspirations?

All at once he found the event unbearable. 'Thank you very much,' he said.

'Are you OK?' Jezebel said. 'You look shaken.'

'I am, but I'll be fine. I appreciate your kindness.'

They walked in silence through the halls with the elk trophies, until they reached the main doors, where Jezebel said:

'I'm delighted to have met you. I wonder if you'd be willing to help me with some research I'm doing for the Honours College? I'm going to be a therapist, you see.'

He nodded, too upset by it all to ask her what kind of therapist she wanted to be.

TWELVE

The Opportunity Must Be Seized

When Melvyn consulted the *I Ching*, he got the third trigram, Resolving Chaos, with a moving fourth line. The oracle proclaimed: *The opportunity must be seized. Don't allow false pride or false inhibition to hold you back*. Did those oriental sages nail it or what?

So he invited Jezebel to the campus Sundoes, bought her a cup of sludge, and mentioned in passing that the following weekend, his wife and daughter would both be away. Jezebel did not take the hint. How could he nudge her, subtly?

'I may get a tad lonely, all by myself. All weekend. Alone.'

Tinker Quick was squeaking about her useless boyfriends on the sound system. Students eyed Melvyn and Jezebel with the curiosity of paparazzi.

'Unless you'd maybe like to keep me company,' he murmured. 'Would you?'

Her answer was startlingly loud. 'I want to make sure I understand. Are you suggesting that I come over to your place and copulate with you, sir?'

Heads turned. Someone took a photo with a phone, he was pretty sure. 'Of course not! Please speak quietly.' In a nearly inaudible whisper, he added: 'I was thinking along more romantic lines, but now you mention it, haha, sure, sex is good too.'

She gave him a clinical look. 'I'll see what I can do, sir.'

'So you'll pass by—Saturday? For um… lunch?'

'I'm busy Saturday. Maybe Sunday? If I can.'

Slack-jawed students gaped after her as she strutted out.

*

Melvyn was on tenterhooks that Sunday morning. He had bathed in Thalia's bubble bath—soaking in the tub, which he had not done for years—shaved with a real razor, and drenched his chin and cheeks with cologne. The house was clean by Shamburger standards, which were far from exiguous, but little could be done about Frida's pagodas of papers and books, rising from tables, desks, floors, and any other vacant surfaces. Melvyn had bought and lit aromatic candles. Norah Jones sang seductively on the stereo. His most daring move had been to defer dressing: instead of his usual professor clothes, he wore only a white towelling robe, and a pair of Aladdin-like red leather slippers. Dr Pound had licensed him to be wicked. But would Jezebel appear? Had her reticence been a deliberate strategy, to keep him in suspense? A bit of sexy teasing? Or might she simply have lost interest in him?

Melvyn prowled around the house, watched curiously by Darcy and indifferently, or scornfully, by Garfield, the corpulent marmalade cat. For once Melvyn did not open his email. Nor did he enter Facebook, where he would see constant updates from Frida, gushing about the powerful, beautiful young women at the symposium, with photos of her glowing like a red traffic light beside other women, all wearing triumphant smiles. Perhaps one of a margarita or a plate of sushi. He turned off his cell phone. It would infuriate Frida if she texted him and he failed to answer, but fuck her. He had withheld the number from Jezebel too, like obvs. So the question was, what could he do until she arrived—if she did?

He was way too excited to write, or even read. What would the Superior Man do? A spot of Tai Chi? He did a sequence, but could not concentrate, and kept forgetting the next pose. He sat on his zafu cushion to meditate. All he could think of were his bare legs, which were muscular and manly, embroidered with a dense, curly mat of dark hair. At their apex was the tabernacle, the holy of holies, the secret, venerable organ, dangling in a state of readiness—a dangerous, mysterious demi-urge. Would it behave? He had his anxieties on that score. He hoped it would spring into action at the first whiff of hand-to-hand combat. As it reposed on the pillow of his balls, he felt its weight: yes, it was satisfyingly, inordinately, unwontedly large. He flipped back the dressing gown to have a peep. Yep, no question, it was a solid-looking member, a veritable African python, thick, long, sinewy, magnificent. It had been such a stalwart, faithful friend. *Where would I be without you, old buddy?* He flicked the sacred serpent back and forth, a contented smile on his face.

And yet his worries interrupted his musings. What time was it? Would the neighbours see her arriving, if she came? They were a nosey bunch, seldom far from the folds of their curtains. And if they observed Jezebel's arrival, would they report to Frida? They ought to have arranged to meet in a motel. No, that would have been beyond sordid. He was not *positive* that Jezebel intended to have sex with him. Bullshit, of course he was. But what if there were some emergency? What if Thalia had one of her panic attacks, and needed to fly home? If she called in desperation and he did not answer? Above all, should he pop a Viagra? No, relax, the python said. It was eleven o'clock, then twelve, twelve-thirty, one. The candles burned low. Norah Jones kept singing. He was getting hungry. Damn her, she wasn't coming.

But just when he was about to give up, there was a timid

knock on the door, not preceded by the whoosh of an automobile engine, or the slamming of a car door.

Melvyn arose from his zafu cushion and slithered over the carpet, watched sceptically by Garfield. Checking quickly that the serpent was concealed behind a flap of the bathrobe, and taking a deep yogi breath, he seized the door handle.

As he opened the door he realised he had forgotten to prepare any lunch.

But there was Jezebel, with her impassive, sculptural face, half-hidden by glasses, wearing the Grecian dress she had worn to receive him at the desolate McMansion, and bearing gifts: some sort of meal, by the look of the Styrofoam boxes, and a bottle of sixteen-year-old single malt Scotch, which she thrust at him.

'Come in,' he said, ushering her inside, and scanning the neighbours' windows for white faces or moving curtains. Nothing he could see, thank God. 'Where's your car?'

'Around the corner. I didn't want to attract attention.'

'You *are* smart.'

'Thank you, sir. I'm flattered by the bathrobe. How thoughtful and sexy.'

'You don't think it's overdone? It's not exactly subtle, is it?'

'Who wants subtlety? You're being confident and masterful. I find that thrilling.'

Melvyn had imagined their passion overtaking them. In his fantasies, he had thrown off his robe, or she tore it off his body, while she flung off her own clothes, and quickly they were fused on the floor. But they had not so much as touched one another. He had forgotten the etiquette, the ritual. *I must be patient*, he thought.

'You've brought a meal,' he said. 'I forgot to get one. Thanks so much.'

'It's Italian. *Pollo a la cacciatore*. Do you like Italian food?'

'Like it? I love it: I am Italian-American, you know. I'll open a bottle of wine.'

He swept three or four towers of Frida's books off the table on to the floor.

'No need to do that, sir,' Jezebel protested, 'you may damage them.'

'It's only my wife's creative writing pedagogy,' Melvyn said, with visceral hatred. 'Some of it written by her. Vacuous baloney. I think I'll set fire to them, actually.'

While Norah Jones warbled, he microwaved the meal, and they drank a plummy Montepulciano. The wine helped him relax. Jezebel nodded with what he took to be philosophical approval as he put the books in the fireplace, and set them alight, which was harder than he expected. The flames only burned the covers and blackened the edges. Obliterating Frida's name felt great, though. As they ate, apropos of nothing, Jezebel said:

'Do you appreciate lingerie, sir?'

'Depends what kind,' he said, recalling Frida's drawers, capacious enough for the hindquarters of a carthorse, and the massive contraption meant to check the uncontrolled swinging of her pectoral appendages. How she managed to funnel all that flesh into those 'cups'—buckets would be a more accurate word—was a puzzle. How did she strap it all together? Frida in her underwear was not a pretty sight.

'You might appreciate this kind, sir,' Jezebel said, lowering her décolleté and giving him the briefest glimpse of a boldly-cut, black lace push-up bra.

'Oh boy oh boy oh boy. God yes. May I see more?'

'Soon,' she said, a drop of red wine on her chin. He ventured to lick it off. 'We don't want to rush things. What about this?' She sat sideways, raised the hem of her long dress with tantalising slowness, until he saw stocking-tops and suspenders, then covered up.

'You are a major genius. Um, would you like to see my bedroom now?'

'Yes, I think that would be appropriate, sir. Let's have a glass of Scotch first.'

'Aren't you afraid you might lose control of yourself?'

'Oh yes, sir. That's precisely what I'm afraid of. Make it a large one, please.'

The whisky was rich, complex, and peaty, with caramel tones. Melvyn flushed as he drank with her. They ascended the stairs, Melvyn kicking piles of Frida's papers out of the way, and found themselves in the bedroom, where Jezebel's Grecian robe dissolved at his touch, magically, leaving her Nike-like body resplendent in the lingerie—black bra, stockings and suspenders, and a suggestion of a V-string. Melvyn's own bathrobe fell open. Jezebel's astonishment at the sight and touch of the python was a connoisseur's, not a virgin's.

She spoke in awe. 'How huge, how… swarthy. This is a black man's penis, sir.'

Melvyn took that as an entirely non-racist compliment. 'Gee, thanks.'

No need for Viagra with a nubile woman, it struck him. He was virile, manly, *huge*. He was a man of the jungle. They crashed down together, scaring off the curious Darcy, and *desecrating* the connubial bed—what a delightful word. Their coupling was athletic, aerobic, a middle-distance run, ending in a sprint neck and neck to the finish. Hardly spiritual, but one hell of a blast. Boy oh boy oh boy, Melvyn had not had such an awesome time in years.

'You're a fantastic lover, sir,' she said as they lay together afterwards. She still had her stockings on. 'Sensuous, but brutal. The perfect combination in my opinion.'

If only Frida could have heard that! Melvyn's pride in himself mushroomed; he grew; he glowed. *And* she believed him to be brilliant!

No one had ever spoken to him like *that* before. 'Do continue,' he said.

'Yes, precisely. Do let's continue. I see you are ready. If you would like to, that is.'

'I sure would,' he said, clambering on top of her again. 'I'm even beginning to enjoy you calling me sir.'

'I'm glad, sir.' But somewhere under her dress on the floor, her phone rang. 'I'm afraid I need to take that call, sir,' she said, pushing him off. 'Please excuse me.'

Well, I'll be darned, Melvyn thought, as she snatched up her bra and dress and left the bedroom, whispering into her phone. What the heck could be so urgent?

He fancied he heard her pronounce the fricative F—maybe Frank?

Surely not. Could anyone take precedence over him, the brilliant writer with the black man's penis, the sensuous but brutal lover? The hell they could! He would show her. He would be masterful again, snatch the phone from her, hurl it away, drag her back to the bed and ravish her. She would enjoy that. But by the time he got down the stairs, she had her ballet flats on and was slipping out of the front door.

'Sorry, sir, I must go. I can't explain now. Thank you, it was beyond my dreams.'

The girl was kind of a nut. Still, he had got his revenge on Frida. No one could take that away from him. What a chick. He hummed the Ode to Joy as he showered. He was *way* too happy to think about tidying up before Frida came home. Unfortunately for him.

THIRTEEN

A Germ of an Idea

A stained glass Tree of Life, a vintage reproduction of the Tiffany original, hung in a window in Huw's study. Behind a slender golden trunk in the centre of the panel were hills, a lake, and a river zigzagging towards the tree. Foliage and flowers filled the lower foreground. In the upper limbs of the tree hung red and orange fruits and purple blooms. Branches trifurcated from the trunk and spread in an orderly tangle, like a Celtic knot, reaching upwards, towards the fruit, the foliage, and the flowers. Gazing at this glowing panel as he wrote, Huw was inside the sap of the tree, his spirit rising, racing through leaves and twigs and petals, into the hearts of those fruits. He was surging, humming, spinning. One with life.

You may imagine he was in ecstasy, filled with mystic joy. Sometimes he was. But not today. Sadness abides in the core of life, in the heart of the oak and the orange tree, in the capillaries of the leaves, in the stamens and pistils of the blooms, in the probing roots, in the deep, dark earth where the worms toil and burrow. Joy animates every fibre, but it is fleeting. The tree carries the knowledge of its own decay and demise. Even at its zenith, in that crown of leaves burnished by the hot liquid light of the sun, it feels the creeping of the rot—so distant and slow that it could surely never reach these heights—and yet it can and it must.

Every evening for the past fortnight Miranda had come home late, often in the small hours. All day, every day, Huw dreaded her planned departure for her own flat. Still, he hoped to persuade her to change her mind. If he could just reassure her that he would give her space, respect her desire for independence, let her 'find herself,' wouldn't she stay with him?

The day before she was due to leave, she came home from work early and agreed to take a short hike with him. 'Isn't this beautiful?' he said on the overgrown trail in the mountains. Now and then he had to use a stick to part the undergrowth.

Miranda kept her eyes on the ground. 'I'm afraid of the snakes,' she said.

'You never used to be. If there are any, they're sure to feel us coming.'

'I'm not so sure. I'm so frigging scared.'

'Just tramp heavily. Like this. They can feel the vibrations.'

He demonstrated but she did not follow his example. 'There might be bears.'

'I haven't seen any signs. And if there are bears, they'll only be black ones. They're just like big dogs. You wave your arms and shout and they go away.'

'If you haven't gotten between them and their cubs.' She stopped dead.

'Come on, Miranda. We've only been walking ten minutes.'

'I can't go on, Huw.'

'You want to go back already?'

Tears glittered in her eyes. She nodded. He sighed. 'Well, come on, then.'

'I can't walk back through that undergrowth. It's infested with snakes.'

'I'm sure it's not. But what are we going to do, then? Stay here?'

'Could you carry me?'

'If you really can't do it, of course I could.' He tried to hug her, but she was stiff as a statue. He picked her up easily—she weighed a hundred and ten pounds.

When they reached the car at the trailhead, he set her down. She was panting.

'All right now?' he said.

She shook her head as children do.

'What's going on? I haven't spoken to you all this week. I don't like that.'

'Don't be so demanding, Huw. I told you I need some me time right now.'

'I understand that. But there's so much me time. I hope we still have a marriage.'

'Of course we do.'

'Even though you're moving out?' She didn't answer. 'And you're spending so much time with the McBanes, too. Is that helping?'

'I guess. Although they can be a tad weird.'

'I've noticed. But how do you mean?'

'You know Matthew's OCD, right? I think he's gotten a bit obsessed with me.'

'Go on,' Huw said grimly.

'He's asked me to tell him each month when I get my period. He insists.'

'What did you say?'

'He's afraid I might get pregnant. He doesn't want that.'

'What's it got to do with him?'

'Well, he's afraid he'll impregnate me.'

'Jesus Christ. Are you sleeping with him, then?'

'Of course not. I think I'd remember if I was.'

'Are you sure?' She was so heavily medicated, he wondered if she would.

'Sure I'm sure. He's a marshmallow man. Physically repulsive.'

'But if there's nothing between you, how could he get you pregnant?'

'He believes he has the power to impregnate me by looking at me.'

Huw had to let that sink in. 'Christ, he's off his head.'

'He's convinced that if he covets me lustfully, I could conceive his child.'

'An immaculate conception? What exactly do you do with those loonies?'

'Talk, eat. Drink.'

'You're not supposed to drink at all because of all the meds you're taking.'

'I know. But Matthew is a doctor. He won't let me do anything dangerous.'

'You're so naive. *He* is dangerous. They're both dangerous. They're scheming.'

'What do you mean, scheming?'

'My guess is that they want to have a threesome with you. I saw how NeAmber ogled you. They're taking advantage of your illness, Miranda.'

'That's a horrible thing to say. But I guess it could be true. They have been kind of creeping me out lately…'

'Really? Then surely you aren't still planning to go to Mexico with them?'

'I have to. I have to see Chichen Itza. Frida's paintings. It's important to me.'

'You don't have to go with them. I'll go with you—as long as they don't come.'

'It's too late. We have the tickets.'

He could not say he knew that already. 'You've actually bought the tickets?'

'We're going at the start of May. You couldn't go then anyways, because of the university exams.'

'Couldn't you change your ticket? I'm afraid you're falling

into their power. And drifting away from me. I feel I'm losing you. I love you, Miranda.'

'I love you too,' she said—glibly, the way children say it when pressed.

'Really?' She nodded, faraway. 'And you'll stay with me?'

'As long as you make me happy.'

'Of course. So long as I make you happy. As you told me a few weeks ago.'

Now, in spite of his anguish, as he sat beneath his Tree of Life, words poured from Huw's pen. His ancestors murmured in his ear: all he had to do was listen. More medium than poet, he wrote, and what he wrote was good. Even so, he shared the knowledge of the tree. Sorrow accompanied the incantation, like the strains of the Bach B Minor Mass. Grief informed the myths of the Mabinogion, even as they blossomed and bloomed and formed wreaths, bright and quick and playful. He was in peril of losing her—and his own life.

That was his secret knowledge, as he composed on the beautiful, bleak morning after Miranda had gone. He had to finish the book and provide for Owen's future. Last night Miranda's brother had come to fetch her. She had taken little: her clothes, her profusion of shoes, a few books and pictures. Miranda's brother was a big man with red hair who so exactly matched a second century statue of a Roman soldier in the Uffizi that he could have been the model. He had said unkind things about Huw which Miranda had reported to her husband. Huw had wondered if he would have to fight him. If the red-haired Roman insulted him, he would punch him, even if it meant a humiliating defeat. Luckily no violence was offered. Huw did not plead with Miranda to stay, so there was no ground for conflict. Brad averted his eyes from Huw's, embarrassed to be there. He hefted the heavy suitcases like playthings. Huw did not offer to help. She was dry-eyed, lifeless as the doll in *The Sandman*. Had Huw fallen in love with an automaton? If so, who was her Coppelius?

Who had created this beautiful automaton? Her mother, her father? The McBanes? Might it be Huw himself?

On the lawn a cardinal pecked at something, and a blue jay bullied the crimson bird out of the way. Huw had left his study door open. Owen paused in the doorframe on his way downstairs, either not noticing the tears on his father's face or not remarking on them out of embarrassment. Indeed, what he said was probably a tactful attempt to distract him.

'Hey, I saw that skinny dude you work with the other day. The one with the punky, chunky wife.'

Punky, chunky. Huw gave Owen a feeble smile. 'Melvyn. Was he with Frida?'

'No, some chick. Quite a hot one.'

'A chick? Melvyn? Are you certain?'

'Dude was in Sundoes with her, near my school. They looked intimate.'

'Really?' That did not sound like Melvyn, but right now Huw could not think about him. He could think of nothing but Miranda's departure.

'I expect he's banging her,' Owen said. 'I would for sure.'

Huw attempted another smile, but did not reply.

'Hey, who was that last night?' Owen asked.

'It was Brad coming for Miranda. She's gone.'

'Oh yeah, I know. We said goodbye. I didn't see Brad, though.'

'Did she say anything to you?'

'Just that we'd stay friends. Oh, yeah. She asked if I'd help her paint her apartment.'

'Did she? Will you?'

'Yeah, probably.'

'Out of friendship? Love?'

'Well, she's cool, for an adult. Also she said she'd pay me.'

'Did she?'

'Yeah, and I could definitely use the money. Well, see you later,' Owen said.

He slammed the door on his way out, and moments later

Huw was on his bicycle, sailing into the street with an abstracted expression. Huw's grief coursed through him. For hour after black hour, no image arose in his mind but Miranda's face, sorrowful, distant, and unreachably beautiful, like a mural of a medieval saint in a Spanish church. Only her face, offering benediction or malediction. But then, merciful as rain, the words began dropping around him, in Welsh and English, a murmuring, a whispering, a rumour, a scratching he saw as well as heard, for he saw the Gothic letters, the calligraphy of the quills, the flourishes, the illuminated capitals, the bold colours and gold leaf. Voices, as bell-like and clear as those of chanting monks, gave him their words. He thanked God for that blessing.

*

He was less thankful for his role as thesis committee Chair at Timothy's defence later that day. His advisee had rejected all of Huw's suggestions for revisions, so the text was littered with wrong collocations, tense switches, clichés, and redundancies. The prose was turgid. Because Timothy had turned in the novel over a month late—with Frida's approval—Huw could not demand changes, so his only choices now were to either fail or pass the blasted thing. He ought to fail it. But that would displease Frida, and might put his promotion in jeopardy, or even his job, at a time when over half the family income had vanished at a stroke. He decided to pass it, since the other committee members planned to. Looking back later, his decision to appease would seem injudicious and cowardly to him.

The atmosphere in the Conference Room was celebratory but nervous. Jorgenson was there. It was not unusual for the spouse of the person defending to attend, but usually the Dean did not. The old man made Huw uneasy. It was the Chair's job to ensure an impartial examination, and how could he, given such pressure? Jorgenson was the kind of older man you found in the *Prairie Home Companion*—big and smug, in a Truman

Capote dickie bow and seersucker suit, with dyed hair and a San Francisco moustache. Timothy pranced and preened among his pals, mostly male, white, and gay, although Charleston and Broome were among them. Timothy had a blonde floppy fringe reminiscent of David Bowie in the early eighties. Like the singer, too, he sported a suit that hung loosely on his epicene frame. Although he neighed at the jokes, his face had the pallor of a pre-Raphaelite princess. As they all took their seats, he cast a pleading look at Huw, who pretended not to have seen it.

The other committee members were Marge, the transgender Queer Studies specialist, and Melvyn, in a pumpkin-colour shirt, grinning like a rapscallion. Lucky Luke was there, in his usual Hawaiian shirt but with a tie featuring fists raising the middle finger, and Rocky sat beside her idol, mimicking Frida's earnest expression and wearing the same kind of purple pavilion of a dress—in fact, maybe the very same one—a vast garment with mysterious folds and flaps. It swamped Rocky's thin frame. Frida was dressed soberly, in a black business suit. Hippo legs descended from a swollen skirt, but her feet, in ballet flats far, far too small for her—had she cut off bits of her heels, like Cinderella's sisters?—failed to meet the floor.

Frida glared at Huw, and if he was not mistaken, at Melvyn too. The gold nose-ring gleamed with menace. Her bristles, surely freshly rasped for the occasion, glinted like rust shavings. The monstrous effort of breathing made her shudder with each exhalation.

Huw sat at the head of the table. He began the proceedings with a quote from Dylan Thomas' 'How to Begin a Story', which, judging from the blank looks of his audience, even the faculty, no one recognised or appreciated. Marge (*née* Marvin—her new name was a tribute to her 'hero' Marge Piercy), broke protocol by interrupting Huw in her baritone:

'Oh puh-lease, spare us the wisdom of your dead white males.'

Rocky's head nodded with manic emphasis. Melvyn audibly

sniggered. At the irony of her berating white males? The fatuousness of the remark? Was Melvyn on Huw's side?

Huw noticed he was slouching and flicking his swivel chair about in a frenzy. He had to pull himself together, or the pack would fly at his throat. He asked Timothy to introduce his thesis. He reminded the audience that the purpose of the Critical Introduction was to show that the writer was familiar with similar works, acknowledging influences and comparing his own text analytically with others, pointing out where it was original and unique, and its merits and weaknesses.

Timothy stood, hands in his pockets. 'I am *beyond* thrilled to see you all here. I love you all so very much. The title of my thesis is *Derridean Rent-Boys*.' No one laughed. 'It's named after French philosopher Jack Derrida,' he sighed, 'who was this awesome Algerian post-modern neo-Marxist guy. But you all know that, right? So I guess I want to tell you how I got the inspiration for this incredibly complex, profound, challenging philosophical fictional novel of mine. Yeah? I know we're meant to read the classics, but that's so old school, right? Like, who cares? All those dead white males,' he said, looking at Marge, who nodded back encouragingly, 'like *whatever*.' He glanced at Huw, who did not nod back encouragingly. Timothy had read none of the psychological thrillers that Huw had recommended to him.

'So in fact my handsome husband had the idea of getting some inspiration from more modern artists, I mean the truly profound pop singers, like Lil Bitch or Meltdown at the Motel. And diverse geniuses like Mustwe East and Benno Venus. That's where I get the hip-hop rhythms from, and the street-cred. OK, cool, but what about the plot and the themes? Well, Jorgen helped me out there too. I must admit I'm a fanatical gamer, I play eight, ten hours a day, and I'm a devotee of the LGBT games especially, like the Assassin's Creed and Borderlands series. Street Fighter, too, which has a transgender hero,' he said, with an ingratiating smile for Marge.

Charleston rolled his eyes. Most of the others nodded gravely.

'And I was inspired by the masterpieces of modern television too, obviously, like Cracking Meth or Game of Crowns. I think you can see that in the really deep philosophy my hero Dominic gets into. I could compare it with The Matrix, but it's on the next level, haha. Sure, *Derridean Rent Boys* is a nail-biting, sexy thriller, but it questions the meaning of existence too. It's kind of metaphysical. Jorgen compares it to Sartre and Camus.'

Although this drivel lacked even the most fatuous post-modern critical content, Huw noted, the earnest faces of Timothy's audience indicated fascination. 'I must admit,' Timothy went on, flicking his hair out of his eyes, 'that at times I gave in to despair, especially when the draft I had poured my heart and soul into was ripped to shreds by *someone*,' he said, casting a baleful look at Huw. 'I knew deep down in my heart that this novel was a masterpiece, as Jorgen said, but at times I lost the track, like that old school Italian dude, you know, the one with the comedy. I was *literally* in hell. Sometimes I wanted to give up, and just drink margaritas on a beach, you know? So I'm so humbly grateful to God, and my dear husband, and the incredible, amazing, brilliant Frida and Rocky and Marge, who were so supportive.' His voice trembled and tears fell. He clutched the leather-bound copy of his manuscript to his chest. Broome, Rocky, Jordan and the youths began to yip and squeal.

'Thank you, Timothy,' Huw said, 'if you've finished. However, I failed to see any analytical elements in your introduction, or even a cursory attempt at a bibliography.'

'Brutal,' someone hissed in a stage whisper. Huw could not tell who had spoken. The frosty silence indicated that most of the audience agreed.

Huw asked Timothy to read from his work. The slender boy smiled self-consciously, flicked his floppy fringe out of his eyes again, and began to declaim in a melodramatic tone, his voice rising at the end of each sentence like a Valley Girl's, his free hand fluttering like a bewildered bird, his hips swinging to the rap-influenced rhythm of his prose, his shoulders shaking with insincere emotion like those of a televangelist. It was mindless entertainment, certainly, and pretentiously mindless entertainment at that, Derridean, Foucaultian entertainment, a detective story with long digressions on the stupidity and bestiality of the cisgender, heterosexual police, ponderously explaining the machinations of the patriarchy who ruled Southern cities, and using its characters as mouthpieces to deliver diatribes against the canon of Western writers. As literature it was inferior even to Savanna B. Manley's, if that were possible. It was, just about. Huw unmoored his mind, let it drift, allowed the words to coagulate, congeal, clot, into a sticky, affected mess, whose import was indiscernible, because it was meaningless, as Jacques Derrida himself might have agreed—and indeed decreed. A beam of sunlight gushed in through the windows, golden and green, filtered by the foliage of the oak trees, and Huw hung suspended in that stream, swimming upon its surface.

And then it happened again: Time stopped.

The moment caught Timothy like a choir-boy, mouth agape, eyes round; Jorgenson beamed with paternal pride, a white hand with slug-like fingers reposing on his paunch. Broome had an index finger thrust inside a warthog nostril. Rocky was staring at her phone. Charleston frowned, possibly deep in Marxist dreams or dialectic. Melvyn Shamburger smiled, yet kept a wary eye on his wife. Lucky Luke was fast asleep. Jordan's bony legs, in black silken trousers, were wide apart. She pouted like a model. No one was listening to Timothy's twaddle, as far as Huw could tell.

Except Frida, perhaps. Her legs resembled the ruined columns of a lost civilisation. The dirigible balloon of her suit floated above the granite stumps. But her squat, stony face, with its gold ring and rust-shavings on the scalp, wore an expression of fierce concentration. Had Timothy offended her? Unlikely. Because he was gay and the Dean's spouse, he had a free pass, although no one would ever admit that. Might Frida be cross with her husband, then? Melvyn had cast sheepish, guilty glances at her. What was going on there?

On this occasion, no cherubim gambolled, rolling and laughing on cushions of cloud; nor did blond angels blast away on trumpets, or massed choirs sing in Latin. This time a massive, darker presence lurked among the treetops outside in the unearthly, roiling light, a figure with a human shape, but with wings, as far as Huw could tell. An angel, or archangel? Once again there was music, a lugubrious organ fugue, with dissonances, irresolution, and ponderous silences. While the pedal notes rumbled in his entrails, the Presence in the oak tree, half-veiled by branches and leaves, raised a sword or lance. St. Michael? Huw heard him intoning verses in Latin: *Non te amat, tempus abire tibi est.* She loves you not, it is time for you to leave. Am I off my head? Huw asked himself. What could be more natural, after all this? Yet again, Huw wondered if this pause had a cosmic purpose. The previous episode had left him with nothing comparable to Jaromir Hladik's respite in *The Secret Miracle.* The novel remained incomplete and he had not given up teaching. Yet in these moments of stillness, he had the certain knowledge of the futility of his job, the triviality of the minds of most of his students, the vanity of his colleagues, the theatricality of the proceedings, and the malevolence and megalomania of Frida Shamburger, who seethed as she faced him. *Te odit.* She hates you, the archangel told him. But like Jaromir, he had no way out but to play the part of enemy. And it was possible that the pause was a mere illusion—because his mind had faltered and failed momentarily. Or was Time the illusion? Perhaps the human brain was too crude to perceive that the eternal moment was the reality. In that case, the chain of events, life itself, was nothing but a dream. *Non te amat.* Miranda loves you not, the Presence repeated.

Frida's tundra-cold eyes brimmed with murder. Huw shuddered. A white whippy thing reared over him, poised to strike. Timothy. His eyes too glared at Huw. Tiny black points—heroin eyes. Of course he was a junkie. The treetop stirred. The archangel wielded his sword. The skirling of the organ culminated in a flourish, a skein of terrifying treble notes.

The music held a warning and a command, but the message was muddied. He heard the ticking of a loud clock and his own voice:

'Thank you, Tim. You may sit down.'

'*Timothy*,' Timothy hissed, but Huw did not apologise.

'Dr Shamburger,' Huw said, addressing Melvyn, 'would you like to comment on Mr Jorgenson's *novelette,* I mean, uh, story?'

Melvyn blushed, stood, fiddled with his tie. 'He evokes Tocqueville well,' he said, pronouncing it Tokeville, as the locals did. 'I mean Tocqueville.' Tockville, Frenchified.

'It's not set explicitly in Tocqueville,' Timothy said.

'I know,' Melvyn said, 'but come on, dude, we all recognise it.' Jorgenson scowled. 'What I mean,' Melvyn went on, 'is that it's so very true to life. Of any Southern college town.' He cast a helpless glance at his wife, who was regarding him with blatant scorn. 'And uh, Tim, I mean Timothy, does a real good job of describing the queer sub-culture of Tokeville—a town like Tockville. The sex scenes are a tad graphic, and some might argue gratuitous… '

'Would *you* argue they're gratuitous, Dr Shamburger?' snarled Timothy.

'Hell no,' Melvyn said, chuckling with embarrassment and turning redder. 'I never said that. They're realistic for sure. You feel the raging lust of the young gay guys. And the philosophical digressions are… how shall I put it? Interesting? I subscribe to post-structuralist theories myself, and I found Timothy's extremely detailed and at times verbose explanations—how shall I put it? Informed? Maybe a tad didactic? As if they were written for Wikipedia or a Young Adult audience. Which is your intended audience, right, Timothy?'

'What*ever*,' Timothy said, disdaining to look at him. 'It's littery fiction.'

'Literary fiction, right. Of course, no one would call it original, but what is?'

'I seem to recall your own fiction was described as 'a long-winded, unimaginative re-hashing of French post-structural philosophy',' Timothy said, 'by a famous critic.'

A ghastly glint appeared in Frida's eyes. 'Sachiko. In the Noo Yorker.'

Melvyn babbled, 'Right, right, but it got awesome reviews too, for instance…'

'Would you mind sticking to Timothy's work?' Huw said.

'Oh sure. What I mean is that, in spite of a few faults, a handful of trivial defects, this is, as my wife Frida puts it, a novel of remarkable poise and ambition. How many students dare to write philosophical gay thrillers? How many are as bold in their condemnation of the canon? How many dare do away with prescriptive grammar, and even conventional English usage and spelling? I can safely say I've never read a novel like this. Well, I guess I have seen a few,' he laughed, 'but not *exactly* like this.'

Basilisk stares met him. Charleston choked with laughter.

'In other words, what I mean is that it was quite good,' Melvyn said. 'In fact, like totally excellent. If you're into that kind of thing. Of course, I wasn't reading for pleasure, but if I had been, make no mistake, I might have enjoyed it. Maybe. Well done, Timothy. Yeah.'

Timothy lurched to his feet, flailed as if throwing a punch, flicked his fringe out of his eyes, loosened his tie as if it were throttling him, and collapsed back into his chair, grunting.

'Thank you, Dr Shamburger,' Huw said, 'for that deft, articulate analysis. Dr Piercing, would you like to add your comments?'

Marge, whose short hair was dyed in the full spectrum of LGBTQ colours, frowned, deep in cogitation. 'It was an awesome read. I mean a real page-turner. Perfect for the beach. I just got back from a long weekend in Cancún with my honey,' she said—she had transitioned from straight male to gay female, 'and boy were those sex scenes hot! Very courageous, I thought, yeah. Props to you, Timothy, for describing the delights of using dildoes. As some of you might know from my prize-nominated, trend-setting blog, *Trans-aggressions,* I've tried my hand at that. To considerable critical acclaim.'

Huw sighed, recalling the sickening detail about her sex life in Marge's blog.

'Very interesting, Dr Piercing, but we're discussing Mr Jorgenson's thesis.'

'Right, sure, of course. What I like most about this marvel of a fictional novel is the ideology. I mean, the whole plot is a clear metaphor for the stranglehold the white patriarchy has over the rest of us. Right? I mean, all the bad guys are white.'

'Apart from the Colombian drug dealers,' Huw said. 'In fact most of the bad guys are brown. The good guys are all white. Didn't you notice that?'

'Oh, sure, I may have been on the beach with my honey, and maybe drinking a few margaritas too many, but I read it real carefully,' Marge said, unflummoxed. 'But the good guys are all gay, you notice that? Very cool. It's the evil capitalists and criminals who are cisgender, heterosexual—I mean hetero*gender*, sorry. Gender is a social construct, as I teach in my classes. Nothing to do with biology. *Everyone* and his dog knows that. You choose your gender and your sexuality. As long as the patriarchy doesn't impose one on you.'

'And yet,' Huw interposed, 'Dominic says he feels like a girl trapped in a boy's body more than once. Doesn't that suggest *he* believes there's a biological element to it?'

Marge snorted; Frida snorted; Rocky snorted; Timothy snorted. Soon everyone was snorting or squealing like the Gadarene swine plunging off the cliff.

'*Hel-lo?*' said Marge. 'This is the twenty-first century, right, Dr Lloyd-Jones? We don't need old-school reactionary theories like that here. We're *Americans*.'

'I don't follow you,' Huw said. 'What do you mean?'

'Like duh. We believe in *equality*.'

'So do I. I just don't think that assigning the status of heroes and villains to entire groups of people aids equality. But we're getting off topic. I take it, Dr Piercing, that your final verdict on the...' unable to utter the word *novel*, he said, 'this mystery, this gay philosophical detective *epic*, was positive?'

'I already said it was awesome. I mean sure, like Dr Shamburger said, bits of it are maybe not so well-written, but who cares? What matters is the message, right? And let's face it, it helps that Timothy is gay. I mean, he's white—which is bad, obviously—but he's diverse. He's a minority. And he's not exactly cis-gender, either. He has transgender leanings. That is *so* cool.'

'You mean Dominic, my protagonist. Not me, surely?'

'Yeah, right,' Marge laughed. 'But we all know Dominic is your alter ego, Timothy. No need to blush, dude. I don't mind what you do with your dildo.'

A ripple of laughter turned into a wave, then a tidal wave. Timothy smiled. Huw did not. Frida was orchestrating the swings of emotion, a potentate on her overburdened swivel chair.

But now the moment Huw was dreading had come: he had to deliver his opinion on the thesis. Everyone looked expectant. Frida's scummy brown eyes burrowed into his. Timothy shivered. Jorgenson glared. Only Melvyn smiled at him, as if egging him on.

'*Derridean Rent-Boys* is a rotten title,' Huw said, 'although it does indicate the themes of the story. As I've said to Timothy, the thesis has its virtues. There's a certain facility with language, self-assured, realistic dialogue, and also, as Melvyn noticed, the setting is evocatively described. On the other hand, as a thriller, the story is slow and clogged with philosophical musing. As philosophical fiction, it's not only puerile and derivative, but difficult to understand—'

'That's because it's so incredibly, amazingly complex,' Timothy said.

'I disagree. Thought should be clearly expressed, as

Schopenhauer held. Muddy expression is infallibly the result of muddy thinking.'

'Why don't you tell us what you *really* think?' Timothy said.

'Sarcasm—that is the prevailing tone of the so-called novel, isn't it?'

'*So-called*?' Timothy's eyes filled with tears. 'Don't you love it at all?'

'It isn't a novel yet. It could be. You have a germ of an idea but you haven't developed it. And it's too disordered. And there are too many egregious language errors. I'm passing it because it's no worse than the usual thesis standard, which is frankly abysmal. But you'll have to do a great deal of revision and editing to stand any chance of publishing this.'

Timothy bit his lip and wept. A shocked hush prevailed. Old Jorgenson visibly trembled with rage. Marge and Rocky gaped at Huw. Frida sneered at him. Lucky Luke snored. Jordan knitted her brow, and Charleston looked as though he were planning the revolution. Broome lumbered to her feet and charged from the room like an enraged rhino. Only Melvyn smiled in weird way. Again Huw wondered if Shamburger was on his side.

There was a groan of stressed steel, followed by a sharp snap: Frida's chair had collapsed. She sprawled on the floor, her skirt torn, revealing frilly bloomers of a quaint, possibly Victorian design. Her short thick limbs flailed helplessly. Rocky, gasping with the effort, managed to flop her idol on to her side, and a group hoisted her up.

Once she was on her feet, Frida directed a venomous look at Huw, uttered what sounded like a curse in a rare tongue, perhaps Uto-Aztecan, and aided by Rocky, staggered towards the door. Although Melvyn had not got up to assist his wife as she lay helpless on the floor, he jumped up now, but Timothy laid a hand on one of his bright orange sleeves, with the grin of drunken peasant in a Breughel. 'Hey, Melvyn, buddy, join us for a drink.'

Melvyn gave him a guilty grin, and made a rush for the door, as if eager to escape. He got there just before Rocky and Frida, practically pushing them over in his haste to get out.

'I need to talk to you,' Frida said. 'Rocky told me she saw you the other day. On the *west side* of the city.'

Instead of replying, Melvyn fled—at least that was the way it seemed to Huw. What was all that about? Frida got stuck in the doorway again and Rocky forced her though it with the loud pop of a cork being pulled, and more curses.

At last Lucky Luke stretched, raised the bill of his cap, and said, 'Is it over already?'

Charleston approached Huw. 'I dig your honesty, prof. You want my opinion, Timothy got what he was asking for, the pompous little prick.'

But Huw wondered if he had overstepped the mark. He feared repercussions, even reprisals, but was not sure he cared. With Miranda gone, his job mattered only for Owen's sake. Huw had failed to rise to the challenge of Whoever was freeze-framing time for him. Twice now. Would such an ellipsis ever occur again? And if it did, would he be ready?

FOURTEEN

Low Animal Cunning

When Melvyn got back from drinking margaritas with Timothy and his buddies, photographs of him grinning like a stoned bonobo were already on Instagram—he had smoked a little Maryjane too—he sneaked inside the house, slipping off his deck shoes at the door and tiptoeing in his socks towards the stairs. He glimpsed Frida, marooned on the settee, her Pearbook perched on the crests of her breasts and belly, a bag of ice draped over her brow. A terrifying noise issued from her throat—*a death-rattle*, he told himself, with a wild surge of hope, but no, that was too great a miracle to ask for. *Please God, if I can just reach my study without waking her, that's all I ask. I managed to evade the inevitable cross-examination by fleeing to Timothy's thesis celebration. She may forget if I can avoid her now. Dude, be a ninja. Move like Garfield.*

He inched his way up with the patience of a cat burglar, and had almost attained the safety of the upper storey when he trod on the step that creaked. He cursed and halted.

'Melvyn, is that you?' The voice was lupine, savage, thick and phlegmy.

Go back to sleep, he prayed. He did not answer.

'I said is that you, Melvyn?' Her voice was louder, and proto-human now.

'No,' he said. *Jesus, did I say that? That was dumb-as-dogshit.*

'Who the fuck is it, then?' That voice might have made a hardened criminal quail. Bumps, thumps, crashes and metallic clicks followed. Moments later Melvyn turned to face Frida, who was at the foot of the stairs, still in the skirt she had torn falling off her chair at Timothy's thesis defence, her forehead bruised and bumped like a boxer's. She swayed drunkenly, and clutched a nasty-looking Colt Cobra snub-nose .38, which, he saw with mounting panic, was pointed at his genitals. She did not look happy to see him, either.

'Haha, joke,' he said quickly. 'Of course it's me. Darling.'

'Don't *darling* me,' Frida said, without lowering the weapon. 'Scumbag.'

'Gladys, I mean Frida, put the gun down. I only had a drink with Timothy.'

Frida lolloped up the stairs, the Colt still aimed at his privates. 'I'm not pissed at that, you slimy snail. I want to know what you were doing on the west side two weeks back. Outside a *gorgeous* mansion. Looking as guilty as *sin*, Rocky said.'

Melvyn feigned incomprehension. 'Uh, Rocky? Why, whatever do you mean?'

'Just move, *buster*,' she said with relish. Boy, had she been bingeing on Turner Classic movies, or what? He turned; she jabbed his back with the barrel.

'You want me to put my hands up?' he said. No answer. 'I have no idea what this is about, Frida,' he stammered, preceding her into the bedroom. 'Oh, maybe you mean that day I visited um, uh, an English professor on the west side?'

'Oh yeah? Which one? What were you up to while I was at the retreat, huh?'

Melvyn assumed his Anthony Perkins expression of

half-witted innocence that, he realised too late, confirmed his guilt. 'The usual. Writing. Tai Chi. Karate.'

'What were you doing right here?' Frida said. 'In our bed?'

'Um, sleeping?' He gave her a weak smile. How could she possibly know?

'Where are the stains, Melvyn?' The effort of holding the pistol up to the level of his chest had tired her, so once again it was pointed at his penis, which shrank and shrivelled, as it did in icy water.

'Stains? What do you mean, Gladys, uh, Frida? I washed the sheets.'

'Yeah, you washed them all right. You think you're real smart, don't you, Melvyn? That's tantamount to admitting you cheated. You think you got rid of the evidence, don't you? Which English professor did you visit?'

'Uh, Cooper.' Damn, he would have to beg Cooper to cover for him now.

She snorted through the thick white rubbery snout. The nose-ring shook.

'So this is the gun I saw in your purse on Sunday before church?' he said.

'Shut up, Melvyn. Don't change the subject. Why did you wash the sheets?'

'Well, haha, I washed the sheets because they uh, looked dirty. Obviously.'

'I bet they were dirty, all right. Real dirty. Like you.'

'I can't see why you're suspicious.' She couldn't prove a thing, he was sure.

'Let's say it's a woman's intuition. Let's have a look in the bedside tables.'

'Go ahead,' he said, relieved. Thank God, she had not a shred of evidence.

She dug through his drawer: smelly socks, gum, expired rubbers, Viagra, ancient after-shave. Nothing incriminating. He was grinning now. 'See, dear?'

Then she stamped around the bed and rummaged through her own drawer.

'Oh, wonderful. Oh, Jesus, yes. Look what I found in this one, Melvyn.'

With her left hand she fished out a tiny scrap of red lace which she held between her thumb and forefinger as if it were toxic. Oh no oh shit oh fuck oh Jesus—it was Jezebel's absurdly miniscule V-string panties. How could she be so damn dumb? Or had she planted them deliberately? Could she be so devious?

'That,' he fumbled, with a nervous giggle, 'must be… uh, Thalia's? Clio's?'

Frida jerked the gun up to head height. She was going to pistol-whip him.

'Don't tell me you're fucking your own daughters, Melvyn.'

'For Chrissakes, no!' he yelped. 'What do you take me for?'

'A dirty slug. You better come clean, Melvyn, or I'll blow you away, I swear.'

'All right, you want the truth? OK, I admit it, I did entertain a—how can I put it? A girl. A woman. While you were at that wacky retreat. I'm so sorry, Frida.'

'A *girl*, Melvyn? What kind of a girl? A stoodent?' Totally East Boston now.

'Yes, a real smart one. And it only happened once.'

'I don't *give* a damn how many times you boned her, you amoeba, or what her IQ is. How old is she?'

'Like twenty-one. Honest. She's an adult, Frida.'

'You call that an adult, Melvyn? Jesus Christ, that's only four years older than Thalia. The *same* age as Clio. It turns my stomach. You are such a filthy pervert.'

'I'm not sure that's fair. It wasn't my fault, exactly. She was hounding me. I kept turning her down. She just wouldn't take no for an answer.'

'You mean you're so spineless she forced you to fuck her?'

'Exactly—I mean, hell no,' he said, as Frida pointed the pistol at his privates again. 'My new therapist said I should, Frida, I swear.'

Frida's features slid into Picassoesque disarray: snout on the side of head, one pink eye migrating to her forehead, the other one next to a pointed ear. 'Say *what?*'

'She said we were both adults,' he stuttered. 'She couldn't see the harm.'

'*She?* A woman said that? Who the *fuck* is this so-called fucking *therapist?*'

'I can't say that,' Melvyn pleaded. 'Confidentiality? You understand, right?'

Frida aimed at the floor and pulled the trigger. A crash and smell of cordite. An elliptical hole appeared in the floorboards, right between his stockinged feet.

'Jesus, Frida, control yourself. Please. Don't shoot me in our bedroom.'

'Next bullet, it's your foot. I'll nail you like Jesus. Who's the therapist?'

'Dr Pound,' Melvyn whimpered. 'Dr Eliza Pound.'

She grunted again. 'What about the *smart girl?* She one of our stoodents?'

'Yes and no. I mean, she is a student at Oxbow State. But not a Creative Writing major. Truth. Believe me. I would never stoop that low.'

'Sure you would. You got the morals of a marmoset.'

'Hey, very witty.' Melvyn tried to laugh. 'Maybe lower than a marmoset.'

'You got that right,' Frida said. 'You know what, Melvyn? You make me puke, spew, barf, heave, gag. You make me chuck my fucking guts up.'

'Boy, Frida, you're a walking thesaurus. What a terrific bunch of synonyms.'

'Don't be a smartass, Melvyn. You're dumber than dogshit.'

'Yeah, right.'

'I mean it. You're *chicken*shit, you know?' She waved the Cobra at his cock.

He hung his head. *Yeah, yellow. Where is the Superior Man?*

'I oughta plug you. Right through your little wiener.'

'Not there, please. Anywhere but my little wiener. That would be a terrible idea.'

'Give me one good reason why I shouldn't shoot you,' Frida said.

She was having a hell of a time playing the tough broad with the gun—he guessed she had been watching Lauren Bacall or Bette Davis movies—but it might not be wise to point that out. 'For a start,' he said, 'you could go to prison.'

'Are you kidding? I'd say it went off on accident. Who would they believe?'

Damn, that was true. 'And I'm repentant. Like a Republican politician caught rogering an intern, or a Catholic priest poking one of the choir-boys.'

'You mean you're a liar and hypocrite, just pretending to be repentant?'

'No, I mean I'm really, really, truly, sincerely, deeply sorry, and willing to debase myself. Demean myself. I'll do anything to prove how sorry I am.'

'Anything?'

'Scout's honour. Cross my heart and hope to die if I tell a lie.'

One of the few benefits of being married to Frida was that her mind worked so sluggishly that it was easy to follow her thoughts as they plodded after each other. She considered his offer. To use one of her clichés, her face took on an expression of 'low, animal cunning'. Actually, she did look remarkably like an animal, and a very low, cunning one, at that. A fox? No, that was way too hackneyed. A sneaky dog? Better. A sly stoat? Hmm. A crafty, wily… hog? *Yeah*, she was probably saying to herself. *It could be kinda fun to debase him, like really demean him, humble him, show him who's the boss. And useful too. He'll be my slave. I can use him for…*

'Okeydokey, then,' she said.

'Okeydokey? I'm in the clear?'

'Melvyn, you're in very deep shit. Let me make this plain. You are not in the clear. I'm gonna make you suffer for the desecration of our marriage bed. In more ways than you can imagine. You're about to experience suffering without end.'

'Oh thank you, dear. Certainly, I understand. It's so generous of you.'

'You're gonna grovel, Melvyn. Big time.'

'More than I'm grovelling already?'

'Way, way more, Melvyn. Mark my words. You just wait, buddy.'

At least she isn't going to blow my pecker off. Nothing could be as bad as that.

Slowly, the barrel drooped to her side. Without the gun pointed at him she was just a battered porker stuffed into torn clothes. Hideous, sure, but nothing to be afraid of. Not for the time being, anyway.

'Dang, Melvyn, what the heck is that smell? Did you just soil yourself?'

Uh-oh—the turd was heavy in his boxers. He smelled it himself now.

'Gee, I'm sorry. I didn't know I had. But you understand…'

She broke into swinish merriment, snorting and squealing with joy. 'That is so disgusting. So perfect. You've made my day, Melvyn. You *filthy* little child.'

He waddled past her to the bathroom. Boy, would she pay for this!

*

Later, long after he had dumped his boxers in a jiffy bag, had a painstaking shower, and endured a period of sober penitence on his zafu cushion in the study, meditating on the Way of the Superior Man, with only occasional fantasies of Samurai vengeance, the deafening roar of the television led him downstairs to the lounge. He found Frida 'reclining'—how refined that made her slumping sound—on her colossal dentist's chair, Upton Abbey on the flat-screen as usual, her Pearbook perched on the St. Michael's Mount of flesh around her middle. She was scrolling through her newsfeed, perusing pictures of the Loathsome Leader, and Meghan, Margaret Atwood and other mavens, Syrian kids, and cute kittens. She was jabbing likes, emoticons with tears and gaping or grinning mouths, in response to each. But he could see she was also 'working', from the pile of coffee-spattered papers beside her, and a book pillowed on one of her knees, whose cover showed a beautiful black woman wearing a tall African headdress and scarf, glaring with penetrating elegance at the camera. Its title was: *Becoming the Brilliant Writer You Are – Effortlessly.*

'Sup?' he said. Had she forgiven him? Would she remind him of his shame?

'Just working on my novel.' Yes and no, then, thank God. 'Such a struggle. The agony of creation. Self-doubt, ecstasy, misery, transcendence. You know?'

'Of course. You might like these, darling.' With the deference of a butler from *Upton Abbey,* he stooped and extended a box of Belgian chocolates towards her.

'Oh Melvyn, how sweet, haha. Did you make sure they're Fair Trade?'

He had not; he had no idea if they were; nor did he give a damn. 'Absolutely.'

'That's lucky. I could never eat all these delicious chocolates if I suspected they were the product of child slavery in West Africa.'

Sure you could. 'Naturally not. Would you like some coffee with them?'

Her cheeks dimpled. 'Are you trying to butter me up?'

By the time he had made it and brought it back into the lounge, where strings screamed over a 'tragedy' on *Upton Abbey,* he saw the chocolate box was empty—she had not left him one. Melvyn set the large bucket of sticky, sweet goo in a cup-holder on her armrest, and turned to dart away on 'velvet paws'. But before he could exit, he heard, above the roar of the television, a sucking, slurping, repulsive noise. By now he should have gotten used to Frida drinking like a thirst-crazed simian. A burp followed the gurgling of the drain, and a sergeant-major shout stopped him in his tracks: 'Hey, was it really a girl you boned, Melvyn? Or like, maybe a dude?'

'Say what?' He turned. She had half-rolled over like a beached whale.

'You're chummy with Timothy. Are you into dudes?'

'Hell no. I'm straight. Heteronormative. You know that.'

'That's so old school, don't you think? Kind of right-wing? Such a drag.'

Was she joking? 'I guess it is. But I can't help it, can I?'

She took another slurp. 'Don't you think you could make more of an effort?'

'Gladys, shit, I mean Frida, what are you *saying*? What *are* you saying?'

'I'm just sayin' you're a cisgender, straight, white, middle-aged *male*…'

'I admit it. But I'm not sure I follow. You're suggesting I should be ashamed of my gender, my skin pigmentation, and sexual orientation?'

'Let's get real, bud. You epitomise the white patriarchy. Not cool, dude.'

'I guess,' he said, hanging his head. 'I'm sorry, I guess.'

'You should be. You are responsible for all the evil in the world, Melvyn.'

'I am?'

'Not just you, dumbass. But your kind. White men. Think of all the people you've enslaved and exploited—all the ethnicities. All the poor *women*.'

'Sure, I get that. I'm a liberal. But it wasn't just me. And white men have done a few good things, right? Think of the glories of Western civilisation. All the art.'

'Dude, give me a break. It was all propaganda. Designed to victimise women and other genders and people of colour. All the so-called art—all that highbrow stuff—it was nothing but marketing. To keep you cisgender white guys in power.'

'Hang on a minute: what about Michelangelo and Leonardo? Bach, Mozart? Homer, Dante and Shakespeare? Kafka and Dostoyevsky? That was all just marketing?'

'Sure, those guys were just ad men. Sidekicks of popes and kings. Lackeys. But it's all over now. It's time for you guys to change. Get with the programme.'

'I see your point—but I spend nearly my entire life apologising as it is.'

'I appreciate that, but it's not enough, Melvyn. That's *so* last century.'

'Well, what should we do? How can *I* make amends?'

'For a start, I think you could do a dude, maybe Timothy or one of his buddies. Or a transgender person. Go gay, Melvyn. Take a walk on the wild side.'

What would the Superior Man say? Nothing, probably. Melvyn wrinkled his nose. 'Just imagining it makes me want to barf.'

'That's a prejudice, though, right? You've been assigned a gender and a sexuality, and you've accepted it like a goddamn moron. But it's your choice. You could change all that, Melvyn. Reinvent yourself. Assert your freedom for once.'

'I totally want to, but hell, not like a pillow-biter!'

'How bigoted. How disappointing. I expected more of you, to be honest.'

It hit him like a karate kick to the temple. 'Frida, are you trying to tell me that you might be bisexual yourself?'

She smiled in a surprisingly natural way, for her. 'Well, I might not use that terminology. But I am totally like polyamorous, Melvyn. And proud of it.'

'Doesn't that basically mean you're a promiscuous slut?'

'Melvyn, you are *so* unhip. No, it means I reject monogamy and exclusivity.'

'You do? So you don't mind that I banged Jezebel? Is that cool now?'

'That was her name, was it? No, Melvyn. You can bang *Jezebel* all you like. Hell, bang anyone you like.'

'Gee, thanks, Frida. I really appreciate your generosity. I might just do that.'

The smile of low, animal cunning reinstated itself. 'Provided you don't mind *me* banging someone, naturally. Tit for tat. Quid pro quo.'

'Mind?' he said quickly. 'I'd love that! I'd adore it!'

'You would, Melvyn? Maybe you'd like to join in, too?'

'You gotta be shitting me.'

'Have I ever shitted you, Melvyn?'

'All the time,' he said. 'So you're seriously saying you want me to join you in bed while you fuck some other guy? I never knew you were such a slag, Frida.'

'Hey, I didn't say it'd be a guy, did I? So here's another big reveal: I'm pansexual, Melvyn. I discovered that at the retreat. Can you handle that?'

'I'm not sure what it means, to be honest.'

'It means I'm into everyone—not just dudes and chicks but *all* genders. According to the Canadian government, there are like sixty of them.'

'Wow. I would never have guessed *they* had so many. Those Canadians.'

'You need a minute to let it all sink in. Yeah? But I sense that you're down with the idea. And you did promise you'd do anything to prove you're sorry.'

'I sure did. Though I'm not certain I need to be so apologetic now.'

'That's the spirit, Melvyn.'

'So let's get this straight: you're inviting me to some kind of threesome?'

'Wouldn't that be awesome? Imagine being in bed with two hot women.'

He did. The trouble was, one of them would be Frida. 'I can't do it.'

'Way disappointing, Melvyn. You're so uptight. But okay, as a first step, how about being a spectator? Like from outside, through a window or something.'

'You mean like a voyeur? I guess I could be a voyeur.' A 'stirring in his loins' surprised him. Oh boy oh boy oh boy. 'Yeah, sure.'

Frida beamed like a hag in a Bosch painting. 'Coo-ul.'

'But wait—who will it be? Oh no, not Rocky?'

'Melvyn, I can't exactly do a colleague, can I? Especially not a colleague lower in the hierarchy. That wouldn't be right, would it? I mean ethical, and all. Huh?'

'I bet Rocky wouldn't mind. I think she'd jump your bones in an instant.'

'Right, she'd be down with it. But *I* might feel badly about it.'

Give me a break. 'You got so many… scruples, right?'

'Calms?'

'Qualms, right. You're so amazingly sensitive, Frida. And articulate.'

'I guess I am, thanks. You know what? It's gonna be wicked *hot,* Melvyn.'

'Sure. But won't you tell me who it is? It's driving me wild imagining it.'

'That's the idea. Keep going wild. No, you'll find out soon enough.'

'I can hardly wait, Frida.'

'Attaboy. Thanks for understanding me, Melvyn.'

Melvyn gulped. 'Did you just thank me—for real?'

Enjoy it while you can, Melvyn. Summer's lease hath all too

short a date, as the bald white dude with the goatee said. You know, one of the old school lackeys.

Like you, Melvyn. Like you.

FIFTEEN

Women and Girls Rule His World

A woman, Huw guessed from the softness and tentativeness of the knock on his office door, if that was not a sexist inference. Theoretically prepping classes, in fact he was gazing with nostalgia at a picture of Miranda in her wedding dress, her brow garlanded with flowers.

'Come in,' he said. 'Door's open.'

In came Jezebel, the girl he had met at the feminist retreat. He wondered what she wanted, not that he much cared. Her face provided no clues. For a student, her clothes were too formal: a black pinstripe skirt suit, with black tights and heels. She carried a briefcase. She wore her hair swept into a ballet topknot, as Miranda often did, which in Jezebel's case emphasised the sharp angles of her face, unsoftened by makeup. She could have been a lawyer. In other circumstances, he might have been intrigued, but since Miranda's departure, having to talk with anyone was a trial. He hoped he could get rid of her quickly.

She shut the door behind her. 'May I talk to you in private, sir?'

As a rule he insisted on keeping the door open, but exhausted and grieving as he was, he simply sighed. 'All right, then. Take a seat.'

She pulled back the armchair opposite his desk, away from him. He understood why when she sat down: she was now far enough away for him to see her long, shapely legs. She crossed and re-crossed them. Her skirt was only slightly above the knee. Even so, it was an impressive display. But perhaps he was imagining things. Her air was professional.

'How are you, sir?' she said crisply.

Because she was a stranger, and looked older than she probably was, he almost confided in her. But if he blabbed about Miranda leaving him, he might end up blubbering. And he could not divulge to a student his anxieties about his job, or frustrations with his colleagues. No, better keep it buttoned-up, the British way.

'Fine,' he said, hands thrust in his blazer pockets. 'What can I do for you, Jezebel?'

'You remember my name. How flattering. Thank you, sir. I believe that's your wife?' She nodded at another photograph of Miranda, on the wall.

'Yes?'

'She looks like that actress. The one in *White Swans*.'

He smiled wanly. 'She does. Although I find my wife more beautiful.'

'You must love her very much.'

'Yes.' And yet she did not love him, the angel had said. *Non te amat.*

'Did she enjoy the retreat with my sister?'

'She said it changed her life.' *And mine, and mine. Tempus abire tibi est.* Had the archangel meant that it was time for him to leave, or her? Would she have left him so abruptly if it had not been for Petronella and her goddamn goddesses? He doubted it.

'That's what most of the women at the symposia say,' Jezebel said. 'Personally, I have my doubts. They feel empowered afterwards, sure, which I guess is a good thing. They often take drastic actions right afterwards. But I'm not sure the transformation is deep. It's not based on self-knowledge so much as obedience. It's a kind of cult. Petronella tells them what to believe, what to do. They exchange one kind of subjection, one kind of conformity, for another. The patriarchy for the matriarchy. Most people can't face freedom. They'll do anything to avoid thinking for themselves or figuring out who they really are.'

Huw listened aghast. Was she as mature as she sounded? Without question she was bright and articulate. He remembered she wanted to be some kind of therapist.

'Have you divulged these thoughts to your sister?' he asked.

'Oh yes. She doesn't disagree. We often laugh about it.'

'I see—so basically, to be blunt, the retreats are just a scam for relieving privileged white women of their money? For milking the insecure and the foolish?'

Jezebel offered him a brief, brittle smile. 'Petronella wouldn't put it like that. They get value for their money. And the symposia are not just for white women. All ethnicities are welcome.'

'I don't remember seeing any other ethnicities in the hall.' She made no reply to that. 'But you still haven't told me why you're here.'

She crossed her legs again, slowly. Her eyes never left his face. She did not smile or flirt and yet he had a gut feeling that she desired him. But if that were so, why would she behave with such ambivalence? Was she so sophisticated that she understood that ambiguity, mystery, and uncertainty, were ways of heightening tension, of stimulating desire?

His intuition told him that she was. Fate was offering him yet another nubile young woman, and unlike Elise, this one was not even his student. If he wished to, he could.

'A number of reasons,' she said. 'For a start I've been reading your first novel, *Ceredigion*. You're a brilliant man. You belong on the shelf with the greatest British writers.'

'That's kind of you.' In his opinion it was not true, but all the same it was touching to hear. 'What did you most like about it?' The psychological acuity, he expected her to say.

'The sex scenes,' she said without a moment's hesitation. 'They're so sensual, and yet rather brutal too. Isn't that the perfect combination? When Blodwyn finds Llewellyn on the beach after his boat's sunk, believing he's drowned, and they make love on the wet sand, while the freezing rain lashes her back—I was practically gasping as I read that one. You understand exactly how a woman feels when she makes love.'

'Do I?' He curbed his amusement. Perhaps she was more ingenuous than she looked.

'Absolutely. Would you mind signing my copy of the novel, sir?'

'I'd be happy to. Do you have it with you?'

'Yes,' she said, but made no move to open her briefcase. What would her next move be? Clearly she had a strategy. He did not. He was only responding to her moves.

After a thoughtful pause, she crossed her legs with a swish of her stockings again. 'Do you remember me asking if you'd be willing to help with my research?'

He did, and nodded. 'No need to keep calling me sir.'

'I'd prefer to. I intend to train as a sex therapist after I graduate with my Psychology degree. My Honours thesis is based on some original research. On relationships between young women and older men. My hypothesis, which of course I'm testing experimentally, is that such relationships may be very valuable for both parties.'

'I see,' Huw said with alarm. 'For the women, for material reasons, presumably?'

'Not at all. I postulate that young women use these relationships to grow intellectually. They learn so much from intellectual, wiser men. Like *Pygmalion*.'

She knew Bernard Shaw; impressive. 'And the standard view is that the men do it simply for the sex—but I imagine you'll tell me that they have nobler motivations too?'

'Not necessarily nobler. Of course they enjoy the sex with the younger woman. But the emotional and spiritual effect on them is far greater than the physical one. They get a renewed sense of confidence, they feel infused with life, they rediscover the selves of their youth—the true selves, the ones with heroic ambitions—that they had to abandon as they compromised with life.'

'That's a remarkable analysis.' And an accurate one: that was exactly how it had been for him when he met Miranda. But however flattering it was that Jezebel was offering herself to him now, as she clearly was, and however tempting it might be to allay his misery with some meaningless sex, he knew he would regret it. 'How did you develop this theory?'

'Partly from reading—not just psychology, but literature, including your own deeply penetrating novels, sir—and partly from observation and experience. But I need to confirm my conjectures, with a careful collection of data. That's where you come in.'

'I'm not sure I follow you. Would you like to interview me? Because I have a younger wife?'

She hesitated. 'To start with, yes.'

'To start with? What else do you have in mind?' Would she proposition him?

'Dr Shamburger is one of my subjects. He has helped me considerably.'

'Has he indeed?' She was skilful at deflecting questions she did not want to answer. But it was odd that she had asked Melvyn, since Frida was not younger. Was he actually having an affair with this girl? Huw recalled Melvyn's blissful reveries, the gloating grins, the guilty glances at Frida, and his apparent flight after Timothy defended his thesis. Huw had seen Jezebel leaving Melvyn's office too, more than once. It all added up. Could Melvyn be having an affair with such a cool, distant girl? It beggared belief but Huw really hoped so.

'Oh yes. I've learned a great deal from Dr Shamburger.

Although he has that somewhat affected New England manner, deep down he's more primitive. I mean that in the DH Lawrence sense. As a compliment.' She crossed her legs again.

'You astonish me.' *And scare me a bit,* Huw did not add.

'And so if you'd be so kind as to answer some questions… to start with. Nothing more. It will be *completely* confidential, of course. No names.'

'I should hope not.' Her request was not precisely improper, since she was not his student or even in his college, but it was questionable in taste, and might be risky. Bright as she was, and professional as she presented herself, he had the sense, in spite of her strictly controlled manner—or because of it—that she was a bit unhinged. Her stare had the intensity of the fanatic's. But what might she be fanatical about? She was unusual—intriguing. Still, his impulse was to refuse. Miranda would strongly disapprove if he told her. Then what made him waver? he asked himself. The very fact that Miranda would disapprove, he realised. It was a way to assert his independence. He remembered the Persian doctor, and a line she had quoted from Hafiz: *How did the rose ever open its heart and give the world its beauty?*

He longed to open his heart, whether he had any beauty left to give or not. 'I could answer a few questions. But I reserve the right not to reply to any that I find indiscreet.'

Jezebel fixed him with a clinical gaze. 'Thank you,' she said, bending to reach into her briefcase, and giving him a glimpse of her bra as her ivory blouse opened. She handed him a first edition hardback of *Ceredigion*, and a fountain pen. He took them and wrote:

To Jezebel, with admiration for your perceptiveness. Just remember that, as Blodwyn finds out in this novel, passion can lead us astray: life should not be reduced to a single obsession. Was that too moralising? Too late to change now, anyway.

'Will that do?' he said, signing it and passing it back to her.

'Wonderful, sir. Wise, as I expected. I'd like us to be very close friends.'

'That's flattering, but probably not appropriate, as people say here.'

'I feel that you have so much to teach me,' Jezebel said, crossing her legs.

'Everything of value that I know is in my novels.'

'Oh no, sir,' she said, standing. 'I know that's not true at all. Goodbye for now.'

She held out her hand; he shook it. Intriguing though the girl was, he hoped he would not see much of her in the future.

*

Miranda's condo was in a complex on the west side of the city, where only white people lived. Although no law forbade African-Americans to reside there, any black male engaged in suspicious activities in the newer subdivisions, such as walking from his car to a shop in a sinister manner, or exercising a dog in a park, or jogging on a public path, was likely to be reported, arrested, pistol-whipped, or shot once or twice, if he were lucky just in his legs, to discourage returning. Huw hated the area and marvelled that Miranda would choose to live there. She had wanted to live in the historic district for its 'diversity', after all.

She opened the door to him with her now customary glazed smile. The product of all the opiates, he supposed. Pink velveteen pyjamas, which did not flatter her flour-white complexion. No make-up. Disappointing, because she had known he was coming.

'It's sweet of you to visit with me.'

Odd though it was to be visiting his own wife, Miranda's formality struck him as odder still. He did not reply. As so often in the States, he felt he had stepped into a TV show. In her lounge, the awful *White's Physiology* was on the screen. Miranda settled on her sofa, so he had no choice but to join her. 'What do you think of my apartment?' she said.

He had been too shocked to notice when he entered, but

now he did. The walls startled him: ochre and magenta, apricot and damson, cherry-red and Prussian blue.

'Did you paint this all yourself?' he said, evading the question.

'I sure did. With Owen's help. He's a great little worker.'

'The colour scheme is inspired by Frida Kahlo's house, I suppose?'

'Spot on. Which I'll soon be visiting in Mexico. I'm so wired about that.'

Posters of Frida's paintings hung everywhere. Above the mantel, Frida's head with antlers, and the body of a doe, stuck with arrows. Was that how Miranda saw herself? As a vulnerable, lovable animal, chased and tortured? On another wall was Frida surrounded by black spider monkeys, one of them clinging to her back, his very long thin arm fondling her breast—Frida, with her adolescent boy's fluffy moustache, in the midst of mischievous emblems of lust. Again, was that how Miranda saw herself? Besieged by little simian men, snatching at her with their phallic arms and prehensile tails? Then there was Frida and the Broken Column: naked from the waist up, nails driven into her face and all over her body, her torso split open to reveal a shattered stone column. She was weeping with tightly pursed lips. In control, triumphing over her pain, glorying in her beautiful breasts, which were similar to Miranda's in size and shape. Yes, of course she identified with her.

'Isn't she great?' she said, following his eyes. 'No, you hate her, don't you?'

'I don't hate her. She was imaginative, and quite accomplished technically—nearly as good as Diego Rivera or José Clemente Orozco. But rather solipsistic, surely?'

'What does that mean?'

'Focussed on oneself. Self-absorbed.' Did that describe himself too? he wondered.

'But you only really ever know yourself,' Miranda said, pushing her hands into the little pouches on each side of her top, which made her look pregnant.

'Yes, that's the philosophical justification. But I disagree. With empathy, you can understand others. And paint them. Rembrandt did. So did Vermeer. Augustus John, too.'

'You're lecturing me again.'

'Just giving an opinion. I don't mean to lecture you.'

'And yet you do. It makes me feel dumb. You see, you would never have allowed me to have these pictures on the walls of the blue house, would you?'

She had him there. 'Well, they wouldn't go with the style of it, would they?'

'You see? It's always *your* vision. What about me? This is me, Huw.'

He saw her point. 'Yes, I'm sorry. If you come back, you can hang your pictures.'

'Gee, thanks.' Her tone was sarcastic. 'All over the house? Or in one tiny corner?'

'How about a whole room? Would that be enough? A study just for you?'

'Who's being solipsistic now? Did I use the word right?'

'You did. Touché.' He allowed her room to submerge his senses: the hot, throbbing hues of the walls, the images of exotic suffering. Immersed in the flood of colour, in Frida's dreamworld, which was Miranda's dreamworld, where women sprouted antlers and arrows, and monkeys patted their breasts, where nails were driven into their flesh and their chests were ripped open, but they kept on their corsets and pursed their lips, he wondered if he had misjudged his wife, underestimated her. What if this bold décor indicated a passionate, creative, sensuous soul? And what if she *were* a bit self-absorbed? Did he have the right to judge her for that? Wasn't he equally self-absorbed? And had that insight come too late?

'I'm sorry,' he repeated. 'I feel like I'm only really getting to know you now.'

She looked up at him with a secretive smile—a *solipsistic* little smile.

'Is it too late?' he said. 'I could change, I swear. Or is it too late now?'

'I don't know,' she said—and settled down to watch the drivel about jealousy among glamorous doctors on the telly. Incited by Frida's monkeys and bare breasts, Huw gave in to the temptation to caress. His hands probed and wandered, from the nape of her neck to the plump swellings beneath the pyjamas—stroking the velveteen, striving to slip under it and embark on pilgrimages to the south—the Eternal City. She did not respond to his advances.

'How could anyone with a modicum of intelligence watch this rubbish?' he said.

'I guess I must be a dumbass, then, because I enjoy it.' She got up, turned off the television set with an exasperated sigh, and put a CD in the mini-stereo.

'Oh no,' he said, identifying the shrill caterwauling of Tinker Quick.

'I like her,' she said, returning to the sofa. 'God, you're like an octopus.'

'I don't use my arm to deliver semen. Not yet, anyway. You really like her—what shall I call them? Her soulless, formulaic, squeaky ditties?'

'You're so judgemental. So patronising. So *superior*.'

'Critical. Discerning. I have impeccable taste.'

'How nice for you.' She did not smile but she did allow him to undress her.

Afterwards, he nodded off. Ideas purled through his dreams. What if the Kahlo obsession were not an index of Miranda's sensitivity, but simply another pop culture trend she was following? Frida was in fashion. Women all over the world adored her. Because of her unashamed narcissism, her obsession with her suffering, which to her was more painful and more noble than all others, and her belief that she was a victim of existential injustice. Naturally women identified with her. Huw did not resent Frida, who had coped as well as she could with a life of physical and emotional pain, but he did resent the halfwits who had turned her into a secular saint, an example of suffering womanhood, persecuted by insensitive men. *That asshole Rivera fucked Frida's own sister! That asshole Trotsky jilted her! Good for Frida for flaunting her lovers, male and female—especially the female ones! You go, girl!*

Frida Shamburger had adopted her first name, Huw understood in the miasma of his dream, to signal to everyone that she was creative and unconventional, wild, uncontrollable, masterful, pitiable, but also formidable, stronger than any mere man, and *way* more exciting.

'What's the matter?' someone was saying. *What's the madder?* Or was it, *Who's the madder?* 'You're grumbling. Snarling. Making fists. Wake up, you.'

No, *Huw*. Tears stood in Miranda's eyes. 'I love you so much, baby,' she said.

So much—an infallible indication of insincerity. This time he was unable to reply.

*

When he got home he had an email from her:

Huw, I've been thinking about our relationship and although I love you dearly I see it isn't going to work. Better if we make the split clean. I could date you but although you say you love me you'd just be 'shagging' me, right? So I think a divorce is best. Don't try to dissuade me. As you know, I'm super stubborn. I've decided. Don't write. I'll talk to you after I get back from Mexico with NeAmber and Matthew. (I'm leaving the day after tomorrow, remember? Bet you'd forgotten.) You'll be fine, you'll find someone. Give my love to Owen.

Randima.

Unable to face the house he had shared with her, or the university, he called in to cancel his classes and drove to the trailhead at Elk Creek for a run. He could either expend energy in fight or flight, or explode. He sprinted off down the trail without a warmup. No one else was running or walking. He flew along, doing six-minute miles: he timed them. His heart pumped like a piston, smacking against his ribcage. He hardly saw where he was going. His feet barely touched the ground. Nearing the bridge at the midway point, he almost stepped on a copperhead sunning itself. Presently a female figure in a tracksuit came jogging towards him. A familiar figure, he was half aware, but he paid little attention to her until she was almost upon him. It was the doctor who had attended to Miranda after her suicide attempt. She glanced at him, but he could not tell if she recognised him. Once again Huw had the sensation that he knew her well, and they had in the past been close, long, long ago.

She stared ahead. She was not going to greet him. That upset him.

He considered calling out to her. Would she respond? Why was she so aloof?

He hurtled towards her. She did not swerve. Set on her course, she would not alter it.

He deflected his own flight somehow. She neither averted her gaze, nor saw him.

But she had to have done. And be impressed by his speed. What a vain, immature hope, he thought as he bolted past.

As he ran, faster still, nails pierced him, the pistons clanked, clattered, and hammered, the pain grew, and some colossal force, a sledgehammer weight, hit him in the chest, knocked the breath out of his lungs—and felled him.

He sprawled on the path, gasping, unable to get any air inside his lungs.

He could not even cry for help. What bad luck that the doctor had passed him.

And that his life was over. He wished he could see Owen before he died.

His lungs had collapsed—he had no lungs.

An age passed. He could not breathe. He was going to die. Then the doctor loomed over him in her olive tracksuit. Kneeling, she held his wrist and listened to his chest.

'How do you feel?' she said in a calm voice.

At last he swallowed a gulp of air. 'Not great.'

'You were running at an insane speed for a man your age.'

'I'm in tiptop condition.'

'Your pulse is too fast.' She smiled—kindly or mockingly? He must have sounded vain. 'Sure you're fit. I can see that. Even so, try taking it a little easier next time, okay?'

'Okay. Do you know who I am? You recognise me?'

'How is your wife?' she said with the same wry smile. 'Better?'

'She thinks she's better. She's going to Mexico next week. She's left me.'

The doctor gave him a sharp look. 'I'm sorry.' Was she upset? Why would she be?

'I wasn't asking for your sympathy. Sorry, I don't mean that. Can I get up?'

'No. You need to rest until your heart rate goes back to normal.'

'Have I had a heart attack?'

'The wound is where the light enters you,' she said, her hand on his heart. 'That's Rumi again, but I guess you know that. You're a professor of literature, aren't you? I don't think you've had a cardiac arrest, but you should see a cardiologist for a check-up. This is a warning. You may have a heart attack if you don't change your way of life. Here's my card.'

'Thank you.' He hoped he would see her again. But that was wrong, wasn't it?

The wound is where the light enters you. The Welsh myths proved that—without suffering there was no learning. All the rest of the day, although his chest burned, Huw felt that a taper was alight there. Inside his heart a new radiance glimmered. He hoped the small flame would not go out.

SIXTEEN

Presumed Guilty Until Proven Innocent

Frida was not just late by faculty standards, or even hers, but insultingly late. Twenty minutes and counting. Lucky Luke had already pulled the bill of his ball cap over his eyes.

'Do you think, like, maybe Frida really isn't coming this time?' Rocky said.

'She said she was on her way,' Melvyn said. 'Right before I came in.'

But he was buzzed anyway. His plot was proceeding according to plan. Not only had he boned Jezebel and got his revenge on Frida, but she had accepted it, and everyone had taken the places he had assigned them. Huw was playing his part as if he were intent on his own destruction. He had insulted Frida's friend, Savanna B. Manley, and defended a womanless syllabus; offended his female students and defied Frida, and trashed the thesis of a vulnerable gay student, in public, and actually made him cry. As an extra bonus he had affronted Rocky, who was dim, certainly, but not too dim to take offence. Could it get any better? Yes, it could: Thalia, who was in Owen's class at High

School, had told him that Miranda had left Huw. For the past few days the Welshman had been stumbling about the campus like a wino, unshaven, muttering some kind of gibberish. Welsh, maybe. The dude had lost it. Totally. His days were 'defiantly' numbered, as most of Melvyn's students spelled 'definitely'. And the purpose of this meeting—if Frida could get off of her fat ass, and Facebook, and stagger here—was to decide the guy's future. Would Huw be promoted?

Melvyn was confident of the outcome. And now that Miranda was available, and Melvyn had recovered his virility so gloriously, he thought he might just bone her too. Why not? For sure he deserved another conquest. His mind drifted off in pleasant pornographic fantasies. Oh boy oh boy oh boy. This position. No, that one. Hell, both. All of them.

Seated across from him, Roquette Rathaus thumped the keys of her laptop. The Conference Room had mahogany tables and glass-fronted bookshelves. Empty, of course. It looked and smelled like a corporate board room, with its leather armchairs, wax polish, and synthetic air freshener. Two twenty-five. Lucky Luke was wearing his standard orange Hawaiian shirt, jeans, and monumental work-boots, lavishly decorated with mud, which reposed on top of the polished table like an art installation by Tracey Emin. Lucky Luke was himself in an artistic pose: tattooed Popeye arms behind his head, baseball cap shielding his eyes, a smile on his lips. Asleep? Or, as student lore had it, permanently stoned?

Stoned, was Melvyn's guess. *And* asleep. If only Melvyn could relax like that.

'Should we maybe adjourn the meeting?' Rocky said. 'Or start without her?'

Melvyn was chairing, and Frida would not forgive him if he did either.

'I'm sure she'll be here directly,' Melvyn lied. 'She's not usually so late.'

Lucky Luke raised the bill of his cap an inch, winked like a crocodile surfacing on the Nile, murmured 'The hell she isn't,' then pulled the bill down again to settle into muddy dreams. Or else he was composing deathless poetry. Rocky glanced at Melvyn with an irritated expression, then returned to her abuse of the keyboard.

A little after two-thirty, the door cracked against the wall with a report like a rifle, and in lurched Frida, panting, red-faced, exuding the fetid fragrance of Sundoe's. Sugar and crumbs liberally dusted her pink LGBTQIA+ tee shirt.

'I am *so* sorry for the delay,' she gasped. 'Something urgent came up.'

Oh yeah? Like an irresistible urge for coffee and cakes?

'No problem,' Rocky said, as the squat figure struggled to drive herself through the doorway. 'We've only been here a couple of minutes anyways.'

'Over half an hour,' mumbled Lucky Luke beneath his visor.

'I *am* the director of the programme, you know,' Frida snapped, collapsing into an armchair beside Rocky, 'and I have a ton of responsibilities. Unlike some of you.' She glowered at Lucky Luke, who showed no sign of having heard.

No hint of anger towards himself, though, for once, Melvyn reflected. In fact she showed no sign of having noticed him at all. She opened her Pearbook, which was covered with stickers of flowers and kittens, and the legend, in blobby pink letters, *Women Rule,* with a decal of a grinning Meghan Markle next to it. With her black goggles on, Frida looked rather like Von Richtofen, the First World War fighter ace. She panted and snorted, her thick nose ring shivering in time with the machine-gun rattle of the keys as she pounded them.

'Now we're all here, the purpose of today's meeting...' Melvyn began.

'Is to discuss Dr Lloyd-Jones' application for promotion,' Frida said. Ack-ack-ack-ack. You could practically smell the cordite. 'Rocky, will you be our secretary today?'

'Sure, Frida, I'd be delighted to,' Rocky simpered. 'I just love to help.'

'Uh Frida, you know I'm the chair of the tenure and promotion committee?'

The goggles swivelled towards Melvyn, her face a murderous mask. She rattled off another burst, typing and snapping like the Red Baron. 'It's obvious from his portfolio,' Frida said, ignoring him pointedly, lifting a folder from a *Save the Whale* shopping bag and hurling it across the table, so that it crashed to the floor, 'that Dr Lloyd-Jones does not deserve promotion. Especially after his shameful humiliation of Timothy the other day. A *gay* student. It was so homophobic and uncaring of him. A display of toxic masculinity.'

Rocky, who had just put on a pair of black goggles too, looked up from her typing. 'We all totally respect your opinion. I'm sure we all agree with you.'

Melvyn crawled under the table for the portfolio, thought, *Screw it,* and left it there.

Lucky Luke raised the bill of his cap, like a yawning crocodile. Would he snap those jaws?

'Let's not jump to conclusions,' Lucky Luke said in his Southern drawl, although he had grown up in Lodi, California. 'We should examine his achievements in each field, right, Melvyn? Teaching, Service, and Scholarly or Creative Work. Surely we want to be fair?'

'Of course we want to be fair,' Frida fumed. 'I'm all about fairness. Like in the courts, I believe everyone is guilty until proven innocent.'

'Don't you mean the opposite?' said Luke. 'Innocent till proven guilty?'

'Yeah, right, except in rape cases—then you have to believe women,' said Frida.

'Right on,' Rocky said. 'Always believe women.'

'We're getting off-track,' Melvyn said. 'Let's discuss his publication record.'

'It's stellar,' Luke said. 'Three novels, all with independent presses, admittedly, but prestigious ones. Gungate, Pepper, and the last one, *Ceredigion*, came out with Blossomsbury. Sachiko gave him a great review in the *New Yorker*. He won the Wholegrain Award and was short-listed for the Brooker Prize. Not too shabby.'

'Yeah, but that was like centuries ago,' Rocky said. 'What's he done in the past five years? That's the period we're looking at. Huh? Zip. Zilch. Nada.'

'Squat,' Frida said.

Melvyn grinned: given her shape, that was funny. 'Diddly-squat,' he chimed in.

'All right, he hasn't published a novel in the past five years,' Luke said, pointing his boots at Frida, 'but who has? We know he's been working on his *Manicomium*, or whatever. And he's published extracts from it in *The New Yorker*.'

'No one cool reads *The New Yorker* anymore,' Frida said. 'Only assholes.'

'Right,' said Rocky. 'It's so elitist—so patriarchal—so *white*.' Her mouth contorted with nausea as she spoke. She poked inside it, making convincing retching sounds.

'Isn't that envy?' Luke said. 'I'd love to be in *The New Yorker*. All that dosh.'

'Luke,' Frida said, 'who cares about money? We're *artists*, not whores.'

'Yeah, what she said,' Rocky added, blazing at the keyboard. 'You go, girl.'

'Melvyn?' Luke said. 'You're a fiction writer. What's your opinion of him? Everyone said he was brilliant when we hired him. Even Frida. Has he lost his touch?'

Damn, this was awkward. Melvyn could not afford to antagonise Frida, but on the other hand he might need Luke's vote when he, Melvyn, came up for promotion himself next year. Besides, much to his surprise he discovered that he had qualms—he still had the vestige of a conscience. And Huw's publication record was way better than his own, not to mention Frida's, which was pathetic by any standards.

'His stories are not so bad,' Melvyn said. 'But he should have published a book recently. Maybe with some small but highly-regarded micro-press.'

'Like yours?' Luke said. 'Or all of ours—mine included? Huw's the only one of us with a national reputation, let's face it. We wouldn't be jealous, would we?'

'Of course not,' Frida said. 'Okay, as a writer I admit he's not so bad. For a straight white male. An *older* straight white cis male. But what about his service record?'

'Stellar again,' Luke said. 'Faculty Senate, University, College and Department committees, many of which he chaired, Editor of the *Starving Artist Review,* judge of national and state literary contests, arts advisor for the Tocqueville City planning committee. He's advised a bunch of graduate theses and organised our Writers-in-Diversity series. He's been on state television and NPR. He's been giving creative writing classes in prisons and mental institutions too. *Pro bono*.'

Rocky wrinkled her pug-like nose. 'Yeah, but he could have done like way more.'

'Have you done more, Rocky?' Luke demanded. Was he defending Huw so hotly out of sheer decency? Melvyn wondered. Could any human be that nice?

'Not in like quantity, I admit. But it's the *quality* that counts,' Rocky said.

'What do you mean?' Luke said.

'Like, what's he done for the LGBTQIA+ community? Or for African-Americans or other oppressed minorities? What's he ever done for *women?*'

'Yeah, what's he ever done for *women*?' Frida grunted behind her goggles.

'He doesn't have the safe space decal on his office door,' Melvyn said.

Luke frowned. 'So what are you saying? He's racist or

misogynist or homophobic? I'm queer and I've never found him homophobic.'

'Luke—we saw him make poor Timothy weep. How heartless of him. Anyway, even if he's not homophobic,' Frida said, 'he is racist and misogynist. Just look at his syllabi.'

'We're discussing his service right now. Can we agree that it's acceptable?'

'Like barely,' Rocky said. 'He might could volunteer at a women's shelter.'

'We're agreed on that,' Frida said, rubbing her stubby pink trotters together.

'No, we aren't,' Luke said. 'At least I'm not. Are you, Melvyn?'

'On to his teaching,' Frida cut in. 'Where there are obvious deficiencies.'

'Not to me,' said Luke. 'Be fair. His evaluations are way above average.'

'But there are lousy ones too,' Frida said. 'I noticed a disturbing tendency for his students to complain of his arrogance and their inability to understand him. Someone rated his competence in English as below average.'

'Does that reflect his competence in English or theirs?' Luke said. 'His English is flawless, you know that. We've all had students who hate us and give us zeros on everything.'

'In any case, we shouldn't pay too much attention to evaluations,' Frida said. 'They're notoriously unreliable.'

'That's the opposite of what you usually say, Frida.' She did not deny it. Luke went on: 'The word is, Huw's an excellent instructor. Tons of students have told me he's the best they've ever had.'

'I don't believe you!' Frida said. 'Students always say *I'm* the best.'

Because you give so many As and tell them they're all special, Melvyn thought.

'And what about this recent scandal over his syllabus?' Frida said.

Rocky nodded *sagely*. Luke indicated puzzlement by raising an eyebrow and bending his knees slightly, retracting the gun barrels of his legs. 'What scandal is that?' he said.

'A student complained to Frida that Huw's novella syllabus only had like *white males* on it,' Rocky explained. 'And he actually said women couldn't write to save their lives. Or ethnic minorities. Or gay or transgender people. He said they all sucked, big time.'

'Nonsense,' Luke said. 'Huw never uses American slang.'

'It's totally true,' Rocky said. 'Trust me.'

'How do you know that?' Luke said.

'Dude, Frida *told* me—*duh*.'

'Holy fuck, Frida, those are serious charges. Are you saying you have solid evidence that Huw made bigoted statements about women and minority writers?'

Frida's nose-ring shook and her scalp flushed crimson. 'I'm not saying I heard it with my own actual ears,' she admitted. 'But I know it's true.'

'So whose testimony are you relying on?' Luke said.

'Can't say. FERPA. Student confidentiality,' Frida said.

'Jeez, Frida, I have to know if you have evidence for those accusations.'

'All right, it was Broome,' Frida said. 'A mature student.'

'In age, yes,' Luke agreed. 'But mentally and emotionally—sweet Jesus. For a start she had the hots for Huw. We all know that. And when he rejected her advances, she turned sour. Second, she's mentally unstable. She carries a loaded pistol in her purse. She actually showed it to me.'

'Hey, so do I,' Rocky said. 'Like *hello?* Women have to protect themselves.'

'Me too,' Frida said. 'All men are rapists—except for gay men, of course.'

Melvyn snapped out of his reverie. Miranda, dressed as a Japanese schoolgirl, in black knee socks, had just laid down, or rather lain down, her eyes drooping seductively.

But Luke accepted the reproach. 'Maybe that's commoner than I realised,' he said. 'But third—well, you must have noticed that Broome is desperate to curry favour with you, Frida. She's looking for fellowships, prizes, recommendations.'

'She has a genuine admiration for me,' Frida said. 'A reverence, you might say. For my scholarly work and my example. I find that deeply touching.'

'Exactly. She's sycophantic, and makes no secret of it. So don't you think she might just be willing to besmirch Huw's name to gratify you?'

'Luke, are you suggesting that I'm biased against Huw?'

'Well, the idea had occurred to me.'

'I'm shocked that you'd consider me capable of bias,' Frida said. 'I believe in humanistic values. I'm a progressive. I fight for social justice. I read the PuffPost.'

'Maybe so. But ever since Savanna B. Manley's reading, when Huw said she was a shit writer, you got to admit you've held a grudge against him.'

'I don't know what you mean!' Frida said.

'Yeah, what do you mean?' Rocky said.

'You took it personally,' Luke said. 'I heard the conversation. I think you've been out to get him since. You want revenge.'

'I never heard anything so insulting, so false—so preposterous!' Frida said.

'Yeah, *preponderous*,' Rocky said. 'Props for the cool word, Frida.'

Melvyn decided to cut short the confrontation. 'I think we've had a very thorough discussion of Dr Lloyd-Jones' portfolio,' he said, toe-punting it further beneath the table. 'And now, maybe we should put it to the vote?'

'Yeah, let's put it to the vote,' Rocky said. 'I'm so like *done* with this baloney.'

For Melvyn, though, it was a tricky decision. He knew his wife would vote against Huw, and Rocky would support her, and Luke would vote for Huw. That made Melvyn's the decisive vote.

If he voted against, the Department Committee disapproved of the proposal, and it was unlikely that Dean Jorgenson, who had been incandescent at Timothy's thesis defence, would gainsay that vote. But if Melvyn voted with Luke, for Huw, the votes would be evenly split, and the Provost and President might give Huw the benefit of the doubt.

The Neolithic hunter in Melvyn wanted to see Huw defeated, thrashed with sticks, pelted with rocks, driven from the warm cave and the comfort and safety of the tribe. And the beta male in him, who feared the matriarch, cowered beside her heaving flanks, grateful for protection, willing to obey. Yet another part knew that Huw deserved to be a full professor—far more than Frida did, or Rocky. So maybe he should vote for him? Against the women? To stake out his independence? Defy the bloated Red Baron crouching with her black goggles on. That was what Dr Pound would urge him to do. But did he have the guts? Did he?

'Clearly we should vote by secret ballot,' he said. Luke nodded.

'Should we like vote by secret ballot, Frida?' Rocky said. 'You're the boss.'

'I'm not ashamed of my opinion,' Frida said. 'Are you ashamed of yours?'

'A secret ballot is the correct procedure,' Luke said. 'As you well know.'

'Votes for Huw's promotion…?' Frida snapped. Ack-ack-ack-ack.

'I do this under protest. Please put that in the minutes,' Luke told Rocky.

'And against…?' Frida said, with a *grim smile of satisfaction.*

Rocky's arm *shot up* like an infant's; Frida's followed at once.

Melvyn was paralysed.

'Are you abstaining, Melvyn?' Frida asked.

Damn, he could abstain—he had forgotten that. Should he? He would avoid having voted against anyone. But no one would be pleased if he sat on the fence. Who was more powerful? That was obvious. *I am a good person,* he told himself. What would the Superior Man do? He had not consulted the *I Ching* that morning, but it would counsel him to follow his conscience. Vote for Huw's promotion. He *would* vote for Huw. He would show Frida.

Feebly, uncertainly, his arm began to rise, then drooped.

'Three votes to one against,' Frida said.

'Are you sure?' Luke said. 'That wasn't clear to me. Melvyn, were you voting for Huw or against him? Could you verify that?'

'*Ich habe durchfall*,' Melvyn mumbled, remembering a phrase from German 101. I have diarrhoea. It was true. If he didn't get to a toilet real soon, he was in trouble.

'What the hell does that mean, Melvyn?' Luke said.

'Is there a motion to adjourn the meeting?' Frida said.

'I vote to adjourn it,' Rocky said.

'Seconded,' Melvyn said. 'I declare the meeting adjourned.'

'No, *I* declare it adjourned,' Frida said, snapping her Pearbook shut.

Lucky Luke mumbled something that sounded like 'hypocritical bastards'. Oddly enough, Melvyn agreed with him, although he had got the outcome he planned. With luck he would soon be the alpha male of the department—but right now he had to reach that toilet.

SEVENTEEN

Heartline and Lifeline

How much worse can my life get, Huw asked himself, now Miranda wants to divorce me?

As it happens, Huw, far worse than you can imagine.

The day had passed quietly. In the morning he was able to write, to his astonishment, and in a final exhilarating spurt had completed his novel. Before lunch he lifted weights in the university gym with ferocious determination. His heart raced, his muscles tearing apart, but he ignored the pain. He ate in the cafeteria, which was unusual for a professor, and afterwards took a stroll in the university nature reserve, an area of prairie grasses and woodland frequented mainly by the amorous: condoms hung on shrubs and strewed the trails.

Sans glasses, he failed to recognise the person he was approaching, but he could tell she was female, and even from behind had a hunch she would be attractive. Her light, balletic gait was familiar: she pranced along, slowly, her feet hardly touching the ground. She wore headphones. The stateliness of her step suggested music. Twice her bare, slender arms rose, unhurriedly, gently, gracefully, as if choreographed. She wore a filmy blouse, a longish skirt of peasant inspiration, but of a more diaphanous fabric than peasants wore, and espadrilles that laced up her brown calves. She had her hair in a ballerina's shiny, tight topknot.

As he caught up with her she twirled, in fact pirouetted, rising on her tiptoes and trembling—smiling with joy and self-confidence, as if she expected applause.

'Elise, how graceful you look, floating along this woodland path like a nymph. You must be a dancer.'

'I am,' she said with pride.

'What are you listening to?'

'Chopin. The *Preludes,* played by Maria João Pires.'

Although his heart was in bits, he smiled. 'How fitting.'

She descended from her trembling points pose and stood squarely before him, far closer than usual for an American. 'Thank you, Huw. How are you?'

Should he confide in her? It might be unseemly to discuss his private life with a student, and impolitic, even though he had no intention of seducing her. But he needed to tell someone, and her use of his first name invited intimacy.

'Rotten, to tell the truth. You may have heard my wife left me.'

She nodded rhythmically, probably still listening to the music.

'She wants a divorce,' he added.

'How *splendid,*' she said, beaming. Huw guessed she had picked up the phrase from Masterpiece Theatre, maybe *Upton Abbey.* 'I mean what a splendid opportunity for you and her, to grow, to find yourselves, to explore new ways of being. It could be awesome, Huw.'

'I daresay that's how she looks at it. I confess I don't.'

'It's natural that you don't right now. But Time will heal you. I foresaw imminent catastrophe in your life, do you remember?'

'Yes, you did, Elise. What do you foresee now?'

'Give me your palm again.'

'Is there any point? You read it so recently.'

'The lines can change. In a remarkably short time.'

He surrendered his hand to her. When she took it in hers, the pleasure was instant—not exactly sexual, but certainly sensual. To be touched by such a pretty sprite was a joy. Women could be kind to men. Some of them still liked men. She stood so close that their bodies nearly touched.

'Yep, it has changed all right,' she said, peering at his palm. 'I saw the rupture in your heart line a few weeks ago, when it was kind of a crack. See? Now it's broken. Sorry.'

'Yes, it's broken. No hope at all, then?' he said, half amused, half wistful.

'You must *embrace* change,' she said. With a hint of suggestiveness? Or was that his imagination? 'Decay and dissolution bring new growth. Go with the flow.'

She said the last words with the glibness of Andie McDowell in *Groundhog Day,* and Huw had to resist retorting with the cynicism of Bill Murray.

'Philosophically, I agree. But my feelings are stuck in the Stone Age.'

She laughed. She smelled of apples and lavender. 'Now look at this, though. See this fork, right here in the lifeline. I don't remember seeing that last time. Maybe it was there already, but not so pronounced. It's crystal-clear now.'

'What does it mean?'

'I think a choice, maybe work-related. To stay here or work somewhere else.'

Tempus abire tibi est. 'Anything else?' He found himself believing her.

'Look here on the heartline: a clear break, but then there's this new line—I think it's new—connecting to the heartline. That could be a fabulous new love.'

She looked up at him and he nearly fell into the clear pools of her eyes. He had to change the subject. 'All I can think about is my old love.'

'Of course you feel hurt now. But you'll rise again—like the phoenix. Hey, I got a new tattoo. Of a phoenix, as it happens.'

Huw despised tattoos but asked politely, 'Where?'

She flushed. 'Close to my lady parts.'

'What a quaint phrase. In that case I don't suppose you can show me?' He was surprised that his tone had come out flirtatious, although he had not meant it to.

'Hell, I don't care,' she said, at once peeling back the brown film of her skirt—down over the flat abdomen, to the tops of her panties, a mere membrane of white cotton. Still no sign of the tattoo. With the titillating skill of a striptease artist—and yet too shy to look him in the eye—she pushed down the top of this garment too, revealing the mythical bird, beak open, wings wide and beating, rising from a pyre of curling flames and an equally thick fire of curling reddish hair. At last Elise dared to look at him. Across her face flittered embarrassment, but also pride, pleasure, and a challenge. It was not the saucy glance of the temptress, but the graver one of the princess offering herself to the prince.

'How extraordinary,' Huw said, embarrassed, because his voice shook.

'You like it then?' she said, still holding her skirt and panties down.

'Oh yes,' he said, far too quickly. 'It's wonderful.'

'I was afraid you might not dig it. A guy your age.'

'Usually I dislike tattoos. As most old fogeys do. But this one was done by an artist. The phoenix is alive—about to take flight.'

'Isn't it, though? It's so cool that you're into it, Huw. You want to touch it?'

A swarm of impulses assailed him, stung him. Of course he wanted to touch it! But no, of course he didn't! What was he thinking? What about Miranda? And Elise was not just a student, but his student! And what if anyone came along? They were standing in a glade of oaks and hornbeam, through which sunlight poured in melodramatic shafts. Luckily, there was no sign or sound of anyone. Just the humming of insects, and traffic not too far away.

'I probably shouldn't,' he said.

'Why not give in to temptation? You may.' Another quaint turn of phrase.

His hot blood often got him into trouble. But he pictured Miranda's face.

He shut his eyes. 'Better not. For both of us.'

'What a shame,' she said, covering up without rancour. Again there was distance between them. What terrible timing. If it had been a year hence, when she had graduated and he had got over his grief—*if* he ever got over it. 'Maybe some other time?' she added.

'I'd better turn back,' he said. It made him feel old, passionless.

'Sure. But before you go, there's something I got to tell you.'

He expected a gauche declaration, or more pressure to succumb to her advances. But she looked ashamed, or indignant.

'It's very hard to say. Maybe I shouldn't. I mean, this is in confidence, right?'

He nodded, fearing the worst. 'Of course. Go on.'

'You can't say I told you, or I'll get in trouble with my dad. Big time. You know the Shamburgers have it in for you, yeah?'

'I know Frida has. But both of them?'

'Yeah, I think so. They're lodging some kind of complaint against you. Because of how you conducted Timothy's thesis defence. Frida was furious.'

'I gathered that. But how do you know all this, Elise?'

'My dad told me—because I'm in your class and I have a major crush on you.'

'Jesus, your dad knows you have a crush on me?'

'No worries, I told him you're irreproachable—which is true, though I believe you could be tempted, frankly. If I work on you a bit more. See, you're blushing. That's so cute, Huw. Anyway, dad told me that Jorgenson and Timothy are making the complaint and the Shamburgers are backing them up. Or vice-versa. I'm not exactly certain. The little bitches.'

'Thanks for warning me.'

'Sure, no problem. Let me know when you change your mind about the phoenix.'

When, not *if*. 'Thanks again, Elise. May your phoenix fly.'

'Oh, it's about to take off, trust me.'

The encounter had unsettled him. On the one hand he was flattered that Elise was courting him, but also aware that his emotions were a bewildering mess of grief, anger, regret, pity, self-pity, confusion, denial and despair, all bubbling and boiling together. And on the other hand, there was Elise's worrying revelation about the plot against him.

But all that was forgotten when he got back to his office and saw the email from Miranda, blaring in caps: RAPE!

The message was incoherent, so he called her. To his surprise, she picked up.

'What happened, love? How are you? Can I come over?'

Her voice was tiny. 'Yes, I'm at home. Thank you, Huw.'

EIGHTEEN

Masterful Melvyn

Feeling as tough as Tom Cruise in *Mission Impossible,* Melvyn put on his burglar gear: black jeans, socks and shoes, a black polo shirt with the NaNoWriMo logo, and its fatuous slogan, *The World Needs Your Novel*, and a black bomber jacket. What about a ski mask? Nope, if anyone saw him, they'd call the cops. *How about blacking my face, then, like Justin Trudeau? People would never forgive me: you have to be the wet dream of liberal women to get away with shit like that.* Still, he had not shaved for a week and the face of a caveman stared back at him from the mirror. No doubt about it: he looked totally awesome.

Should he drive or walk? Each option had drawbacks. Even the smaller of the Shamburger SUVs was identifiable by the array of stickers: *I'm with Her, LGBTQIA+ Alliance, Teach Tolerance, Hillary for President, Black Lives Matter, Thank a Teacher,* and many more. On the other hand, the citizens of Tocqueville regarded pedestrians as tramps, malefactors, and madmen, and some hick with a BB gun or even a shotgun might well snipe at him from a dormer window as he walked past. Jezebel's strategy was best, he decided: he would drive to within a block of the address Frida had given him in the Historic District, then slink under the shadows of the oaks and maples on foot.

On the way out, with his heart thudding as though John Bonham were using it as a kick-drum, he picked up a pair of binoculars, and a natty device which he strapped to his temples. Garfield watched from the upstairs landing, peering through the banisters with an expression of undisguised scorn. Melvyn dismissed the fancy that the cat knew what he was up to and would confabulate with Frida later. Darcy wagged his tail hopefully.

Melvyn patted his head. 'Tough luck, pal. This one's for the dawgs, dude, not the dogs.'

Then he sprinted to the tank-like purple jeep, and vaulted up into the driver's seat. He set off, gripping the wheel, imagining machine-gun fire raking the road at any moment, and listening to *The Eye of the Tiger*. He sang along about the will to survive and the thrill of the fight. Tocqueville slashed by his windows, a Southern Gothic city, old wooden houses with porches and turrets lurking between trees, hounds howling at the moon. He left the car in the unlit parking lot of The Seventh Day Adventist church, in a deep pond of shadow.

As he flitted between the trees, crossing his fingers, he considered Huw's fate. Timothy had lodged a formal complaint, first with Frida, which she had supported with enthusiasm, then with the Dean, Jorgenson, who had naturally endorsed it, and thus it had reached the President, who had sent it on to the Board with reluctance and anger, so he had heard. The university lawyers were meant to be in discussion with him and the Board of Directors, right now, in an emergency session, as Melvyn stole towards his destination. Huw would be fired for sure, tenure or no tenure. If he were lucky, they might just castrate him, metaphorically speaking—force him to make a grovelling apology, which would leave him impotent in all departmental matters, a minion of Frida's. Melvyn preferred that possibility. *Because of my innate kindness and humanity*, he told himself. *I'm not such a bad guy. Not like Frida, who's evil.* After tonight, if his dreams were realised, he would turn the tables on the lot of them. *He* would for sure soon be the alpha male in the department. Oh yeah.

He crept up to the house like a panther, not on all fours, but with the stealth of one. It was a white nineteen twenties Arts and Crafts home, with a porch on which stood a rocking chair, a derelict sofa, a coffee table, ashtrays, beer bottles and cans. Screwed into the siding was a metal plate emblazoned with an axe-wielding warrior and the legend, *Go Goths!* The football team of an adjacent state, he remembered. Melvyn edged around the side of the house. Who *did* it belong to? Some slovenly student. Or an equally messy professor. Lucky Luke? No, he was gay; an unlikely lover for Frida. Still, anything was possible these days. The crickets and katydids chirruped, covering his almost soundless approach. A bat skittered above his head, making him duck and nearly cry out. An owl screeched as he took up his position at the back, behind a bush close to the French windows. The scene was just what a third-rate writer like Frida would come up with. The bedroom on the other side of those windows was brightly lit, as she had promised. Melvyn had no need of the binoculars. A huge sleigh-bed, with a poster of dubious taste—atrocious taste—hanging above it. A sexy squaw, built like a glamour model, with a fierce expression, carrying a bow and arrows, surrounded by friendly wolves and bears, in moonlight, with dramatic snowy mountains in the background. Dream-catchers hung over the bed, which was empty.

For now.

No books on the bedside tables—so the resident was not a literary person. Next to a vast flat screen television hung a poster of a sultry Tinker Quick, her long legs wide apart, in thigh-high boots, her arms akimbo, her black hair flying in the wind, an expression of triumph on her heavily made-up face.

Evidently the tenant was a student, or an immature adult.

More evidence for this hypothesis was the profusion of Goth

garments scattered on the floor and hanging from the furniture: black leather pants, spike heels, fishnet stockings, suspenders, a brassiere fit for a Valkyrie, a corset—man, did women still wear those?—and a spiked collar and a riding whip. Real kinky. The wait was unbearable. It was seven-thirty, the time Frida had said. So where was she?

From deep inside came a cacophony, some kind of music—not Tinker, but Metal. A guttural, growling voice, the clanking of heavy machinery, the pounding of jackhammers, drums, guitars, shrill, hysterical solos. Melvyn smiled: Frida hated this kind of music. Despite the volume, he heard a feminine shriek, of laughter or pain, it was impossible to tell. Who could the mystery paramour be? Marge, maybe, the trans professor? Melvyn's mind boggled, ran riot, imagining all possible anatomical permutations. Oh boy oh boy—or oh girl oh girl.

However, when the bedroom door opened, with a tsunami of metallic din, it was not the Queer Studies professor who entered: this woman's hair was long and black. Otherwise, since his wife's bulk nearly hid the other figure, entangled as they were, all he could see was that she was also 'large', and taller than Frida. The women crashed about in the throes of passion, but Frida's paramour somehow kept her back turned towards him. She was wearing a black leather sleeveless jerkin with a skull in studs on the back; a black leather skirt, wider than it was long; fishnet stockings and suspenders, which slightly attenuated the chubbiness of her legs, and the black jackboots of an SS officer. A spiked collar. From behind she looked familiar. She had Frida in a combination of a bear hug and head lock. Was the woman a professional wrestler? Frida's copper scalp barely came up to her shoulder blades.

Nonetheless, Frida was impelling the pair towards the window, in her hideously short purple minidress, staggering as if her ankles were cuffed together with chains. Damn, they *were* cuffed together with chains. Only when the couple stumbled to within a foot of the pane did they pause, still kissing, or was it biting? Frida knew she had an audience of course. What about Alaric the Goth? Melvyn guessed Frida had discussed her fantasy with her 'mistress'—and had her consent. Maybe she was an exhibitionist too? Only now did Melvyn remember the action camera strapped to his forehead, and turn it on. Would they realise they were being filmed? And if they did, would they cease their lovemaking? He would just have to risk it.

Neither of them gave any sign that they were aware of his bearded head poking out of the bush, beyond the extraordinary violence of their kisses. It was a relief, but also a slight—was he too insignificant to notice? Besides, what did he feel, watching Frida? Horror, sure, but arousal too. Melvyn had rejected her invitation to watch lesbian porn with her, but Sapphic love turned him on, he knew now, even in the guise of bull hippopotami in combat.

But the tableau was changing with breath-taking speed. The living sculpture writhed and wrenched itself around, so that the women, who were not ten feet away, presented their profiles to him. The woman gripping Frida in strong, if flabby, arms, was none other than their 'mature' student, Broome. His first thought was that he had been right that the tenant was not a literary person: though a creative writing major, Broome preferred trash television and video games to books. His second thought was: a *student.* His third: *Frida's* student. As that sank in, Broome broke free—maybe he had been wrong about who was clasping who or whom—and ripped off Frida's dress, thrust her face down on the bed, snatched up the riding crop, and lay into the vast Gorgonzola backside as if she were giving a public flogging in Saudi Arabia. Whack! Thwack! Swish! God, it was good! He was invisible, invulnerable. Had he orchestrated it himself, it could not have been more perfect. Doubtless Frida had wished to demean him by making him watch her with a lover, but with each of Broome's brutal blows he became more aroused, more potent. The whip whistled above the death metal—he could not hear it of course, but he *saw* and *felt* it whistling—and Frida squealed, or was that Dimebag Darrell? Nope, he would know that sow-like panicked squeal anywhere.

In the interest of decorum, what happened next should be elided from the record. It should be, since this is not pornography, but a work of serious literary fiction, as any discerning reader will agree. But we must remember that Melvyn's camera was recording every nanosecond. So, however offensive it may be, there is a record extant, and thus we are with regret *forced* to dwell upon the squalid incident a little longer, as judges and juries must when trying unspeakable crimes, regardless of their inclinations. *We could at least speed up the video, though, surely*? we seem to hear the more delicate readers among you pleading. Very well: clothes flew off and fell in a flurry of leather and lace. Broome and Frida engaged in acts of—ahem— 'oral love'. Broome spanked Frida with her blacksmith hands, then again with the whip. Frida threshed and wobbled. Heads shook and nodded. Mouths gaped in terror, and delight, to shout, to imprecate, to implore, to slobber, gnaw, suck, and bite. Melvyn stifled the urge to rush in and join them. Broome seized a fearsome mauve cudgel—in fact a dildo, a *circumcised* one—Jesus, were there special Jewish dildoes?—and looking as cruel and triumphant as Tinker Quick, committed an unspeakable act on Frida, who screamed above the cataclysmic noise.

You go, girl, Melvyn urged the savage Goth. An eardrum-perforating screech accompanied each jab of Broome's brawny arm. What could diminish Melvyn's joy? Only the realisation that never again could he possibly be so happy. He gave thanks, to God or the Goddess, Whofucking*ever*. His life was complete. This was nirvana, the purest ecstasy.

It ended abruptly. Broome snatched up scraps of leather and fled. Frida floundered on the bed in a state of shock, her back bruised, cut, covered in welts, Melvyn was delighted to see. When she rolled over, wobbling, quivering, and shaking, mascara and tears streaked her face. Superb, very gratifying. And then it happened: she broke the fourth wall. As she levered her squat body into a crouch on the bed, she looked out of the window—directly at him.

Could she see him? It was bright inside, dark outside, and on an instinctive reflex he ducked back into the foliage of the hibiscus bush. Still, her face, with the gold ring dangling from her snout, stared straight at him, and her expression dumbfounded him. She tried to smile, but the effort was too much: her lips contorted into a sneer, then a snarl. If it was not love her face showed, it was *something* erotic or pseudo-romantic. Or plain perverted.

Unable to contain himself any longer, he burst from the bush, heedless of whether his wife would be angry that he had not waited, and heedless of his swollen member. Would she notice that, concealed within his pants? He sure hoped so.

Melvyn tapped his watch, and beckoned to her to follow him. For once he knew she would do his bidding. He sprinted round the block to his car, hardly caring now whether the neighbours might see him and phone the police, or blast away at him with their semi-automatic weapons. He raced home like Vin Diesel in *The Fast and the Furious*, yelling.

He was right: he did not have to wait long. He had just checked that Thalia was still out, bribed Garfield with a saucer of milk, and swallowed a stiff Scotch, when Frida's SUV screeched into the drive. The car door thunked as if an Olympic weightlifter had slammed it.

Battered, bloody, her dress in shreds, a ghastly grin on her face, Frida looked more fearsome than a Russian weightlifter when she came in. It was a decisive moment. He jumped on her, pushed her roughly up the stairs into the bedroom, swept the mewling Garfield off the bed, and deposited Frida on it. He tore at her garments as Broome had done. Her dress disintegrated.

And then—well, dear reader, you can guess what he did, and how. He proved himself a *man*. Or rather, a Silverback gorilla, an alpha male, just as he had hoped earlier. For once Frida was not on top in any sense. And for the first time in many, many years, he enjoyed it.

'Wowee,' Frida said afterward. 'I never knew you could be so… *masterful,* Melvyn.'

'Neither did I. To be honest.'

'But what's that weird flashing gadget on your forehead?'

'Oh, this? I forgot to take it off. Just a light. For seeing in the dark.'

'Right. Genius. You are smart.' For once, Frida was happy, relaxed. *Nice.*

'I feel fulfilled,' he said truthfully. 'I never dreamed I could want you so much.'

'Oh Melvyn,' she moaned. 'It was all for you, sweetie. I *love* you.'

He had not heard that for a decade or two. Did she mean those gooey words? In her Disney-distorted mind, maybe. He did not repeat the formula. *No need. I have all the power I could ever desire, right here, digitally saved. My Third Eye. From now on she can never bully, browbeat, humiliate, or degrade me. She can never scorn me or scoff at my words. All these years she's been the boss. Now it's my turn.* As he lay on his back, with Frida's bruised flesh flopping over his chest like a burned omelette, Melvyn considered revealing what he had done. Not yet, he decided. Even so, he could not resist teasing her about Broome:

'I have to admit the identity of your lover surprised me.'

Frida's gaze was adoring. 'Because she was a woman, you mean?'

'No, because she's a student. One of *our* students. That's risky, surely?'

She chuckled. 'Don't worry. I'm pretty powerful at Oxbow State, Melvyn.'

'All the same, you'd be fired in a heartbeat if anyone found out.'

'But Broome will never tell. And I know I can trust you.'

He smiled *duplicitously*, as Gardner and Chandler might have put it.

'Sure you can trust me, honey,' he said, smirking with his secret knowledge of the footage. *Blackmail*—what a cool word. He had turned into a *film noir* tough guy, like Humphrey Bogart. And Lauren Bacall was awaiting him in the wings.

NINETEEN

The Voice of God

Oh dear, the poor old Welshman. Even by the standards of his *annus horribilis,* Huw is having a rotten day. Let us divulge, lest the reader despair, that despite the slings and arrows of outrageous fortune, and his own *hamartia* and *hubris*, our handsome dark-haired Celtic hero will receive another chance to save himself. Already Time has twice churned to a halt for him and yet Huw has gone back to his stale old life. Will he have the wisdom to seize his last chance?

Here he is, at Miranda's front door, frantic after the email titled 'RAPE', his heart racing, having sped in his car and sprinted up the stairs. He is sweating, panting for breath.

Miranda has accused him of arrogance and self-centredness, of superficiality and insensitivity. We have seen him struggling with that knowledge—recognising the truth in her words, yet, so far, failing to change much. And from folk tales, including the Welsh ones, we know that the man who cannot change is doomed to an inferior existence, or punishment. We know too that the hero only has three chances. Huw is no boy—his hair is greying at his temples. And yet he is not yet fully grown up. The dominant myth of his time is that one need not mature, ever, that it is more fun to be a boy, to play, to evade responsibility, live a life of fantasy. Huw has accepted this creed, like most men. Only now is he starting to question it.

He knocks. No response. He tries again. He's heard something inside—a monotone nasal squeak, some announcer on a television, or an irritable seal—and a shuffling noise. He imagines Miranda in her fluffy pink slippers and pyjamas. Is she hurt? Is she still in danger?

He does not suspect that his own life is in danger.

From our Olympian halls, we observe as he confronts his fate. Will he understand in time that fate is not the same as destiny—that destiny is what one makes of one's fate? He has not avoided the catastrophes, cannot avoid them, but he could find self-knowledge, wisdom—and face his troubles with dignity, like the heroes of ancient Greece and Wales.

'Miranda?' he calls. No response. 'Are you there? It's me.'

He sat down on the top step to wait. His ears whistled, his left arm ached, his jaw and the left side of his face ached, and the pressure in his chest mounted. *I should go to the hospital*, he thought. *But I've got to see Miranda first. If I can just hold out until then.* He wanted to lie down but forced himself to sit up.

At last the door opened, very slowly, silently. 'Huw?' a tinny voice said.

He jumped up to fling his arms around her—but seeing her in her pink fluffy slippers with the pom-poms, as he had guessed, and the pink pyjamas with a design of teddy bears, her hair uncombed, lank and greasy, her face bare of makeup, and yet as white and blank as a geisha's, he restrained the impulse. If he touched her, she would crumple like cardboard.

'What are you doing here?' she said. Her face was not anguished, but blank, numb.

'You know what I'm doing here. You told me to come. You

said you've been raped. Oh my God, Miranda, I'm so sorry. How are you?'

'All right, I guess. I know I look like shit. What do you want?'

'For God's sake, you invited me. Just now. I'm worried. Can I do anything?'

'No. I don't think so.' She did not move aside for him to enter.

'I love you, Miranda.'

'I love you too,' she said mechanically. *Non te amat,* the choirs had sung.

'Will you let me in?'

'My apartment is a trash-heap. You'll have to wait while I have a bath.'

'I don't care what you look like.'

'Wait in the living room. I can't talk to you till I'm clean.'

On the television, a woman with blonde hair and the manic smile of a patient in an advert for dentists was talking in sotto voce squeaks with a rodent-faced politician. Huw sat on the sofa, clearing a space among the medical books, health magazines, medicine bottles, and a menagerie comprised of a stuffed toy poodle, a panda, a duck, and the Pink Panther. They looked brand new. More disturbingly, amid the detritus was a carving-knife. From the bathroom he heard the hissing of water. Miranda's shower lasted half an hour. Then she padded to the lace-and-satin bedroom, where she cloistered herself for another half an hour.

She emerged in full regalia—dressed rather like the TV announcer, in a royal blue skirt-suit, her hair curled and blow-dried, her lips scarlet. Only the celebrity smile was missing. She sat in a pine-framed armchair, crossing her slender, stockinged legs, obsessively rather than seductively, despite the stiletto heels. Behind her, Frida Kahlo with antlers and arrows in her body frowned down on him.

'Why have you gone to such trouble dressing up?' he asked her.

She shrugged. 'You expect me to look nice.'

'I expect nothing of the kind. Don't you believe me? I love you.'

'Me or my body? Would you love me if I were fat and ugly?'

'Oh no, not again. Won't you tell me what happened? From the beginning?'

'I told you, he raped me.'

'Who did?'

'Matthew, of course. McBane. My fucking boss.'

I knew it, he almost said. 'Go on. Where? When?'

She spoke with the detachment of a perfect witness. 'Last night. Their house. I drank a ton of wine at dinner—he kept refilling my glass, although I told him not to—and they led me to a bed, so I could rest, they said. They put out the light and I fell asleep. When I awoke I found them on each side of me, stroking my body. Both of them. I told them to cut it out, but I was still plastered. I stumbled out, half-dressed, intending to drive home. But Matthew caught up with me, and pushed me into a dark room.'

She stopped as though someone had punched her in the gut.

'Was NeAmber with him too?' Huw asked.

'No, he was alone. He said he needed me. He said I had to help him. Only I could save him. He said I couldn't tell anyone. He tore at my tights. Then he did it.'

'He raped you.'

She gulped. 'Yes. Digitally.'

The computer meaning struck him first. Had McBane hacked her laptop? No, she meant with his fingers. She was speaking clinically, as the traumatised often did.

'I'm going to kill him,' Huw said.

'Please don't. I've lodged a complaint with the police. I did a DNA test. I can nail him, Huw.'

'Good. But I still want to kill him. Or at least beat him to a pulp.'

'I beg you not to. He needs to be shamed. To lose his job.'

'Yes, you're right. So what do you want me to do?'

'Just be here for me. And try to be more understanding.'

'I am trying. I'll try harder, I swear.'

'The sea-monsters say I need to affirm my independence from men. Do you realise, I got married when I was nineteen, and apart from the two years after my divorce, I've been married ever since? To *men.* I don't know who I am. I've spent my life pleasing men. Being what they want me to be. I need to find out if there's anything inside of me.'

She glanced at Frida Kahlo split open. Then at two seated Fridas, holding hands. Each had her internal organs revealed, her chest dissected. The Fridas all gazed coldly back at her.

He did not know how to answer. Was there anything inside her? What did he love? Had he fallen in love with his own image of the perfect woman? A picture?

'If I don't exist, I figure I may as well kill myself,' she said. 'Right?'

'You do exist. Please don't hurt yourself.'

'I'm not sure, Huw. Most women don't exist.'

'You mean they simply perform functions and roles, don't you? Like that woman with the glazed smile on the screen, talking to the squeaking rodent.' She nodded. 'If you need to divorce me to find yourself,' he went on, 'I will accept that. I have thought about it. I just want to be in your life, somehow. Help you if I can. And see justice done. Retribution.'

'It's coming. The sea-monsters told me. He'll be swallowed up. Believe me. Leave me now. If you don't hear from me again, remember that I will always love you.'

As he drove home, his chest still hurting, in fact hurting more, the song with those lyrics, which he had always hated, bellowed hysterically, swooped like a sick swallow in his brain. I-ee-ay, will always love you—oo—oo—oo-oo—oo. Hold tight, Huw, boyo. Be brave.

*

Instead of going straight to the hospital, as he knew he should, why did he decide to ride his bicycle to work, when a heavyweight boxer was punching his chest, he had pins and needles in his left arm, and his jaw ached and throbbed, right up to his left eye? He knew it was daft. But there he was, flying under a canopy of oaks and maples like Geraint Thomas again, head down over the drop handlebars, quads and calves taut, sweat streaking his face, mind empty as a Zen monk's. As he neared the final intersection before the campus, a series of mishaps befell him. Three dogs tore out from a porch and chased him, barking and snarling at his heels; next, a pick-up truck brushed his elbow, with drunken boys hanging out of the windows, screaming and making him swerve; then a pink Corvette barrelled by, piloted by Rocky, who was staring at her mobile phone. At the red light, she kicked the brakes, and Huw, already off balance and too far from the kerb, hit her back bumper.

He performed a gymnast's stunt—clinging to his handlebars, upside down—then the tarmac rose to crack his head and knee and elbow, and he lay tangled beneath his bike. A car door thunked shut. *Rocky will help me up,* he told himself. But no—she only inspected the back of her car for damage, muttered about fucking jerks, and got back inside, without so much as a glance at him. Possibly she had not recognised him. As she drove off he read her bumper stickers: *A Woman's Place is in the White House. Practice Compassion. Be Kind.*

Someone lifted his bike off him. The sky pulsed around the white-hot heart of the sun. Long legs, disembodied, rose out of suede ankle-length boots and ascended like temple columns towards the empyrean. Gentle hands touched his face, held him under his armpits.

'Don't lift him, Elise. He could be injured.' The voice was Charleston's.

'Sir? Huw?' Haloed by a corona of sunlight, her face floated among cirrus clouds. 'Are you OK?'

'I think I'm having a heart attack. I'm pretty sure I am.'

'Oh man, this sucks,' said Elise.

'It's probably a mild one,' Huw said. 'Don't worry.'

'Shit,' Charleston said. Huw still could not see him. Where was he?

Huw closed his eyes and flew off among the clouds. The pain would soon be over. People shouted, cars passed. Charleston gave directions to the emergency services. Elise unfastened his helmet. The strap had been tight around his windpipe. Someone wet his lips with water. He was dying, he suspected. He did not mind, although he wished he were not in an untidy heap like this, bleeding, one leg buckled under him, among people who did not love him. If only he could see Owen one last time, and Miranda. Would he last long enough to say goodbye to them? That was all he asked. The novel would have to fend for itself. The hardback drifted into the sky, trailing clouds of glory, as medics lifted him on to a stretcher, shovelled him into the ambulance and strapped him in.

A blue light pulsed, a siren wailed, and Whitney Houston kept bawling that she would always love him. Was he imagining that? He could *not* die listening to Whitney Houston. Someone held his hand. Miranda? No, Elise.

'Thank you,' he said.

'Hey, no worries.'

Charleston chuckled.

He passed out, or was sedated. When he came to, he was in bed in a blinding white room. God's voice blared above him, loud, authoritative, deep and confident. What was he saying? Or was it a She? Had he made it into heaven? Or was this place purgatory? As Huw's eyes focussed, he saw that God was black. A black woman. She spoke in orotund tones, to polite applause. She wore her hair in a shoulder-length bob. Her face was smooth, and a marvellous coppery colour. She was promulgating laws, commandments, something about *freedom*, *dignity*, *humanity*, *sisterhood*. He could not follow what she was saying. His eyes hurt so he shut them. When he opened them again, God's face was on the TV screen, and she was Obadiah. Her guest, she said, was a great musical genius: Mustwe East.

Huw wished he could lower the volume of the voices, and dim the dazzling light. His weariness overpowered him. If only he could sleep for centuries and wake up in Carreg Cennen, with Owen Glendower beside him, and his own son Owen. A harpist would play Welsh airs and a bard would recite the Mabinogion in Middle Welsh. *He* was the bard. It was his voice. He recited to his dear son and the last native Prince of Wales. He was fulfilled. Joyful. *That* was how he should live.

*

'What's that you're saying? We can't understand a word.'

'I'm not surprised,' he murmured, opening his eyes. 'I was speaking Welsh.'

An olive-skinned woman leaned over him. She had noble, intelligent features, which expressed a gravity Huw was unused to seeing.

'Welsh? Don't the Welsh speak English, Dr Lloyd-Jones?'

'Most of us can if we want to. Am I alive? What happened to me?'

'You had a cardiac arrest,' she said. 'Two of your arteries were blocked. You've undergone surgery. I've given you a couple of stents. Yes, you're alive, luckily. You didn't take my advice to consult a cardiologist, I suppose? You certainly didn't come to see me.'

'I'm afraid I didn't. I should have. Are you the surgeon?'

'Yes, I am.'

'Thank you for saving my life. We keep meeting, don't we? Is that fate?'

She murmured something. 'That means, Who knows God's purposes?'

'What language is that? May I ask where you're from?'

'I'm a US citizen. But I was born in Isfahan, in Iran. I spoke in Farsi.'

'Persia: the land of Hafez and Firdaus, Rumi, Omar Khayyam.'

She susurrated a few more words in Farsi, presumably. 'Is that Rumi again?'

'Omar Khayyam. You look tired. Sleep if you can.'

'Could you do something for me first? Turn off that bloody racket, please.'

'You don't like the television? All Americans love it.'

'But I'm not American, see you. I'm a Welshman. And I loathe it.'

'So do I,' she said, silencing it and dimming the lights. 'I'll drop in on you soon.'

'I shall look forward to that. May I ask your name?'

'Nasreen Shirazi.' She did not hold out her hand but she did smile at him.

He closed his eyes and was soon paddling a hide coracle along the River Teifi. Whenever he paused it turned in the current, like a leaf. It was soothing. The little leather boat drifted downstream. Life could be like that. No need for worry or strife. He cut and peeled a hazel wand, like the wandering Aengus, and hooked a berry on a thread, and dropped it into the water. He caught a silver trout, which turned into a glimmering girl with apple blossom in her hair. She called his name and ran and faded through the brightening air.

He woke up, old and weary from wandering through hollow lands and hilly lands. Owen was sitting beside him, not in his usual hoodie, but a smart blazer and chinos.

'Owen, lad,' Huw said. 'I'm happy to see you. I will find out where she has gone,'

'Miranda, you mean?' Owen said. He had grown up overnight.

Huw smiled and went on reciting. 'And kiss her lips and take her hands.'

'You're a bit delirious. I told her that you'd had a heart attack.'

Stuck in the poem, he could not stop. 'And walk among long dappled grass...'

'I told her to come and see you. She said she would if she could.'

He shook his head, laughing. 'And pluck till time and times are done...'

'But don't count on it. She's been so weird lately,' Owen said. 'Dad?'

'The silver apples of the moon, the golden apples of the sun,' he finished.

'A gorgeous girl was here a minute ago,' Owen said. 'Elise something.'

'What about Miranda? Is Miranda coming? I love you, Owen.'

'I love you too,' he said, sounding embarrassed.

'I must live differently,' Huw said. 'No more bloody silly games. I need to listen to more classical music. Write more. Go home to Wales. Drink more single malt Scotch.'

'Dad?' Owen said. 'You got a call from a woman in New York. Your agent, I think. Sherry Glass? Is that right? It sounded like a joke. I started laughing.'

'That's her real name, believe it or not. What did she say?'

'Something about an auction. An advance? Does six figures sound right?'

Huw whistled. 'I'm going to have another heart attack.'

Nasreen Shirazi entered as he spoke. 'Please don't make so much noise.'

'Sorry,' Huw said. 'But we've got something to celebrate: a publishing deal.'

'Congratulations, Huw. But the main thing to celebrate is that you're alive. Don't forget that. Worldly success is unimportant. You are *alive*. Be aware of that.'

'You're right.' The way she had pronounced his name, with a slightly guttural consonant, was enchanting, and he was touched that she had called him by his first name. All the same, he ached to see Miranda. Would she come? Alive, the doctor said—and he knew she was speaking not of his body alone, but his spirit.

Everyone visited: Lucky Luke and his partner, an ex-Marine, who talked only of catching alligator gar; Cooper and Burd, who brought books by Dylan Thomas and Richard Hughes; and many students, Elise and Charleston, and Jordan and Nutmeg, who held hands and announced that they were engaged, and Truman, who had once been Trudy, and needed a shave; and Walt, who gave him a box of chocolates and, incredibly, the selected verse of Rumi; and even Frank, or Hank, who with a grin left a *Playboy* on his bedside table. Huw longed to see Miranda, but she did not appear, even when Owen returned, as he did every day. On the other hand Nasreen often looked in on him. Apart from using his first name, she avoided familiarity, indeed was formal, but always recited a verse for him, and gave him her deep, melancholy Leonardo smile. He looked forward to her visits and Owen's most of all.

Less welcome was the visit Frida and Rocky paid him. Long before they entered his room, where he was reading John Cowper Powys, he heard the brassy blare, the trombone of Frida's voice, and the trumpet of Rocky's. Even though he was clutching a copy of *Owen Glendower*, dread gripped Huw. He simply could not face them yet. He shut his book and his eyes, and pretended to sleep. The horns gusted in, their boots beating a dirge-like rhythm.

'But what about riding, Frida?' Rocky said. 'I don't know how to teach creative riding.'

'Haven't you read all my books yet, Rock? There's nothing to it. You just tell the students they're all talented and special. Positive reinforcement. Give them As, as long as they condemn right-wing values. Our job is to mould the next generation. That's all.'

'Gee, Frida, you're so inspiring. I always feel so like uplifted after we speak.'

'Thanks, Rock, because I value loyalty above everything. I'm a leader, but I don't lead by fear like some goddamn fascist. I'm kinda like Michelle, or Meghan, or Obadiah. I want my followers to think for themselves. And you do that, Rocky. I know I can trust you. In fact we should think about promoting you. Women should be in charge, right?'

'Are you shitting me?' the trumpet sighed. 'Gee thanks, Frida. I love ya to bits.'

Snuffles and sighs indicated a tearful embrace. The women hurled their chairs at the wall with a crash. 'We better end our visitation,' Rocky said. 'Dude's asleep, anyways.'

Frida dropped her voice to a whisper. 'So I heard it was your car he ran into, right?'

'Uh, yeah. Thing is, I was tweeting with Sheena Grayham, you know her?'

'No way! Sure I know her, she's a genius. The creator of *Bitches*. Very cool.'

'Right, so like I never saw him. Then when I slammed on the brakes and I felt him crash into the Corvette, I never realised it was Huw laying in the road. Like honestly. I just thought it was some fucking jerk.'

Frida laughed. 'You got that right.'

'Haha. John Cow-per Powys,' said Rocky. 'Who's that, some dickhead phallocrat?'

'The hell I know,' Frida said. 'Some dead white male no one gives a shit about.'

'You got that right.' Their boots beat a tattoo on the floor, a rattle and a snare drum snap, and the horns receded, the trombone sliding, the trumpet blasting brief treble bursts.

Not only were they gone, thank God, but Nasreen was coming in.

'Who were those, er, ladies?' she said. 'Relatives? Friends of yours?'

'More like enemies, I'm afraid. Colleagues from the university.'

'I'm sorry. Is your work environment stressful?'

'You could put it that way.'

'You must change that. I noticed they didn't even speak to you. Not once.'

Had she been listening? Did she care enough to do that?

'They never speak to me if they can help it. And when they do, they don't listen to what I have to say. If you don't agree with them, you aren't merely misguided, you're scum, beneath notice. That's what's wrong with academia—with our society as a whole. No one is listening to anyone else. They talk about freedom, but they don't understand it.'

Nasreen shook her head. 'I know what you mean. When people find out I'm a Muslim, they nearly always ask how I can accept the domination of men. It's no good trying to explain that I don't. They've already made up their minds. Those poor women.' She spoke not with scorn but pity. She was a different kind of woman altogether—one who not only spoke of compassion, but practised it.

He knew he would miss her when he left the hospital. However, he was convinced that she would play some part in his future life. But he tried not to think about that. Hurt though he was that Miranda had not visited, he had to see her and ask for another chance.

TWENTY

No Laffing Madder

Melvyn was in an annexe of one of the classrooms in the Harriet Tubman Building, a kitchen intended for grad students, although he had never seen them, or anyone else, use it. The room had become his private domain. He would sneak in to scoff chocolate chip cookies, his secret vice, and watch porn on his tablet—his *top* secret vice. The 'actress' in the video reminded him of Jezebel, which gave him an idea: what if he lured her here for a quickie? The risk would be an aphrodisiac. She would be up for it, he was sure. Oh boy oh boy oh boy.

To enquire what he was doing while engaged in his viewing would be indiscreet, and indeed vulgar; in any case, female voices in the adjoining classroom interrupted him. As there was a door, fortunately locked, into that room, he could hear every word, and since the voices were as harsh and loud as foghorns, he knew he was eavesdropping on Rocky and Frida.

'I gotta tell ya, Rocky, I'm real worried. The Board still hasn't decided if they're going to fire Huw. What if he gets off scot-free, after bullying Timothy so shamefully?'

'We can't let that happen. But like, what more can we do?'

'Remember what we discussed the other day?' Frida said in an affable voice.

'Accusing him of sexual harassment? That'd be awesome. Then he wouldn't stand a chance. Trouble is, he hasn't like actually sexually harassed anyone, right?'

Melvyn's mind did a backflip. Was Frida so malicious and devious? So evil?

'Oh, Rocky, you're so innocent. You can fabricate evidence. In fact, guess what? I caught him holding hands with Elise, you know, the President's daughter.'

Oh boy, Frida was *evil.* Huw and Elise, though? Really? Melvyn was envious.

'You did?' said Rocky. 'That's not like fake news? Gosh, sorry. You did?'

'You bet. They said she was reading his palm, telling his fortune—a likely story! But here's the snag: Elise won't back me up on it. She says he never touched her.'

Melvyn closed his tablet with a sigh and adjusted his dress. He was glad Huw had not banged Elise. That would have been unbearable. Oddly, he was relieved for Huw's sake, too.

'That girl's no feminist, Frida. Too pretty. No solidarity. Got any other ideas?'

'As a matter of fact, yeah, I do. Broome.'

'Are you shitting me? Huw boned Broome? For real?'

No way! Melvyn nearly yelled.

'Between you and I, Rock, no he hasn't. He hasn't laid a finger on her.'

'Right. But isn't that kind of like a problem?'

'Not really, Rocky, because Broome is willing to testify that he harassed her.'

'You mean she'd lie through her ass just to fuck Huw over?'

'Let's not put it like that. I wouldn't call it lying. It's more like metaphorical language. Because she feels he would like to sexually harass her. At least *she* would like him to. Get it? It may not be strictly true, in the literal sense, but it's figuratively true. In her mind. She fantasises about it. And reality's subjective, like Derrida says. See what I mean?'

'You mean if she lies it's like a poem, right? Basically flowery bullshit?'

'Exactly. You over-exaggerate a tad, but it's the lie that tells the truth. In a way.'

Silence followed. Melvyn imagined Rocky's perplexed expression: the knitted brow, the pursed lips, the murky eyes. 'Yeah. Coo-ul, I guess.'

It sounded fool-proof. Huw would lose his job, Frida would invite Holly Tuwuwanda to apply for it, and Melvyn would be appointed Director of the Undergraduate Programme of Creative Writing. Since his recent gold medal performance in the bedroom, Frida had mostly been pleasant. He might not even need to leave her. After all, she had assured him he could bone whoever he liked. He could openly continue his affair with Jezebel. And maybe start one with Miranda too, now she was available? The only trouble was that Melvyn felt sorry for Huw now, just when the finish line was in sight. *Damn my conscience!* he thought.

Melvyn heard muffled words, and pressed his ear to the door. Frida spoke slyly:

'Don't forget you're going to be Director of the Undergraduate Programme, Rocky.'

What the fuck? She'd shaft me like that? Frida had assured Melvyn that the post, with release time and more money, would be his, if they could get rid of Huw, the natural choice.

'But like, what about Melvyn?' Rocky said. 'Won't he expect to get the job?'

'Oh screw Melvyn,' Frida said, with a peal of laughter. 'I mean, he may be a tad disappointed, but he's obedient. Spineless. Kind of a chump, to tell the truth. I got him wound round my little finger. Once Thalia's gone off to college, I'm gonna move a lover into the house. Then we can have a ménage à trois. Melvyn hasn't got the guts to object.'

Are you crazy? Melvyn's mind screamed. *With that freak?*

'Melvyn's in my good books at the moment. He's even been kind of a good lover for the first time in like forever. Still, you gotta remind them who's boss, right? He's just a *guy*. Like I said, I got the jerk wound round my little finger.'

That's what you think, bitch. Melvyn had been obedient—and what had he got out of it? Nothing. Well, the worm was turning.

'Just wait and see,' Frida said. 'It'll all turn out the way I plan. It always does.'

Over my dead body, Melvyn swore.

*

Later, at home in his study, where Melvyn was pecking at his keyboard and wishing he could write like Huw, a sudden corvid screech of alarm sent chills down his spine.

'Mel—vyn! Get your caagh-caagh ass down here! Like this caagh minute.'

Fuck you, I'm not your flunkey anymore, Melvyn mouthed.

He went on typing and slurping toxic Sundoes slush. He heard a crash, a curse, and the thump of feet on the stairs, then stertorous breathing, coming in thick pants, with a wheeze and a whistle and a cracking sound. Frida was wedged in the doorway.

'Melvyn, brace yourself. I've got bad news and worse news. The worst.'

'Oh God—not Clio? An overdose? *Another* drunken fuck with a linebacker?'

Frida struggled to squeeze herself through the frame. 'Caagh—no—caaagh.'

'Don't tell me Thalia self-harmed again and bled all over the Turkish carpet.'

'Worse than that.' Finally she squeezed in with a plop. '*Way* worse.'

He was in a sweat. 'What could possibly be worse than Thalia cutting herself?'

'Try this: those goddamn attorneys say we don't have a case against Huw. Can you believe it?'

Melvyn sighed. 'Well, that sucks. I am glad Thalia's fine, though.'

'One goddamned lawyer said the charge of bullying and homophobia was sheer bullshit, and he had the gall to tell me not to get on his ass about stuff like that again.'

Melvyn wished he had been there. 'Were those his exact words?' he grinned.

'Of course not. He said it was a frivolous accusation. Completely unfounded, the hick said. Just because he's a man. He had the nerve to suggest Timothy and I were delusional.'

'Hmm, he has a point,' Melvyn said. *Rub it in, dude. Look at her face now!*

'What the hell do you mean by that? You hate Huw as much as I do. More.'

Melvyn got out of his chair and stood very close to her, so she had to crane her neck to look into his face. He was a foot taller and she disliked him towering above her. But it was time to show her she was no longer the boss. 'We should re-evaluate our strategy,' he said.

Frida was speechless—which was unprecedented for her. He went on:

'I admit I was jealous of Huw. Still am, to be honest. But don't you feel sorry for him at all? I mean, the guy's just had a heart attack and Miranda wants a divorce. He has to be worried about money, big time. If you get him fired, how's he going to support that kid?'

'He has plenty of money, and unfortunately he's about to get much more.'

Melvyn pressed his point, without asking her to explain. 'We've gone too far.'

'Too far? We haven't gone far enough. That bastard deserves

to lose his job. You're way too tender-hearted, Melvyn.' Frida snorted, her flanks shuddering. 'Tomorrow I'm going to tell the President that Huw has been hitting on Broome.'

'Are you crazy? It's not even true,' he said, forgetting to put it as a question.

'Well, not in the literal sense, no. I bet he'd like to, though.'

'God, I doubt it. Huw can do way better. Anyway, it won't work. Broome is one of Elise's sorority sisters. I'm sure Elise would tell her father that the allegation is nonsense.'

Frida stepped back. 'Give me a bit more space, I can't breathe. Damn, I don't know what to do. We *have* to fire his ass. The Provost won't give us a new tenure line, so we can only hire if we fire. We need more diverse faculty. We could do with an African-American. Preferably a woman. Maybe gay. Trans would be cool, too.'

Melvyn advanced on her again. Frida flattened herself against a bookcase. The appeal to her better nature had not worked, predictably, because she did not have a better nature. She was fond of cute pets, it was true, but then so was Hitler. No, he would have to appeal to her self-interest.

'Do we really want to fire him now, right after his heart attack? It wouldn't look so good for us. For you. You'd look heartless, Machiavellian.'

'I don't *give* a damn what anyone thinks.'

Melvyn echoed what Luke had said. 'Are you sure? Besides, he's kind of a brilliant writer. Original, bold. Incredible gift for language. James Steele said in the New Yorker that he's the most exciting stylist alive. He makes the programme look good. And us, Frida.'

She shut her eyes. 'Yeah, maybe, but he is a white male. Hetero too.'

'At least he's not a dead white male,' Melvyn said, pleased by his own wit.

'Not yet. Oh my God, that's it! That's the solution.'

Melvyn shivered. 'Surely you aren't saying you'd rejoice if he croaked?'

'Well, let's be honest, it would be convenient. Painful, maybe, but hey, you can't have everything. If only that heart attack had killed him. It would have been perfect.'

Would Huw's death have made *him* happy? Maybe. But a smidgeon of pity surprised him again. Like Chandler's hard-boiled detectives, he actually did have a conscience. Weird.

'Anyways, you said you have bad news and worse news,' he prompted her.

'Yup, there's more. Wait for it. According to Lucky Luke, Huw's been offered a contract for his novel by Sloane Square, after an auction. Apparently all the major houses wanted it. It's even in *Publishers Weekly*. I've never heard such shitty news.'

'Geez, isn't Sloane Square the most prestigious house in London?'

'You bet. Holly Tuwuwanda publishes with them. All the best black and gay writers do. And what's more, it's going to come out simultaneously over here with Brooklyn Books. Obadiah is bound to have him on her show. What can we do?'

Melvyn was envious, and filled with schadenfreude. '*You* must be devastated.'

'He's going to overshadow us all. Especially *you*, sweetie.'

What a bitch. 'You sound jealous yourself, *sweetie*.'

'You know me better than that. There's not a jealous bone in my body. I'm totally delighted to see a colleague's success... But it wouldn't be right if the programme became famous just for his work, would it? With him being a man and all. What kind of example does that set? What if all our MFA candidates are white dudes from now on? What would that do to our diversity ranking and funding?'

'Our candidates are more likely to be straight chicks, you know. Our female students find Huw pretty hot—he's got a Chili pepper on *Rateyourprofessor.com*.'

'That is so gross. I mean, what about *me*? Broome says I'm super-hot.'

Melvyn coughed hard. 'Sure, honey, you are sexy as all get-out. Anyway, the question is, what can we do about it? Nothing. I guess he's getting a big advance?'

Frida wept. 'Six figures, Luke said. Or was it seven? I told you he has money.'

'Holy shit. Well, we can forget getting Huw fired. He'll be outta here, pronto.'

Frida fell into the recliner. Springs bent, boinged, and broke. 'I'm so bummed.'

'Look on the bright side: if he resigns, you can hire Holly Tuwuwanda at last. I remember seeing her on Obadiah recently. She's quite the celebrity now.'

'Sure she is. She's African, queer, and HIV positive.'

'Ticks all the right boxes, then. What more could anyone want?'

'She's also drop-dead gorgeous. *And* wears those super-cool ethnic clothes.'

'On the other hand, she can't actually write, can she? I know she's published a couple of derivative novels. But she's not much of a writer. In fact she sucks. Big time.'

'That's subjective, Melvyn. And a tad racist, homophobic, and misogynistic. I think she's a significant voice. In fact I'm writing a piece about her for *Saloon* called 'Black. Queer. Pos. And Highly Significant.' '

More of the usual, then. 'Significant? What does she signify?'

'Well, you know—oppression by the white patriarchy, and all that.'

'Yadda, yadda, yadda. Same old, same old.'

'Melvyn. Get a life. Dude, you are so out of touch.'

'I don't think I am. I'm all for equal opportunities. Sure we should be inclusive. But must we exclude all white men now? How inclusive is that?'

As she shifted, Frida's belly made a weird noise, like a new tyre inflating and popping on to a wheel. 'Melvyn, you're clueless. *You*'ve excluded *us* for centuries.'

'OK, men have. Granted. Not me. And that was wrong. Men had prejudice against women. And gays. And different races. And now we recognise that all forms of prejudice are wrong—except for the prejudice against white men. That's fine, right? No one questions it.'

'But Melvyn, that's not a prejudice. It's just common sense. I mean it's only fair we get our own back, right? And besides, the science backs us up.'

'What science?' It irked him that he was being reasonable again.

...Since she was not. 'Social scientists agree on this. They all say men are evil.'

'I know they do—but do they have any evidence at all to support their claims?'

Frida attempted to lever herself out of the recliner. She propped her heavily-cushioned elbows on the armrests, leaned forward, screwed up her face, and strained like a toddler evacuating her bowels, then crashed back into the chair.

Melvyn laughed. Loudly, openly. At last he let the hellhound off the chain.

She spoke pure East Boston now. 'What are you laffing at? This is no laffing madder. You goddamn misogynist homophobe racist—you're such a goddamn big *man*, aren't you?'

'I can see we're going to have to buy one of those recliners with a motor that tips the chair forward when you want to get up. You know, for geriatrics and *obese* people.'

'That is so mean. What's come over you? I hate you. Help me up.'

This was fun. 'What if I don't want to?'

'Are you losing your mind, Melvyn? Remember, I *own* you. I made you.'

'You need to ponder *your* position. In fact you depend on me, fatty.'

'If you don't get me out of this chair, I'll—I'll tell Thalia. I'll tell *Clio.* She'll be pissed, Melvyn. And she's got a new knife. A real big one. Practically a machete.'

'Clio thinks you're a goddamn pain in the ass. She can't stand you.'

'What? My dear daughter? Melvyn, you get me out of this chair this minute. Or I'll tell Rocky you were fucking that student. The smart one. So help me God. And Rocky will tell *everyone.* As you know.' She grinned as if she were holding a straight flush in poker.

'What if I tell Rocky you've been fucking Broome? How'd you like that?'

Her astonishment was as exaggerated as a ham actor's. 'You'd never dare.'

'Wouldn't I, though? I know you're planning to promote Rocky. Over me.'

'How the fuck do you know that? Did that dumbass redneck tell you herself? Anyways, Rocky will never believe anything bad about me. She's loyal. My minion.'

'She might believe this,' Melvyn said, with grim satisfaction. He sat down at his desktop, clicked on a file, and played the video of Frida and Broome. From the recliner came the kind of moans large female mammals make when they give birth.

'You wouldn't. You couldn't. You wouldn't, Melvyn, would you?'

'Oh wouldn't I? Think how you've treated me all these years, Frida.'

'What do you mean? I've always treated you with love and affection.'

'You've treated me like a piece of shit. Consistently. Like an inferior.'

Frida chuckled. 'I gotta be honest, Melvyn: you *are* inferior.'

'Oh yeah? In that case I'll send this to Rocky right now.'

'Melvyn! Please! I beg you. I'll do anything. Anything! What do you want?'

What did he want? Freedom, peace, respect. Someone who actually *liked* him. Good sex would not hurt, either. But of course he was not going to get any of that from her.

'Independence,' he said, moving to the door. 'The end of your tyranny.'

'Melvyn! Don't you dare leave me in this recliner. I'll—hey, it's not tyranny, it's benevolent despotism. I love you, sweetie. I do. But if you don't help me, I'll, I'll … '

'I will do such things—what they are, yet I know not,' Melvyn said, recalling the lines from *King Lear*. 'But they shall be the terrors of the earth. Yeah, yeah, yeah.'

Frida gasped and pushed, fell back and fumed. 'That's what I'm talking about,' she said, sweating. 'Huw needs to die, all right. And you do, too, Melvyn.'

'You're losing it, *sweetie*,' Melvyn said, shocked by her words but not taking them too seriously. Empty threats. Hysteria. 'You're getting deranged.'

'Deranged or inspired? You remember *The Maenads*, right? You don't realise what a group of strong women can do.' She made one last heroic effort to lever herself up out of the chair. She leaned forward, pressed her hams into the chair's arms. She screwed up her face, panting and grunting. She kicked her tiny feet. Her flesh wobbled, shook, shivered. She fell back and broke wind.

Melvyn laughed again. 'I'll leave you to consider your options, then,' he said. She sobbed as he left the room. Darcy came towards him on the landing, wagging his tail.

Melvyn patted him gently, picked up his cell phone, and called Jezebel.

'How about now, babe?' he said, his voice rising like a lark's. 'Your place?'

'I'll kill you!' Frida shrieked. 'I'll kill the pair of you!'

TWENTY-ONE

Taking the Plunge

It was perfect weather for a picnic: sunny but not sticky. No Mitsubishi Zero mosquitoes whined in the air. Even so, Huw's uneasiness about taking part in the picnic was growing. When he had received the 'invite,' as even faculty called it these days, on a card decorated with Pooh bears and red hearts, Huw's impulse had been to bin it, even though the picnic was ostensibly in his honour, to celebrate his book deal and recovery. That was hypocrisy, of course. Since his return to work, Rocky had told him she was delighted he was back, and tried to deny that it was *her* pink Barbie Corvette that Huw had run into on his bike. But she had missed him so much, really. Everyone adored him. And everyone said he was a genius.

Rubbish—but in the end Huw decided to go for Owen's sake. It would be a while before he saw the advance for the novel, so he could still not resign. Besides, he owed his presence to his students, who apart from Elise, knew nothing of the plots against him.

As Huw arrived at the trailhead with Miranda, who had

agreed to come reluctantly, Melvyn jumped down from the colossal Shamburger Hummer, which was painted a nauseous purple. Melvyn was wearing his pink *I'm With Her* polo shirt and the khaki shorts of a Raj policeman, circa 1923. Frida did not descend from the armoured car and Huw guessed why. Melvyn smiled when he saw Huw—not that Huw trusted him much more than he did Rocky.

From the rear of the car, Melvyn took out a step-ladder, a pulley, and a coil of rope, which he rigged up by Frida's door. He busied himself with the rope.

'Gee, Melvyn, your shorts are so *short*!' screeched Rocky, in a camo dress and combat boots. Was she packing her Beretta too? 'You'll creep out all the women.'

Melvyn glanced at his chicken thighs with a fond smile, and grinned at Miranda, who had just got out of the car. Was his recent friendliness genuine? Huw wondered. Or did he have an ulterior motive? Frida abseiled to the ground, half-falling, half-bouncing off the steps of the ladder, banging it against the bodywork. Somehow Melvyn managed to catch her.

No sooner had she alighted—outfitted in a canvas cape, a skirt the size of a spinnaker, rainbow tights, what looked like deep-sea dive boots, and a broad-brimmed hat, trimmed with ostrich feathers—than she uttered a pterodactyl scream: 'Miranda! I'm *beyond* thrilled to see you!'

So she did not have the courage to address him yet. Since getting back to work Huw had managed to avoid talking to her, or even being in the same room.

The programme writers, students and faculty, and a number of guests—the enormous female vicar Huw had seen at the retreat, who was talking to Rocky, and also, he was surprised to see, Petronella herself—were milling around a minibus and cars, with coolers, picnic hampers, rugs, folding chairs and tables, gas stoves, and enough provisions for a safari. Frida stormed across the piles of food and furniture, paying no attention to anything that her dive boots smashed or squelched. Each footfall was a leaden clump. Chairs splintered or snapped as she stamped on them. Cakes and quiches splattered into mush. She looked as intrepid as Allan Quatermain in *King Solomon's Mines*—a short, inflated, nose-ringed Allan Quatermain. In drag.

Miranda awaited Frida's approach with the passivity of a pawn. Melvyn came up too.

'You like my new hat, Miranda?' Frida gasped, planting a kiss on her cheek.

'It hides the sunburnt skinhead scalp nicely, right?' said Melvyn, smirking.

Taking the piss out of Frida was not like Melvyn, it struck Huw. Had he become more assertive? Or had their relationship changed? Frida glowered—but there was something pitiful and imploring in her expression too. However, she addressed Miranda, not Melvyn.

'It's a *statemen*t, you know what I'm saying?' Frida said. 'A political one.'

'Oh no,' Melvyn said. 'Spare us your sophomore pretensions, please.'

'Meghan Markle wore one like it,' she panted. 'I bought it in solidarity.'

Miranda frowned. '*Solidarity?* You mean, with the British royal family?'

Frida chuckled. 'Meghan's a minority, right? She's black, right, Miranda?'

'Yeah, sure,' Miranda said, with glazed eyes. 'Biracial, anyway.'

'You're not actually black, Frida,' Melvyn said. 'Have you noticed that yet?'

He grinned at Miranda in a new way, even as he spoke to Frida. It was a matinee idol smile—suave, debonair, confident. Something must have changed him.

'Not in the lideral sense,' Frida admitted, in hurt tones. 'Not in like actual pigmentation. But I do have the soul of a black woman. Big time. I'm a soul sister.'

'Cultural appropriation,' Melvyn said. 'Very tacky, Frida.'

'You hear me singing Aretha Franklin in the shower, right? I should have been born black. I wish I was an African-American rider. Or an Asian rider. Why couldn't I have been a cooler colour? White is so goddamn *meh*, right, Miranda?'

'I guess,' Miranda said. 'I just feel guilty for being white, you know?'

But Melvyn would not let Frida off the hook. 'Let's get this straight, honey. You're telling us you identify with Markle because you have a black woman's soul?'

'No, dumbass, I identify with her because I'm an oppressed minority too.'

Melvyn sniggered. Miranda, who without a trace of makeup seemed transparent, stood by, inert and expressionless as a China doll, her mind elsewhere or switched off.

'You got me confused, Frida,' said Melvyn. 'I mean, Meghan was a celebrity before she married Prince Harry, and now she's a member of the British royal family. That's oppressed? And how the hell are *you* oppressed? Your crime boss dad was loaded, you have a doctorate, you live the American dream. You live a life of white privilege, Frida. We all do.'

Frida's lower lip quivered. 'Right, but I'm a woman too. A *pansexual* woman.'

'I'm not sure you need to boast about that,' he muttered. She glowered at him.

Meanwhile Rocky was stamping across the debris left by Frida, leaving very little of the picnic, and enfolded her in a python's embrace. Broome, in a somewhat fey Goth outfit of black lace, leather, and chiffon, joined them. So did the vast vicar. It was a living sculpture, similar to the Laocoon, the four figures showing signs of intense emotion, ecstasy or perhaps agony, all writhing together, caught in the coils of the serpent. None of them had the athletic physiques of the classical originals, but in sheer mass they outdid the Trojan priest and his sons. They must have looked heroic or maybe just 'bizarro' to the students, who surrounded them, snapping pictures with their phones. They were all there: Charleston and Elise, Walt, Truman, Jordan, and Nutmeg. Even Frank or Hank, who had no interest in writing. His presence was explained by Elise's: he never left her side. Timothy was absent, thank God. Only Lucky Luke failed to join the melee. He sat on a rock smoking a herbal roll-up with a suspicious odour. In a mini-skirt and above the knee socks, Petronella swaggered over and drew Miranda aside too. They whispered together as if they were intimate, Huw noticed.

'Let's get going,' Frida said. 'But I warn you, I can't do a huge hike.'

'It's half a mile,' Melvyn said.

'That's what I said: how do you expect me to hike a long-distance trail?'

The party made off, entering a sandy trail among pine trees. Everyone but Frida carried a backpack. She huffed and puffed in short, agonised wheezes.

When they reached the bluff where they planned to have the picnic, Frida sat down on a rock overlooking a lake and miles of mountain and forest. The women spread out the remnants of the picnic on tablecloths, and, while the men busied themselves with drinks and the stove. Frida lost her balance and sprawled, limbs flailing, like an overturned insect.

Rocky tried to get her arms around her but could not, and failed to wrench her up by lifting under her armpits. She seized her hands, and bending her knees and leaning back, with a weightlifter's groan, managed to lever Frida into a sitting position.

'Congratulations, Rocky,' Melvyn said. 'That was quite the feat of strength.'

'What the hell are you grinning at?' Frida asked Melvyn.

'*Du bist scheisse*,' he said. You are shit. Frida huffed, nonplussed by his German.

Broome grabbed Frida's left armpit with both hands. Rocky seized the other side. The vicar thrust her hands under her backside. 'One, two, three, *lift!*' Rocky said. Somehow, they got her up. She wobbled, but with their help, she waddled over to the picnic site.

She kept away from Melvyn, and did not sit down—there was no picnic chair large enough for her to fit in—but propped herself on a rock, beside Broome and Rocky.

The vicar talked to Jordan and Nutmeg, about their upcoming wedding.

Huw found himself beside Melvyn and Elise, on the edge of the cliff.

'Oowee!' said Elise, laying a hand on Huw's arm. 'Just look at that view.'

'We must be four hundred feet above the lake,' he said.

'Celtic hyperbole,' Melvyn said. Whatever had come over him? It wasn't like him to take the piss.

All three stood on the edge and gazed down: far below, the lake swirled and foamed beneath a cataract. Beside the water was a massive slab of rock.

Over his shoulder, Huw saw Miranda frowning at him, as she talked to Petronella. What was that about? Had she arranged to meet Petronella here? Or were the sea-monsters bothering her again? More hallucinations or delusions? Huw was about to go over and comfort her when he caught Melvyn winking at her. Abruptly leaving Huw's side, Melvyn strutted towards her, stiffly as cockerel. Curious, Huw decided to wait a few moments. Hank or Frank was opening brown bottles, and pouring their contents into paper cups, which Elise was receiving. Further back, Lucky Luke was smoking, probably wacky baccy, with Walt, Truman, and Charleston. Jordan and Nutmeg giggled with the vicar to Huw's right. Frida, Rocky and Broome were sneaking hits on a silver hip-flask and making gecko-like screeches. Huw saw the curling lips and imagined a conspiracy. Nah, he told himself, don't be paranoid.

Elise handed him a cup. 'Beer?' he asked. 'Is that allowed?'

'A malted beverage,' Hank or Frank said. 'Don't tell anyone, prof.'

Huw sipped it, looking uneasily over his shoulder again. Melvyn was grinning at Miranda, and touched her bare shoulder. She shrank from his touch. Petronella spoke, saying something cutting, probably. A flotilla of clouds sailed across the sky, hiding the sun.

Then it happened again: Huw heard eerie music, violins like crying children. A deep sawing sound, double basses, sinister. Timpani, French horns, a choir. A baroque requiem. He looked over at his wife again. He could not hear their words, but he lip-read Melvyn's.

I like you, Miranda. Or was it *I love you?* Petronella snapped a phrase at him.

Huw told Elise about the music. 'I hear it too,' she said, close by his side.

'Really? Be careful. You're too close to the edge.'

She smiled at him. 'Live dangerously, right, Huw?'

'We are. Look over there: Melvyn's flirting with my wife, but for some reason I just feel sorry for him, maybe because I can see he's no match for that woman, the feminist guru. And over there, the three witches. What's happening? Tell me. You're our Cassandra.'

Elise shut her eyes and pursed her lips. 'A tragedy is imminent.'

Melvyn stumbled back towards them, with a downcast expression.

'What kind of tragedy?' Huw asked Elise.

'Is there more than one kind?' Elise said.

'For the Greeks, the tragic hero is a victim of the gods. He or she might be anyone. But in Shakespeare it's the hero's character that impels the catastrophe.'

'Boy, you really live in your head, don't you, Huw? You need to listen to your body more. Your feelings and intuitions. Your life might depend on it.'

'You're way too close to the edge, guys,' Melvyn said as he came up to them.

Frank or Hank put his arm around Elise, drawing her gently but firmly away.

And yet Huw remained where he was, on the very edge of the precipice, and Melvyn stood right beside him, with the air of a kid who has been dared to show his courage. Kettle drums beat below the mixed choir. Shadows skipped over the rocks. Huw felt no rancour towards Melvyn. He spun round. 'Who is that?' he said, glimpsing a shape that melted into the shadows. 'See him by the trees? Tall bloke, dark, Van Dyck beard. Do we know him?'

Melvyn followed his gaze. 'I think I saw him earlier. Must be a hiker.'

Frida got to her feet with the help of her friends, lowering her head, as if she were about to charge. A hand signal of some kind passed between her and Broome and Rocky. They all stood. They stared at Melvyn, who began whistling—embarrassed or ashamed.

'I believe Frida is planning to kill me,' Melvyn said. 'And you too, I'm sorry to say.'

'What are you talking about?' Huw said. The women formed a circle, holding hands, and turned, with odd chirping noises, keeping their eyes fixed on the men.

'Look at them,' Melvyn said. 'See how they're staring at us? The question is, what would the Superior Man do? Know what I mean? I just wish I had consulted the *I Ching*.'

'You can't be serious, mate. In broad daylight? It would be insane.'

'You might not have noticed, but they are batshit crazy. And look at Miranda: she knows.' She had clapped her hands over her ears. Her mouth opened in a silent shriek. 'Strange woman, your wife,' Melvyn said. 'She looks like that Munch picture.'

This is it, Huw knew, *my last chance. The critical moment of my life.*

Now the women formed a line, Rocky and Broome on each side of Frida, hands joined, trotting towards them. Broome and Rocky were squealing like teenage girls.

'Should we move? Could it be a joke?' Huw said.

'That's what they'll say,' Melvyn said. 'If they succeed in pushing us off.'

The women lumbered towards them in a sort of slow stampede. Jordan and Nutmeg laughed, obviously thinking it a prank. The vicar looked aghast, and Elise signalled frantically to Huw to move, but for some reason he could not. He had to face them, even though Elise yelled at him to get back—which Miranda did not do. It was clear now that Frida *was* charging, her face ferocious, tattooed arms thrust out, to push him—or Melvyn?

'Yes, they mean to kill us,' he said. Thunderheads rose in mauve-black columns.

It all happened very fast. Frida lurched to her right, barging into Broome, who plunged towards Melvyn and Huw. Rocky made a grab for Frida, who was off balance, but only caught her cloak. Frida was about to crash into Melvyn, but at the last moment he twisted away from her on the lip of the cliff on one leg, in the Crane pose.

Soprano voices shrilled in Huw's ears. French horns brayed. Trumpets blared. The charging women reminded him of the rugby field, when, once again, as he knew it would, Time juddered to a halt. *Tempus abire tibi est,* the choir sang. It is time for you to depart.

Miranda's hands no longer covered her ears, but her eyes. Petronella had her arm around her. *Non te amat,* chanted the voices. Seeing him shattered on the rocks or drowned might shock Miranda, but mostly, Huw knew, she would just feel sorry for herself.

She had seen, but not warned him. She loves you not. Knowing it was a relief—it ended the uncertainty. Why hadn't he believed the warnings? Time to leave. *Non te amat.*

What if he used this pause to take evasive action, like a lucid dreamer? He tried to move but he was paralysed. When he looked at Melvyn, he saw he was exultant.

The music thundered around the mountain, male voices

predominating now, basses and baritones, in a kind of dread-filled requiem, and a mighty drummer thrashed the timpani. A shape was so close that Huw smelled the acrid odour of their sweat. The colossal figure was no longer holding hands with Broome and Rocky, but reaching out to push him over. The brass and woodwind whirled in a spiral of hectic sound. Instinctively, Huw side-stepped.

He grabbed the strong, satanic arms, twisted around, and flung the figure behind him.

Time was flowing again, slowly, but accelerating. Figures seethed around him, yet Huw saw everything clearly. The satanic shape he had grappled with turned into Frida, who flurried between the two men, head flung back, scrabbling at the air. She spun and grasped Melvyn on the lip of the cliff, her back to the abyss, overbalancing, her arms attempting a sort of butterfly stroke, fury and panic on her face. Did Melvyn push her? If he had, it was too swift to register. Rocky clung to Frida's cloak, in peril of going over too.

Lightning lit up a black and crimson face, with white teeth. The devil was still there. Thunder tore open the sky. The mountaintop shook. Frida lost her toehold and overbalanced.

The violins teetered at the top of the E string, vibrato, the timpani thumped, the thunder crashed and cannonaded off the cliffs, the sopranos shrieking as they plunged into the bowels of hell. *Gloria scriptori.* Glory to the author, they sang. *Scribe, scribe, scribe.* Although it was dark as night, with another lightning flash Huw saw Frida's body dangling, her claws clutching one of her husband's arms. Melvyn stood with legs apart, wrenching backwards. Trying to heave her back over the brink, or just save himself? Rocky had let go of Frida's cloak and seized her arms, but she was kneeling, off-balance, slipping slowly over as well. It was like a modern ballet in which dancers leap then freeze in sculptural formations.

Will Rocky and Melvyn manage to pull Frida back from the brink? Huw wondered.

He hoped not. He wanted to see the devil fall.

Forked lightning split the purple sky, thunder shook the mountain at the same moment, and in the blink of an eye Rocky tumbled off the cliff, and was clinging to Frida's back, her arms around her boss's neck. Broome dived headfirst into the abyss. Frida slipped out of Melvyn's grasp but clutched at an outcrop of rock beside his feet. The agony on her face as she tried to hoist herself and Rocky up to safety was indescribable. Melvyn bent over as if to save her. But as the cymbals and the thunder crashed and the wind screamed, and rain lashed them in torrents, he straightened up, stumbled, and the next thing Huw saw was Melvyn's hiking boots on Frida's fingers. Was that an accident? Melvyn looked serene. But he did grind those chubby fingers with his steel-capped toes. Hard. Was it an accident?

Then he *stamped* on her fingers. But he might have slipped. Possibly.

Frida let out a heart-splitting shriek, the music stopped with a peal of thunder and a final thump of the drums, and she plummeted, her cloak fluttering around her. One after the other, Broome and Frida splashed into the lake.

Melvyn looked down. 'Man, was that intense,' he said—with relish, Huw thought.

Elise flung herself into Huw's arms. 'The tragedy I foretold. But you saved yourself!'

Hank or Frank shook his head. 'What were those ditsy chicks smoking?'

'Shut the fuck up, Hank,' said Elise.

'Frank,' said Frank. 'I'm Frank, don't you remember?'

Jordan and Nutmeg wept in one another's arms, although Jordan was also giggling hysterically. She soon had her phone out and was taking pictures. The vicar had her hands together in prayer. 'Heavenly Father, I mean Mother,' she said. 'I mean, Heavenly Parent: you have not made us for darkness and death, but for life with you forever.'

Miranda was in a foetal position, Huw saw as he prised Elise off himself. Petronella had one arm around his wife, and with the other was stroking her hair and murmuring to her.

In moments, everyone was on the edge of the cliff, gaping, gasping, shouting.

'It was a terrible accident,' Melvyn said. 'It may have been some kind of prank that went wrong. A true tragedy. The worst of it is, they weren't even taking a selfie.'

'Are they all dead?' said Elise. She too was already taking pictures.

'Broome never surfaced,' Melvyn said. 'The fall must have broken her back. Sadly, it's clear that Frida has passed too. I believe she's in a better place.' He spoke in pious tones, as he would later at the memorial service, Huw supposed. He spoke like the Superior Man.

'What happened to Rocky Rathaus?' Lucky Luke said. 'Is she dead too?'

No one knew. Peering over the edge, secured by the surprisingly strong arms of Elise around his waist, Huw scanned the foot of the cliff. Nothing. Then he surveyed the cliffside, and discovered Rocky on a ledge, fifteen feet or so below. She had wrapped her arms around the trunk of a young pine growing out of the rock and clung there with her eyes shut tight.

'You bastards,' she whimpered. 'None of you loves Frida like I do.'

Elise got spectacular footage of her weeping on the ledge, and of herself, heroically throwing a rope down to her. She shared the videos and selfies on her page, and in an hour racked up 17,453 likes and over two thousand shares. By late afternoon it had gone viral. That night she appeared on Fox News and CNN as 'the glamorous girl hero of the Westmoreland Gap tragedy.' The following day she had offers from three modelling agencies, and Hollywood scouts calling her. She was an instant celebrity.

Huw drove home later, shaken but feeling free. Miranda had

not spoken to him once since their arrival, and did not speak to him again. Petronella said she would drive her home.

Huw's destiny had been fulfilled, he sensed, except for one thing. But what was it?

He knew he had to do something, but it took him months to figure out what it was.

Envoi

'It's incredible they survived such a high fall,' Nasreen Shirazi was saying as she examined Huw in her office, six months later. On the walls were several framed Persian miniatures and a large reproduction of Leonardo's *Adoration of the Magi*. The scent of flowers pervaded the room—not cut flowers, but potted plants. Orchids, pink roses, poinsettias, and African violets. She had just taken his blood pressure, which was healthy. 'You say they fell two hundred feet?'

'A hundred and seventy. They were lucky to fall into the deepest water and not hit any rocks. Frida was very badly injured. She's still recovering, I hear.'

Nasreen told him to open his shirt, and listened to his heart with her stethoscope. 'That's fine. Vigorous—my, it's beating hard. Are you excited about something?' He was too embarrassed to answer. Smiling, she went on: 'What happened to them? The newspapers said there were charges of attempted murder.'

'I dropped them on a lawyer's advice. Impossible to prove, she said.'

'Didn't I read that your boss accused her husband of attempted murder, too?'

'Yes, initially. But she dropped that as well. In return for being allowed to keep her teaching job. There was an almighty scandal. Elise wanted her father to fire her.'

Nasreen placed her palm flat on Huw's chest—not seductively, but he sensed that she enjoyed touching him. She pressed hard, gazing steadily into his eyes. Her hand was cool and strong. 'She did lose her position as director of the programme, though, didn't she?'

'Yes. Melvyn, her husband, took over. They switched roles. Ever since her fall, Frida has been quiet, almost sweet. She behaves exactly the way her husband used to. She never contradicts him or votes against him, although she's still a bit peevish. I never thought I'd see such a transformation. And her disciple, Rocky Rathaus, changed in just the same way.'

Nasreen threw back her head and laughed. 'In Farsi we have a word to describe women like that. But I had better not say it. So Frida continues to teach with you. She must hate Melvyn as much as you. Isn't it very uncomfortable?'

'It is,' he said, buttoning up his shirt. 'May I tell you something in strict confidence?'

'Of course you can. I'm your doctor.'

'I feel a certain guilt about her. I was to blame for her fall.'

Nasreen frowned. 'What on earth do you mean?'

'Frida thought it was her husband who grappled with her and swung her and made her lose her balance. But actually it was me.'

Nasreen's face paled. 'You struck a woman?'

Huw's gaze wandered to Leonardo's painting. 'You won't believe what I have to tell you. But I believed I was face to face with a demon. I didn't exactly strike her, either.'

'Go on.'

He told her how he had heard the celestial music, with the angelic choirs, the counsel in Latin, the kettle drums, the sinister sounds, the archangels, and that day, the mysterious shape of the bearded man whom Huw had glimpsed several times, a man of immense height, who had an acrid smell; he spoke of the three occasions when Time had stopped, and of Elise's warning of an imminent tragedy, and her advice, to heed the voice of his intuition.

'When the three of them were almost upon us, I swear that that devilish figure was among them. At least I thought so. His arms reached out to push me and I felt his hands on my chest, shoving me backwards, into the abyss. I didn't think. I acted. I didn't hit him, but seized his arms and swung him around. It's a move I did once in a rugby match.'

'And what happened?' Nasreen's had changed; she no longer spoke with anger.

'It all happened in a moment, you have to understand, it was confusing, with women shouting, and losing their balance, and slaps and punches and kicks. But I think that…'

'What? Just say it.'

'The devil turned into Frida. I know it sounds like a lie, or lunacy.'

Nasreen sighed. 'Far from it. That was just what happened.'

Huw laughed nervously. 'You can't be saying you believe me, surely?'

'I believe you. It was no hallucination. You fought with a djinni.'

'You believe that? Is it possible?'

'I'm absolutely certain. You fought a djinni and you won, may God be praised. It was his will.'

Huw shook his head. 'I'll have to think about that. Thank you.'

Nasreen shook her head too. 'God bless you. And what now? What are you going to do?'

'I've given my notice at the university. Finally. Next semester will be my last. I'm going to dedicate myself to writing. Sink or swim.'

'I hope you will succeed.' On her lips, it did not sound an empty phrase.

His heart beat harder. 'I wonder if you'd have dinner with me one night?'

Her face darkened—with anger, plainly. 'Aren't you still married?'

'Not any more, no. My divorce came through a couple of months ago.'

Her mouth softened. 'That is sad. I could see that you loved your wife.'

'Yes, I did.' It embarrassed him to say so, but he had no desire to mislead her.

'You speak with sorrow. You still love her.' It was not a question.

Although his momentary impulse was to deny it, he had to be honest. 'I'm not sure you ever cease to love someone you have truly loved. I do still care about her. And I'm happy that she has found peace and happiness in San Miguel de Allende.' *Even with Petronella.*

'Is that in Mexico, the home of my poinsettias?' she said, glancing at them.

'Yes. She followed her dream, see you, a dream of Frida Kahlo.'

'Like a Disney princess,' she said, with amusement and maybe disdain.

'She went with a woman named Petronella Pikestaff. Do you know her?'

'Ah, the famous feminist. I read about her in a magazine. So many American women are confused. I know it's politically incorrect to say so. Do I offend you?'

'Very little offends me. You aren't a feminist, then, I take it?'

'I am a woman,' she said, almost fiercely. 'I believe in equality, of course. I'm not an idiot. But few American women understand what it means to be a woman. Or is that just my backwards Middle Eastern mentality? What do you think?'

'It intrigues me. I don't think you're backward. I hope you'll tell me what you believe in much more detail. You still haven't said if you'll have dinner with me.'

'You need another check-up in six months' time. Earlier if

the results of your blood tests don't look good. Your cholesterol remains a little high. You should eat more anti-oxidants. Eliminate the stress from your life, if you can.'

She was evading the invitation again. He would have to try once more.

'I am trying. I've resigned, and am no longer living with a disturbed wife.'

Nasreen gave him a long, hard look, gauging whether he was really relieved. 'What happened to her boss? You told me he raped her, didn't you?'

'Did I really? That was very indiscreet of me. Perhaps it was the drugs I was on after the surgery. Yes, and he lost his job over it. Dr Gneiss saw to that. But Miranda didn't press charges. She foresaw ugly cross-examinations and knew she would go to pieces in court.'

'So how is she living? In Mexico?' She tapped a pencil, impatient or nervous.

'Her partner runs self-fulfilment feminist retreats. For white Americans.'

'Of course. And Miranda helps her, I suppose? She's very pretty, isn't she?'

Was there a twinge of jealousy in her voice? Huw hoped so. 'She is.'

'And didn't you tell me that this Petronella's sister used to assist her?'

'You have a remarkable memory. I must have done. And it transpired, in the welter of accusations and counter-accusations after the incident on the clifftop, that Melvyn was having an affair with her. The sister. She called herself Jezebel, like the temptress in the Bible.'

'Oh no.' Nasreen steepled her hands. Her eyes were merry, though.

'She's doing a Master's in Psychology at Cornell now. She aims to be a sex therapist.'

'And how would *you* know that, Huw?' Nasreen's voice was sharper.

'She told me,' he said sheepishly. 'I think she may have been after me too.'

'I bet. Sex therapist, indeed. We also have a word in Farsi for women like that.'

'I can imagine.' Her intimate tone encouraged him. 'And another scandal that started to break but somehow didn't was that it turned out Frida was sleeping with her student, and mine, Broome—the other woman who tried to push us over the cliff.'

'It gets crazier and crazier.'

'I believe Frida is still seeing her. And Melvyn is still seeing Jezebel.'

Nasreen shook her head. 'I don't want to hear more about these sick people.'

'All right. So—will you have dinner with me? Do you like Indian food?'

'I love it. But you aren't ready to date me yet, Huw. I can see that.'

'I think I am,' he said at once, but unsure of himself.

'No, you aren't. Take it from me. We'll wait six months. Then ask me again.'

'You'll have dinner with me in six months? Do you promise?'

'I told you to ask me again then. *If* you are over your grief for Miranda.'

He saw she would not be swayed. He stood and held out his hand, which she took firmly. She did not shake it, but held it in hers. He wanted to take her in his arms, but knew she would not let him, even if she were feeling the same desire. 'I shall look forward to my next appointment,' he said.

'So shall I,' Nasreen said. 'Behave yourself meanwhile.'

'What do you mean?'

'Don't give in to temptation with that model. The one who's in California.'

'Elise? How in the world do you know about her?'

'How do you think? Her father is my patient too. I can be quite jealous, you should know. Like most Middle Eastern women. Dr Goldsmith told me she has a crush on you. I know she's beautiful. It would be fun for you—but not healthy.'

Huw reddened. He had considered giving Elise a call and more than once had got as far as picking up the phone. 'I won't go near her,' he promised.

She susurrated a few words of Farsi. 'Goodbye for now, then.'

It was hard to let go of her hand, which she still held, as people from the Middle East often did, without embarrassment or sentimentality. It obviously betokened something stronger than friendship. Would it be foolish to fall in love with her? If she were to return his love, would she love him forever, or would her love be in vain, as Miranda's had been? As he looked into Nasreen's grave eyes, those deep, deep pools, he saw she was a different kind of woman altogether. And he had become a different kind of man. He would not expect her to comfort or reassure him. Nor would he ever take a woman's love for granted again.

For now, he had a happy day ahead of him—and that was enough.

The End

ACKNOWLEDGEMENTS

I wish to thank the following friends who generously read drafts of this novel, critiqued it and encouraged me greatly:

David Joiner
Jacqueline Newman
Jack Gaiser
Jemima and Rupert Copping